INSTINCTS
THE NEW HAVEN/POINT HOPE INCIDENTS

Instincts: The New Haven/Point Hope Incidents is a work of fiction. References to real people, events, establishments, organizations, or locales are intended only to provide the sense of authenticity and are use fictitiously. All other characters, all incidents, dialogue are drawn from the author's imagination and are not to be seen as real.

Copyright © 2019, 2022. All rights reserved.

Lost in Shadows: Remastered and *Instincts Point Hope* are available individually through paperback, eBook, and hardcover.

The Pleasured Killing available digitally on darktitanentertainment.com.

Also available in paperback.

Paperback ISBN: 979-8-9866393-5-2
eBook ISBN: 979-8-9866393-6-9

Published by Dark Titan Publishing. A division of Dark Titan Entertainment.

Dark Titan Noir is an imprint of Dark Titan Entertainment.

darktitanentertainment.com

WORKS BY TY'RON W. C. ROBINSON II

BOOKS/SHORT STORIES

DARK TITAN UNIVERSE SAGA

MAIN SERIES
Dark Titan Knights
The Resistance Protocol
Tales of the Scattered
Tales of the Numinous
Day of Octagon
Crossbreed
Heaven's Called
The Oranos Imperative
Underworld
Magicks & Mysticism

SPIN-OFFS
In A Glass of Dawn: The Casebook of Travis Vail
Maveth: Bloodsport
The Curse of The Mutant-Thing
Trail of Vengeance
War of The Thunder Gods

ONE-SHOTS
Maveth, The Death-Bringer
Mystery of The Mutant-Thing
Shade & Switchblade
Retribution of Cain
The Mythologists
Ambush Bot
Kang-Zhu
Cheeseburger Man
Tessa Balthazar
Elite 5

COLLECTIONS
Dark Titan Omnibus: Volume 1
Dark Titan Omnibus: Volume 2
Dark Titan One-Shot Collection
Dark Titan One-Shot Collection II
Dark Titan Universe Saga Spin-offs Omnibus: Volume 1

THE HAUNTED CITY SAGA
The Legendary Warslinger: The Haunted City I
Battle of Astolat: A Haunted City Prequel (KOBO Exclusive)
Redemption of the Lost: The Haunted City II
Helper's Hand: A Haunted City One-Shot

SYMBOLUM VENATORES
Symbolum Venatores: The Gabriel Kane Collection
Hod: A Symbolum Venatores Book
Symbolum Venatores: War of The Two Kingdoms
Symbolum Venatores: Elrad's Chronicles

EVERWAR UNIVERSE
EverWar Universe: Knights & Lords
EverWar Universe: Avior vs. Dekar

PRODIGIOUS WORLDS
Mark Porter of Argoron
Raiders of Vanok
Praxus of Lithonia

FRIGHTENED! SERIES
Frightened!: The Beginning

INSTINCTS SERIES
Lost in Shadows: Remastered
Instincts: Point Hope

DARK TITAN'S THE DEAD DAYS
Accounts of The Dead Days

THE HORDE TRILOGY
The Horde
The Dreaded Ones

OTHER BOOKS
The Book of The Elect
The Extended Age Omnibus
The Eleventh Hour: A Chevah Mythos Story
The Supreme Pursuer: Darkness of the Hunt
Massacre in the Dusk
Venture into Horror: Tales of the Supernatural
The Universe of Realms Omnibus: Book 1
The Universe of Realms Omnibus: Book 2

THE DARK TITAN AUDIO EXPERIENCE PODCAST
Season 1: Introductions
Season 2: In a Glass of Dawn
Season 2.5: Accounts of The Dead Days
Season 3: Battle For Astolat
Season 4: Hallow Sword: Cursed

INSTINCTS
THE NEW HAVEN/POINT HOPE INCIDENTS

TY'RON W. C. ROBINSON II

CONTENTS

LOST IN SHADOWS: REMASTERED
1

THE PLEASURED KILLING
201

INSTINCTS POINT HOPE
211

LOST IN SHADOWS: REMASTERED

CHAPTER 1

New Haven Detective and U.S. Marshal Preston Maddox drives down a pair of narrow streets as he's on the search for Jonny Cartel, one of the top drug lords of New Haven, Connecticut. Preston, who's wearing his casual suit attire, drives through the quiet streets of New Haven. He turns a corner that heads toward Orange Avenue, around the West River.

"I take it he's around this area. Somewhere."

He turned a corner, which was leading him into a dark pathway. On the other side of the street is a small warehouse covered in rusted panels. Preston drove closer to the warehouse and spotted a white van on the left side. Preston noticed a group of guys standing by the van, wearing all black with their faces barely covered, stacking what appears to be bags of marijuana and cocaine in the back. Preston also noticed a black SUV beside the van with one man coming out, wearing a white suit with slick hair.

"There's the son of a bitch." Preston said as he sees Jonny Cartel.

Preston slowly put the car in park and turned off the vehicle. He exited out of the car and began walking toward the scene. As he walked closer, one of the men spotted him and started yelling. The other men looked up and see Preston. Jonny turned and stared at Preston. Preston does the same.

"Well, looks like the Instinct has found me." Jonny said. "What's the next step, Detective? I hope you're not here for a license plate or sticker check on my SUV here."

"I'm here to take your worthless self to prison. Unless you have another option of a location you'll like to take you?"

Jonny laughed as he looked toward his men. They laughed along with him, until Preston glared at them. Jonny turned back to Preston, looking at his clothes before keeping his attention focused on Preston.

"Look here, I got an hour before I leave for Miami. So, do me a favor, Maddox. Get a change in style of clothes for once. This whole intimidation approach isn't quite working for you when you're wearing only slacks and a casual jacket."

"I appreciate your generosity in the apparel department, Cartel. Though, I can care less on how you perceive someone's clothing. Anyway, that's not why I'm here and you know why I'm here standing before you and your pack of goons."

"OK, so what can I do to change your mind? Hmm? Give you some profit on the side? Hand you one of my nice fine women to keep you company for the time being?"

"I can care less about your greenbacks or your filthy whores you have stashed back at your place."

Preston held his ground quietly.

"I'm giving you a few choices to make. Either you can come with me, get in my car and I'll ship you off to prison or we can have ourselves a classic standoff where you and most of your men here are killed on the spot. Your decision, not mine."

Jonny stood quietly, not making a sound. Only staring at Preston. Preston kept his eyes locked on Cartel, not making any facial expressions of any kind.

"Tongue turned to lead, Cartel?"

Jonny walked toward the van. He tells his men to pack up whatever they had in their hands and told them to leave the area. The men toss whatever they have into the van and they drive it off into the darkness of street. Preston and Jonny are the only two men at the warehouse.

"Alright, Maddox. Now you have a choice to make and make it right for yourself."

"OK. What are these choices you have in mind for myself that would make me accept them and leave you here to continue your pathetic way?'

Jonny moved his right hand to his side, revealing a revolver under the side of his jacket. Preston noticed it and looked up at Jonny.

"You sure you want to play this little round? I told you already. You want to go that route, you'll end up dead and possibly some of your men too."

"There is no other way around all of this. Now, you can choose your choice. Either you can go ahead and leave this area and don't make a second thought or I could just shoot you on the spot and leave your body to rot."

"So, if I choose the first one, I assume I'll live. If I take the second option, you're going to put one in me. Is that how this is going here?"

"You're smarter than how you dress yourself, Marshal."

"Funny. The decisions you've just gave me are similar to the choices that you gave to that woman I suppose."

Jonny stood frozen still, having what appeared to be a confused and worried look on his face. He shook his head before staying still.

"I'm afraid I don't know what you're talking about, Marshal."

"The woman, whose body was found in the river a few weeks ago. I know you're aware of the case. Only her torso was found floating in the water. Her lower body was discovered across town at some cannibal site where they were partially eating off of it. They eat mostly the thighs and some of the calves. Other than that, they still left some over for anyone to share."

"Holy shit Holy shit! God damn it! If you knew how she behaved and how she acted, you would know deep down that she deserved it, *Instinct*!.."

"No, I don't know why. Probably will never figure out why you had her killed and fed to cannibals. But, overall, why did she deserve it? Is it because she didn't have enough federal reserve notes to pay her remaining price off?"

"She was nothing but a traitorous whore. Sneaking behind my back, working for that Ray Colby guy from Jersey since he just opened ship down here in my town. My town! That kind of shit doesn't play fair in my world of business, Maddox and you understand that don't you."

"I do. But, its none of my concern how you run your business. My concern is stopping your business and putting you in a cell or maybe six feet under."

Jonny started to shake, he held up the revolver, pointed at Preston. Preston stood still, starting at Cartel.

"You know what, I've just had enough of this! I have a plane to catch, Marshal. Big business meeting tomorrow. So, if you'll excuse me."

Jonny started walking toward the SUV. Preston stood his ground, with his right hand to his side. Jonny, still pointing the revolver, gets to the driver's seat of the SUV. Preston stared at Jonny with his hand still to his side. Jonny paused and shut the door as he started stomping toward Preston with the revolver.

"You take one step, you son of a bitch and I'm going to blow your fucking brains out all over this place, Instinct!"

"I wouldn't try that, Cartel. You wouldn't want to make a big mistake by killing a United States Marshal and ruining your world of business for a very long time to come. Even if you have a plane to catch for a supposed big business meeting. I'm sure your other clients and partners will understand what you've been through and will find a way for their business to continue in their eyes before they're caught on their own soil."

"I'll spell this out for you once and only this once. The only way I'll ever lose this business is OVER MY COLD, DECAYING, CORPSE!!!"

Preston pulled out his gun and fired shots toward Jonny in the chest a consecutive three times. Jonny slowly fell to the ground, dropping the revolver in the process. Preston walked toward Jonny, who's trying to reach for revolver while lying on the concrete pavement., Preston kicked it away from Jonny's hand. Jonny bled from his chest as his blood flowed around his body, soaking his suit.

"From the look of you on the ground holding your chest, you didn't listen to my warning, Cartel. I told you not to try anything like that."

"It doesn't matter, Marshal. Maybe I deserved to die. Maybe this is where my journey ends and all. But, soon, there will come a time where you are on the opposite end of a gunshot such as this and you'll be on the ground gasping for your breath. When the day comes that it happens, you'll know what's to come afterwards."

"I highly doubt your kind and strong prophetic words." Preston said with a smile. "But, whenever that day does arrive, I'll be in this same position and the other will be in the position that you're currently lying in."

Preston reached into his pocket, pulling out his black and silver Blackberry. He dialed 9-1-1. The phone started ringing and the 9-1-1 Operator is on the other end.

"9-1-1. Please state your immediate emergency."

"This is Preston Maddox. U.S. Marshal and secondary detective over at the New Haven Detective and Marshal Agency. I've called because I'm currently standing around the West River, close to Orange Avenue at a warehouse. I need an ambulance and a coroner right away."

"An ambulance is on its way, Marshal. Should I assist backup as well?"

"No need for that ma'am. Just the ambulance and coroner will do just fine. I appreciate it and thank you."

He hung up and placed the smartphone back into his pocket. He walked over to Jonny. He kneeled in front of him as Cartel continued to gasp for his breath.

"Don't worry, Jonny. Ambulance is on its way. They'll do what they can for your sake."

"What about the coroner? Don't think I didn't hear that part."

"That's just in case you die here. Which is the most probability."

"Just go to hell, Marshal. Go to hell and burn for the rest of your eternal days."

Jonny's head cocked over as he exhaled his last breath. Jonny died on the spot as Preston only stared at his deceased body. He nodded and walked back to his car, leaving Jonny on the ground for the ambulance to find.

In a suburban neighborhood lies many homes of which families and friends live among each other. One of the homes has its lights on and inside of the home's kitchen is a forty-year old mother washing the dishes as her sixteen-year-old daughter sat in the living room in front of a fireplace watching the TV.

"What are you watching over there?"

"Just some random show. Nothing much on tonight, so I figured I would just watch something that grabbed my interest."

"Seems to me how you're pretty quiet over there that you're either in deep of the show or your bored by it."

"It's interesting so far, mom."

The daughter turned and looked toward the door. Hearing a tapping sound coming from outside. Noticing that the room is quiet except for the TV and her mother washing the dishes. She sat up from off the couch and walked slowly close to the door to see if the sound was coming from outside. The sound started again, this time alerting the mother. She looked over and turned to her daughter, who continued to approach the door.

"What was that outside?"

"I'm not sure. Sound like its right next to the door. Do you want me to go ahead and check it out?"

"Since you're already on your feet, I suggest you could. Just be cautious. There's no telling what that sound could be. Especially in a city like this."

The sound faded away as the daughter inched closer to the door. The mother continued washing the dishes as she glanced over toward her daughter and looked at what was playing on the TV. Hearing no sound, she looked at her daughter.

"Everything alright over there? You seem to be a little nervous?"

"I'm doing fine. Just taking precautions, that's all."

The daughter placed her hand on the doorknob and slowly turned the knob. Opening the door slightly, it gives a chilling creak as she opened the door. Upon seeing nothing or no one by the door, she releases a sigh of relief. The mother walked over toward the living room, seeing her daughter looking out the door and she went back to the kitchen.

"Haley, is everything alright? What are you doing?"

"I'm-"

As she responded to her mother, a hand covered by a black glove quickly reached in from the open creak on the left side of the door. The hand snatched Haley by her jaw and held her mouth shut. She tried to release a scream to gain her mother's attention. Hearing a series of bumping sounds coming from the front, the mother dried her hands and walked out of the kitchen.

"What in the hell are you doing in here?"

She stood in a frozen state as she saw Haley fighting off the black glove. Haley trued kicking out of the door at the individual's body, but the black glove held Haley tightly and slammed her head into the wall. Her mother stood covering her mouth with tears beginning to flow from her eyes.

"Oh my god. Haley, I'm coming."

As she took a step, another black glove reached out from behind her as it appeared the individual came through the back door nearby the kitchen. The intervals entered the home, their bodies appeared to be fit, wearing all black with their faces covered with solid black masks, to where even their eyes aren't revealed. The two individuals throw Haley and her mother against the walls and begin to pummel them to the floor. Both scream for help as they're being beaten.

CHAPTER 2

Officers arrived at a suburb home in the New Haven neighborhoods. They are heading through, going back and forth in and out of the home. An ambulance and coroner arrived on the scene as well. The paramedics entered the home with a stretcher, as do the coroner. A black car pulled up and out came Preston. He walked toward a fellow officer. The officer turned and was immediately what some would call star struck.

"U.S. Marshal and fellow New Haven detective, Preston Maddox." The Officer said. "It's an honor to meet you."

"It's an honor to meet you as well. So, what's the situation here, officer?"

"We received a call from one of the neighbors that something suspicious was occurring late last night at this house. From what we know, there were two females, one adult, the other, teenager. It seems that they were both murdered."

"Just being curious here, but, how were they murdered."

"I'll show you.' the Officer said. 'Follow me."

Preston followed the officer into the home. Inside, the home looked like your typical standard suburb home. A nice leather couch in the living room with a flat-screen TV, a beautiful kitchen with nice shiny tiles on the floor. The home currently filled and surrounded with officers, coroner, and forensic scientists. Preston looked inside the kitchen, to the left and seen the adult woman lying on the tile floor with her head severed.

Preston turned and said to the officer, "So, this is the mother. Couldn't really tell from a distance."

"Yes sir, the teenager is in the laundry room. Follow me, Marshal."

They walked into the laundry room, which is on the left side of the kitchen. Preston looked inside and noticed something red leaking from the dryer. He looked over to the officer and pointed to the dryer.

"Wait. Hold on a quick second. Please do not tell me that she's in there?" He asked.

"Marshal, I'm afraid she is." the officer said.

Another officer walked in and opened the dryer. The door widely opened as an arm flopped out, covered and dripping with blood. They looked inside and see that the teenage girl was shoved into the dryer and stayed inside while it was operating, in which tossed her around and killed her in the process. Preston and the officer left the laundry room, returned outside to their cars.

They walked out of the front door as Preston turned to the officer.

"What was the relationship between the adult and teenager?"

"They were mother and daughter. It was just them in the house at the time. The mother divorced a few months back and took the daughter with her."

"Should we contact the father of the daughter regarding this incident?"

The officer turned and looked toward Preston and said, "I think its best we do that after we get the bodies out of the house."

Preston walked toward his car, but the officer called him back, he walked over to him. The officer looked at little nervous, as if he's about to ask a unusual question.

"Marshal, I have a question to ask you." The officer said enthusiastically.

"Go for it, officer"

"Why do they call you "*The Instinct*" exactly? I never understood the reason for it."

Preston smiled, rubbing his chin and turning his head, looking in another direction. He exhaled slowly before turning and looked at the officer with a mild smile.

"Look at it this way, everyone has instincts in their own sense of perception. It's what makes us do what we do. I just tend to use it all the time. If not most of the time. No hesitation in place of my career. I don't second guess, unless it's confuses the living hell out of me."

"I've always been curious of why you're called that. It must be cool to have a nickname in this line of work."

"Not exactly. From my perspective, nicknames today are now overrated. Don't have any sense of meaning to them."

"Really?" said a voice from behind Preston.

Preston turned and saw his boss, Eldon Ross, the chief commissioner of the New Haven Marshal and Detective Agency. Eldon is a man in his early fifties, wearing a button-down shirt with a nice tie and slacks. Eldon looked at Preston with a glare as he turned to the officer.

"You really believe what Preston's telling you, officer? Because if you are, that just makes you nothing but a rookie in this field."

"Well, sir, he's the Instinct." The officer said without hesitation. "I meant to say, yes sir."

"The Instinct. The only thing Preston could possibly be is a hard-headed guy who doesn't listen to the instructions he's given. Instead, he makes up his own schedule of work and does what he wants whenever he wants. Try convincing me that he's using his gut to make those decisions."

"Eldon, what have I done this time for you to arrive here like this and call me out?"

"You know what you did. So, don't play those childlike games with me, Maddox. Your little incident from last night is quickly spreading around the entire agency and somewhat across the city. This isn't going to go well for you, me, or the agency."

"Eldon, let me explain the situation to you. A few weeks ago, I gave Cartel a choice to leave New Haven or he would meet us end by my hand. After those weeks had passed, I confronted him at one of his hiding spots, smuggling drugs. We talked for a bit as I gave him a short amount of time to leave and he made his decision right there. Besides, I've been on his trail for a few months now and it was getting tiresome."

Eldon shrugged his shoulders. "Yeah right. What else you have in terms of defense? Did you plan on talking him to death?"

"It was self-defense as well." Preston said. "He pulled first, and I fired the first shot. Which was the last shot before I called the police and coroner."

Eldon looked down and around the area as he rubbed his bald head. Glancing at the officers exiting the home. He looked at Preston. "Ok, once you're back at the office, we'll discuss all of this thoroughly and we'll find some way to get through your mess. alright."

"I'll see you back at the office, Eldon." Preston said as Eldon walked away from the area.

The officer walked over to Preston and said, "Jonny Cartel? The elite crime boss, Jonny Cartel."

"What about Cartel is getting you hyped up right now?"

"So, you really shot Jonny Cartel? You killed the bastard. How did it feel accomplishing it?"

Preston stared at the officer. He showed a faint smile before walking away.

"Something just had to be done about the man. That's all I can possibly say on the matter."

Preston walked to his car, gets inside and leaves the neighborhood, going to the Agency Office.

CHAPTER 3

Preston arrived at the New Haven Marshal and Detective Agency. He walked into the front doors. Preston looked around and spotted everyone staring at him. Preston walked to the elevator and pressed the button. He stood waiting for the elevator door to open, so he can leave the lobby. One gentleman, wearing a grey suit walked by and looked at Preston. He does the same.

"Is there a problem, sir?" Preston said.

The gentleman turned his head and continued walking. Preston smiled as the elevator beeped and its door opened. He walked in and pressed the button for the third floor. The elevator door closed. He reached to the third floor and sees Eldon waiting for him in the head office. Preston walked toward the office as he passed by other detectives in their offices solving their own cases. Eldon sat behind his desk, surfing through the internet. He heard a knock on the door.

"Come on in, Preston."

Preston opened the door and walked in. "How did you know it was me that was walking through?"

"I can sense you from the elevator. Anyone can tell if you're in the building or not"

Preston smiled. "Funny. I'm sure you could. What did you need to talk to me about exactly?"

Eldon turned to Preston from the computer screen and looked at him with a gaze. Preston glanced his eyes a bit across the office.

"The reason why you're here Preston is because of the actions you took by killing Jonny Cartel. You know what you did was a big mistake?"

"Are you sure it was a mistake. Because from my point of view, the man had to be stopped one way or another."

"Well, this agency doesn't go by your point of view, it goes by its Chief's point of view. Meaning me."

"I got that well enough."

"So, because of your actions. With a lot of thought and right timing as well. I've decided that you need someone to watch what you're doing on these cases."

"Wait a minute. Just hold on a second. What exactly do you mean someone will be looking out for me? Are you implying a suggestion that I might have a partner?"

"Yes, Preston. That's exactly what I'm suggesting. Look, this is how I see it. You shot Jonny Cartel out in the open with no hesitation. So, if you were to come across someone with a similar history, you would do the same to them. If not worse."

"Of course, that's the way I do my job. Besides, Eldon, I already told you that it was self-defense. Cartel pulled out his weapon first, he also threatened to kill me. So, what else was I supposed to do."

"You could've called backup you know."

"Call backup?" Preston said. "It wasn't that big of a deal. We were the only two there after he commanded his guys to leave."

Eldon leaned back in his chair, rocking in it to relax himself and feel comfortable. "So, overall, what's the big problem about having a partner?"

"My last partner worked on both sides of the law and to make it even crazier, the guy was a snitch."

"A snitch you say. Good thing your new partner only works on one side of the law. Our side of the law and I'll also add that she's very good at what she does anyway."

"Wait. She?" Preston said with a raised voice.

"Well, of course, Preston. Your new partner is a she. There's not a problem is there?"

Eldon looked at the door and waved his hand, signaled someone to come in. The individual walked in and stood by the door, just a few inches from where Preston sat. He hasn't looked behind him yet to see his new partner.

"Preston, here's your new partner. In the flesh I should say."

"Preston smirked. "Really. Let me get a good look at her."

Preston turned and sees his new partner. He looked at her from head to toe. She had nice straight blonde hair that reached near her shoulders and she wore a pair of blue jeans with a white buttoned-down shirt and a brown leather jacket to go with it. Preston smiled at her. She showed no emotion toward him, but only gave him a significant stare. As if she had no trust in him of any measure. Preston turned back to Eldon, smirking.

"This beautiful young woman is Emily Weston. A fellow United States Marshal and Detective from Newark in the state of New Jersey."

Preston turned again. "It's a pleasure to meet you, Ms. Weston."

"Same here." Emily said. "You look different than what I've heard."

"Do tell what you've heard about me. I'm sure the tales were pleasant enough to share to everyone, meaning me, myself, and I."

"Just that your what they call an angry man whose hell bent on claiming justice and changing the ways of civilization as we know it. Using your gun as the holy grail."

Preston laughed as Eldon chucked a bit. Emily stayed quiet with only a face with no emotion of any kind. Preston stopped laughing and noticed Emily's face. Eldon gave one more chuckle before glancing at Emily.

Emily is in her late twenties and her confidence gave her the shine of a woman who stood independent, able to get the job done. She looked toward Eldon.

"I've heard quite enough information about the murders that occurred in the neighborhood last night. I was only wondering how the investigation is currently operating?"

"The investigation is currently ongoing." said Eldon. "But, since you asked about it, you and Preston can go to the neighborhood and asks some of the neighbors about anything unusual that occurred that night."

"That's interesting enough to hear."

Preston looked at them both with a grin. Thinking to himself if he should give some words toward them. As the words near his tongue, he decides otherwise not to speak them.

"Um, pardon me, Eldon, I was planning on going over to a location where I know some answers could be currently available."

"That's Great. Even a better idea I could add to that. Since you brought it up and you apparently want some company, why don't you go ahead and take Emily with you on this."

"She can't go with me on this one." Preston said while smiling. "Besides, she's a well-established novice here in New Haven and no offense to her, but, I don't play well with others when it comes to the law and my tasks."

Emily turned to Preston and stared him in the eyes like a predator inching for a bite toward its prey.

"I could say the same about myself. In Newark, I did most of my work alone and had some help in some cases. So, look Preston, unlike some of the women that you've come across and met in your days, I'm not one of them. Nor do I fit in their caliber in any way, shape, or form. I'm just a woman that gets the job done whenever I can, however I can. With or without your assistance."

"Really?" Preston said. "You're saying you're some type of new breed of female detective. I'm sure I could dig up something from your past back in Jersey that could shake you up a bit."

"Not exactly. You'll hardly find anything on me that could lead to your gloating habits."

Emily turned to Eldon and asked for the address to the murder location. Eldon gave her the file of the location. She walked out of the office. Preston stood up and watched as Emily walked to the elevator. She turned to Eldon. Eldon is smirking at Preston.

"Listen, just try to work with her Preston." Eldon said. "Just try, please."

"Sure thing, I'll try. But, I won't like it." Preston said.

Preston left the office as Eldon goes back to the computer, still smiling about Preston's attitude toward Emily. Preston is outside as Emily waited for him at his car. Preston slowly walked towards the car. He sees Emily standing by the passenger's seat. He pointed at her and the car.

"Mind if I ask where's your car?"

"I thought I'll ride with you if you don't mind me." Emily said. "Don't want to waste gas on mine. You should be alright with that I presume."

Preston looked with a glint and said, "You have a nice valid point there."

Preston took out the keys and unlocked the car. Emily sits on the passenger's side as Preston sits into the driver's seat. He started the car and they left the office, driving to the neighborhood.

"Though, I hope you're standing next to the car when I unlock it. So, that way I won't drive off without you and you can call on a cab to pick you up and drop you off."

As they drove down the streets, Emily turned and stared outside her window at all the locations around the area that they've passed by. Preston noticed and slightly turned toward her direction and watched her as she glanced the surrounding locations. Many vehicles are passing by as Preston entered onto the freeway. The number of passing and surrounding vehicles gives Emily a questioning though.

"Looking for something out there?" Preston asked. "You seem very on point looking at these places is all."

"No. I just never knew that New Haven was this crowded." Emily said. "Though it would be much smaller than what I'm currently seeing."

"We have our moments. Some days are good while the rest are bad. We get through it all. So, what brought you here to begin with?"

"Things became quiet around Newark, so I began looking for another location to work. Later, the agency began recruiting and some of the new detectives went to Newark and I was moved here."

"By the look on your face and the tone in your voice, you don't sound to happy about your transfer. Are you happy?"

"Honestly, I didn't expect to come here." Emily said. "I'm one of the best US Marshals in this country, so I believed they would send me to bigger places like New York, L.A., Miami, Las Vegas, Houston. Just somewhere big."

Preston smiled.

"Very soon, Ms. Weston, you'll realize that New Haven is bigger than it looks to be."

Emily looked. "Can't wait for that."

Currently at the New Haven Airport is Billy Bronson, a scruffy, scrawny, slim man who's wearing a flannel shirt with jeans and a denim jacket, also wearing a baseball cap. He walked towards the tunnel, seeing a lot of passengers walking in and out. He stood at the tunnel, scouted the area looking for someone. He caught someone from a distance and started straining his eyes to get a better look.

"Please let that be him." Billy said.

He finally sees the individual he's come to pick up. Billy walked over to him.

"There's my guy!"

The individual is known as Hoyt Bennett, a man in his late thirties, whose slim with bold features and hair that looked as if it's never been washed or combed. He's also wearing a long-sleeved buttoned shirt with jeans and black dress shoes. Hoyt walked over to Billy, smiling.

"Well, isn't it the great Billy Bronson. We meet once again in this crazy nonstop lifetime of ours."

"Hoyt Bennett. How long has it been, pal?"

They shook hands as Hoyt hugged Billy and patted him on the back. Billy decided to do the same. Hoyt picked up his bags as they walked through the airport.

"How have things been in New Haven since my little departure?"

"You know how this place works. The same old situation with the same old people. Sometimes, even new folks that comes across these ways."

"Billy, I'll say this. It's time to get things going since I'm back in town."

"How so? What do you have planned already?"

"In short words, Billy, it's time to blow some shit up."

Hoyt continued to smile as he started walking toward the exit doors of the airport Billy slowly followed him outside. Shaking his head in uncertainly as to what's being planned in Hoyt's head.

CHAPTER 4

Preston and Emily arrived in the neighborhood. Preston parked the car in front of a blue and white wooden house that's across the street from the murder house. They exit out of the car and walked toward the front door, going up the short steps. Preston knocked on the door. They hear someone on the other side of the door.

"Who's there." said a voice from inside.

Emily said, "The US-" Immediately, Preston cuts her off from speaking to the individual on the other side of the door.

"The US Marshal and Detective Agency."

Preston said. "We were hoping you could speak with us about the murder that occurred across from your home."

The door opened and an African American male is on the other side. He allowed Preston and Emily inside of his home to discuss the murder.

"We would just like to-" Preston said, before Emily cuts him off and smiled toward him.

"We would like to only speak with you, sir. About the incident."

"Come in." the man said.

Preston and Emily walked into the neighbor's home as the door closed. Preston glared at Emily.

"How's it feel to be on the other end?" Emily asked.

Emily walked into the living room as Preston stared at her.

"She's learning." Preston said as he walks inside behind her.

In the countryside of New Haven, Coover and Rusty Bronson, the two older brothers of Billy Bronson sit inside their small home. They are sitting around the kitchen table, counting loads of cash. Coover sniffed the cash as Rusty continued counting.

"Why are you sniffing the money?" Rusty asked. "You know how many germs and possible diseases have touch and rubbed against those dollars."

"It's a sign of good fortune, brother." Coover said. "I wouldn't give two shit loads of coke to avoid the smell of a pack of paper."

"Now, Coover, you need to make sure that no one knows what we've currently have up our sleeves." Rusty said.

"What do you mean? What's up our sleeves?"

"The plans? You remember? The plans that we're supposed to follow courtesy of our boss?" Rusty said.

"Oh, yeah. I haven't forgotten that." Coover said. "Speaking of plans, you heard about that double homicide that happened in that neighborhood area?"

"Of course. What's the big fuss about it."

"It had to be fun you know. Killing those two bitches. A mother and a daughter. It's like a double birthday gift to me."

"Yeah. You have your ways with that distorted mind of yours, little brother. Hopefully, you won't have to put it to great use when a particular time comes along."

Rusty grabbed several stacks of money and started placing half of the money into a brown leather suitcase. Coover, on the other hand, started placing some of the money in his jacket pockets.

"You can keep doing what you're doing, Coover. We need to deliver the rest of this money to the boss?" Rusty said. "He wants it as soon as possible."

"You want to deliver it now?" Coover said. "While it's still in the early hours of the day."

"Why else would we wait. Because you're too lazy to get off your ass for a change to do a proper delivery."

"I got you, brother. Lazy my ass. I can get a large amount of jobs completed whenever the situation fits perfectly."

They get up from the table and started walking towards the front door. They walk outside towards their grey F-250 truck. Rusty placed the suitcase in the back of the truck, covering it with a black sheet made of cloth. Coover opened the door and sat in the passenger's seat. Rusty walks to the side of the truck and gets into the truck and started driving down the pathway.

Back at the neighborhood, Preston and Emily continued speaking with the African American man about the double murders across the street. They are sitting in the living room. Preston and Emily on the blue couch and the neighbor sitting in a wooden chair.

Preston told the neighbor, "We're here on business, sir and because of that we would like to ask you if you've seen or heard anything about the murders that occurred last night across from you."

"Well, officer, I came home around 11:50 and went straight into bed." the Neighbor said. "Though, I did see a black van with two individuals. They were wearing black as well, from head to toe. They came from the back of the van."

"So, is that all you saw before you went to bed?" Emily asked.

"Yes ma'am. I thought they were just stopping by or playing a trick on someone. That's what it looked like to me."

"Another question, if I may." Preston said. "Did you catch the license plate on the back of the van?"

"No, sir. It was too dark for me to see." The neighbor said.

"Are you sure it was too dark, or you just didn't want to look?" Emily asked.

"Excuse me, but, are you assuming that I knew what they were up to?" The neighbor asked.

"No, I'm just assuming that you saw something unusual and you don't want us to know about it." Emily said.

"Sir, with all due respect, she's my new partner and she's new to the town." Preston said. "She hasn't learned much since being here for a short time, so, don't mind her."

Emily gave Preston a deep glare. He sat quietly and gave her a smile. She turned her attention towards the neighbor.

"I'll tell you this, officer. You should get rid of this bitch and find yourself a much more worthy partner." The neighbor said.

Emily gets up from the couch and stood over the neighbor. Preston also stood up and started tapping her on the shoulder to get her attention. Which, he does. Emily gave him another glaring look.

"What?" Emily asked him.

"Just sit back down. We're here on business." Preston said.

Emily continued to stare at Preston. He's silent as a beeping sound is heard. It's Preston's blackberry. He pulled it out of his jacket pocket and answered it. On the other side of the phone is Eldon.

"Maddox." Preston said.

"Preston, I need you and Emily to get back to the office as soon as you can." Eldon said. "We have more things to discuss."

"We'll be there." Preston said.

Preston hung up the phone and placed it back into his pocket. He looked over at the neighbor and told him that it was nice meeting him and thanked him for his cooperation. The neighbor thanked him back and they left the house and get into the car, heading back to the office.

"Where are we going?" Emily asked.

"Eldon needs us back at the office. Something's come up I suppose."

Meanwhile, at a local bar in town, Hoyt and Billy are sitting at the bar, drinking shots of whiskey. Hoyt drinks his and puts the glass down. Billy tried to drink his glass, but can't bear the taste of it. Hoyt watches him calmly as he tried drinking the glass of whiskey.

"I sense there's a problem, Billy?" Hoyt asked. "You can't take a shot of whiskey?"

"Sorry, Hoyt. It's just too strong for me." Billy said.

Hoyt looked toward the female bartender, he gets her attention and pointed to the bottle of vodka on the shelf. She grabbed the bottle and placed it in front of Hoyt.

"Please pour my good friend here a glass of this wonderful vodka you have here." Hoyt said to the bartender. "From our he's looking, he could surely use it right now."

"I'm not sure about that, Hoyt." Billy said. "Vodka isn't my type of drink."

The bartender poured the vodka into another glass and she handed it to Hoyt. He took the glass and turned to Billy. Billy glanced at him, then glanced at the glass. Hoyt smiled.

"You are a twenty-eight-year-old man that working for the local trucking company and now, your closest friend has finally made his return home. The best thing you could do right now is have a decent drink with him."

Billy looked at Hoyt and turned his attention toward the glass. He took the glass and held it up. Hoyt kept his smile as he watched Billy with the glass in hand.

"Hoyt, if it's for your hometown return and to have you here safe and sound, I guess I'll drink to that." Billy said as he drank the vodka from the glass.

Billy's facial expression changed after drinking the vodka and looked as if Billy smelled manure close to his nose after drinking. Hoyt looked at him and smirked. Hoyt's expression showed he became proud that his friend decided to have something like vodka to drink for a change. Hoyt is now happy and turned to the bartender.

"Dear sweetheart, another round, please" Hoyt said. "My friend and I are going to have some fun around here. This is what I'm talking about."

CHAPTER 5

At the city bank, Coover and Rusty parked, wearing all black with their faces covered with ski masks. Rusty gets out of the truck, while Coover stayed inside to watch the area. Rusty went ahead and walked into the bank. Once he entered the bank, seeing the people setting deposits and some even cashing their checks, Rusty started shouting in a high grumpy voice for everyone to get down. The people in the bank get down and hide under tables and around walls. Rusty is carrying a brown gym bag on his left side and a magnum gun in his right. He walks toward the counter and slams the bag onto the counter and points the gun at the banker.

"Alright, little smart boy. Start placing the money in the bag right now!" Rusty yelled. "Come on, you asshole, we don't have much time to spare with your slow packing speed."

The banker is highly afraid and started placing tons of money inside the bag. The people watched in fear. Another banker, whose hiding behind another counter, pulled out a shotgun. He placed the shotgun in gear and stood up, pointed it at Rusty. Rusty sees him and the shotgun goes off, Rusty ducked quickly to avoid the shot. Rusty ran over to the banker and shot him in the head as blood splattered across the golden-brown wall. The remaining civilians run out of the bank to avoid being shot themselves. Coover, still in the truck, sees the number of people running out of the bank. He used the door mirror to see if one of them could be Rusty.

Rusty is still inside the bank, collecting the remaining amount of money on the counter. He looked at the banker and asked him if he was done. The banker confirmed that he was finished as Rusty ran out of the bank, heading for the truck. People continue to be scattered around the entire interior and exterior of the bank. Rusty tossed the bag in the back of the truck. He turned and waved his hand toward Coover.

"Coover! Now's the time." Rusty yelled. "Load the damn thing, will you."

"Right away, brother."

He exited out of the truck, carrying a rocket launcher on his right shoulder. Coover slowly aimed the launcher toward the front of the bank and fired it. The rocket soared through the midair as it smashed itself into the bank, causing it to explode. Fire rises from the shot as they get back into the truck and drive off, leaving the bank in a sea of flames.

Preston and Emily arrived back to the agency. They walked toward Eldon's office and inside they noticed Eldon in the boardroom, speaking with a young man. The young man is wearing a red shirt with brown slacks. They walked into the boardroom and Eldon sees them.

"I see you've made it." Eldon said. "I take it there were no problems speaking with the witness."

"No problems there in that situation. So, you called. I guess there's a situation that we should know or something in that area?"

"A mighty situation. Mainly for you and your concern for New Haven. I thought you should know that your old friend is back in town." Eldon said.

"What old friend?"

"You remember that Bennett fellow, don't you?"

"Which one? The older brother or the younger brother?"

"Can't figure out which one. The two of you were friends at one point before both of you went on different paths in life."

Preston looked confused. "You mean Hoyt? Hoyt Bennett? The Hoyt that was sent to DC because of his previous actions in this town."

"Yes, apparently, Hoyt's back in town and he was last seen at the airport." Eldon said.

"What's the big deal with this Hoyt Bennett?" Emily said. "Terrible individual?"

"Hoyt is a highly-known criminal that has caused major chaos across this city. Apparently, he was caught and sent to prison in Washington D.C. But, now it seems that he's been released and he's back in town." Eldon said.

"After a while, me and Hoyt were great friends. Until I left for bigger things and he stayed and dove into obstacles that allowed himself to gain the attention of the law. After a series of events that featured banks, churches, and stores blowing up, he was arrested and sent to DC."

"So, there's no telling what he'll do next." Emily said.

"I'll visit the bar to check up." Preston told Eldon. "I have a feeling he'll be there."

"Ok. If you truly feel that's the case here."

Preston looked behind Eldon, seeing the young man. Preston pointed at him and looked toward Eldon. Eldon only glanced at Preston before centering his full attention toward him.

"While I'm at it, may I ask who's the young man over there? He looks like a kid. You're brining in kids now, Eldon?"

"He's not a kid. He's only in his early twenties. No big deal."

"Early twenties you say. To me, the boy looks like he's in his mid to late teens. You're sure you got the age correct?"

"I'm positive, Preston. Just don't bother the fellow."

Eldon turned and allowed the young man to walk forward. He walked with a sense of determination.

"Preston, Emily, this is Cody Aries. A young man who's highly trained in this field. He will be operating here from now on along with us in the agency."

"Highly trained you say?" said Preston.

"Yes sir, Marshal." Cody said toward Preston. "I'm a highly trained marksman and I've been training for years."

"Really. You're looking at the same here."

"I trained in sniper. Near and far distance from the target."

"That's an impressive feat. But, firing shots from afar is not my cup of Joe."

Emily walked forward and extended her hand to Cody. They shook hands and smiled toward one another. Emily welcomed him to the agency. Cody said it's a nice honor to meet the other marshals. Eldon walked over to Preston as Emily and Cody spoke with one another.

"So, what were you and Emily doing before you came here?" Eldon said. "If I may have the privilege of asking the two of you."

"We visited the murder neighborhood and spoke with the neighbor who lived across the street from the home." Preston said. "He spoke to us and gave some information regarding the murder victims as well as the supposed murderers."

"Ok. Get any information?" Eldon said. "On who the culprits could be?"

"Not exactly. Though, he did mention a black van with two individuals wearing black. He couldn't see any faces sense they were wearing masks. I believe ski masks for certain."

"Did you get the license plate numbers?" Eldon said. "Did he see it?"

"No. He said it was too dark for him to see." Preston said. "Only saw silhouettes of the two culprits and light reflecting off the van they got into."

"We'll be on the lookout for any black vans with two individuals." Eldon said. "Especially if they fit the size descriptions that were given to us by other neighbors in the area that spotted them."

"Sure. Speaking of looking out, it my break time." Preston said. "So, if you don't mind me."

Preston left the boardroom as Emily and Cody continued speaking with one another. Eldon prepared to leave the boardroom, but Preston walked back in. Beginning to speak to Eldon.

"Oh, one more thing while I'm standing here."

"Ok, Preston. What is it?"

Preston looked at Emily and pointed toward her. She looked at him and so does Eldon.

"Not on me or any of my own thoughts. I'll just have to say you're going to have to do something with her. From my point of view in this field, she's a bad cause."

"I would say the same about you." Emily said. "No need of going over to Eldon to talk him into releasing me from the agency."

"Very well, Watson. It was nice meeting you, Cody."

Cody waved to Preston as he left the room. Emily looked over at Eldon. He shrugged his shoulders and left the room.

"Don't mind Preston. He loves to talk bad about others before they can get a word out about himself."

Hoyt and Billy are still at the bar, though it seems that Billy is drunk from the distorted look on his face. Hoyt smiled as he sees how happy Billy appears to be from drinking the amount of alcohol.

"Billy, how are you feeling right now?" Hoyt asked. "You look like you're feeling fine."

"Better than those murder victims from last night that's for damn sure."

The word *murder* caught Hoyt's derived attention. He wanted to hear more about the murder. So, he inched closer to Billy and turned toward him, beginning to ask more questions about more details involving the murders.

"What do you mean murders?"

"I forgot to tell you while we were leaving the airport. Probably couldn't talk about it there because the TSA and other officials would've arrested both of us as suspected terrorists. But, a mother and daughter were found murdered this morning. But, the murder occurred sometime around last night0. Possibly after midnight."

"May I ask how they were murdered? There had to have been some description on the bodies."

"You sure you want to know? Because it's very graphic in nature, the two bodies. I mean completely graphic. It could make your stomach turn circles."

"Just tell me how the bodies looked, Billy."

"Ok. Fine. The mother's head was severed completely from the body and the daughter was found contorted inside an operating dryer."

"Good lord. Do they know who the murderers are? Are there any traces toward them? Any significant features of any kind?"

"Not, not as of now." Billy said. "Though, though, that Marshal agency group now have a hot female detective on the case along with that Preston guy."

"Preston? Sounds familiar to me. What's this Preston guy's last name?"

"Um… *Maddrops, Maddcocks, Maddtops.* Something along that category. Not sure on what it actually was."

"Madd? Its *Maddox.*"

Billy turned and looked at Hoyt with a confused gaze. Billy shook his head as Hoyt only stared.

"Ok? Its Maddox. So, what's the big deal about this guy anyway? Is he a cold case or a no-good asshole?"

"The big deal about him, Billy, my good friend is I know Maddox very well. We have a large past with each other and since he's still here, I've just conjured up an idea that will shake the foundation of New Haven as we know it. It will cause Maddox to go insane."

"What is it, this idea of yours that will shake up the city and that Maddox fellow?"

"I'll tell you once we leave. We can't risk the chance of someone hearing what we're talking about in this place. There's no telling what could happen if someone were to hear it."

"Well, let's leave now and you can tell me in the truck. If that's how you really feel about this situation."

Hoyt stood up from the barstool and handed the bartender a one-ounce silver eagle. She took it and looked at Hoyt.

"May I ask what this is?"

"Just a little something to remember me by sweetheart."

Hoyt blew her a kiss and gave her a wink. She smiled and walked to the back. Hoyt and Billy left the bar.

Back in the countryside of town, Coover and Rusty are at their home. They counted the money that was stolen from the bank. The money was scattered across a wooden table with a couple of dollars falling on the floor. Coover looked at Rusty with a concerned look. Rusty looked at Coover. "What's the look for?"

"Are we giving all the money to the boss?" Coover said. "Because, I would like to keep some it to buy someone equipment for our projects."

"No." Rusty said. "There's no way I'm doing that. The money in the suitcase will go to him. The money from the bank belongs to us."

"Good. That's good." Coover said. "Oh, you have any possible idea where "Little bro" might be?"

"He's probably handling something for mama." Rusty said. "She loved him the most you know."

"Yeah, she really cared a lot for him." Coover said. "What does that say about the two of us."

A knock on the door is heard and Coover goes to answer it. He opened the door and it's their boss, Ray Colby, a crime lord originally from New Jersey, wearing his black suit with a red shirt. Rusty comes from the kitchen to greet him.

"Mr. Colby, sir." Rusty said. "We didn't expect you to be here."

"I'm here for my money." Colby said. "Now, do you have it for me?"

"Yes sir, we do." Rusty said.

Rusty walked toward the kitchen and rolls out the suitcase. He opened the case for Colby, revealed to him the money inside. Colby smiled and looked at the two brothers. He patted them on their shoulders as he stood up and walked toward the front door.

"You boys are doing a fine job." Colby said. "Don't let that go to your heads or you won't be having a job."

"We try our best, boss." Coover said.

"Sure, you do." Colby said as he left their home.

CHAPTER 6

Hoyt and Billy are sitting on the outskirts of town inside of a small cabin-like house surrounding by a few trees that stood up in the backyard. The front yard is covered with small bushes and short grass. Inside the house are mounted heads of deer on the walls and stuffed bears in the corners. Billy looked at the surroundings and turned to Hoyt.

"Hoyt, what's in this place if I may ask you?"

"This place, my good friend, was one of my old hideouts we had to keep ourselves from the law in any circumstance. It's just a little something I left behind before they were carried off to D.C. Fun times this place was."

"From the look of this place, it damn sure looks as if some rough-ass hunter appeared to be living in here. No offense, Hoyt, but, you're not exactly a hunter."

"I haven't hunted in quite a long time. Though, this cabin here, it belonged to my brother Darren. I guess you could consider him a rough-ass hunter. Seeing as he was always the one going out and catch us some deer, fish, elk. Hell, even one time, he brought home a total of eight squirrels for us to eat since he couldn't find any deer to track."

"Sounds like a good brother to me."

"Speaking of him, how's he been with me being absent and such?"

"From what I understand, he's still working in the mechanic areas across town. Stays to himself as usual."

"That is my brother's way of living a peaceful life. I rather not bother him in such a time we're in."

Hoyt walked toward the kitchen area, where he noticed a small closet. He walked to the closet and pulled out a key. Billy walked around the home, looking at its details left and right. Billy walked over to where Hoyt was located.

"So, the law couldn't find you here? In this little shack."

"No, they could not. The damn officials couldn't even find a trace that lead here."

They later hear a knock on the door. Before they could turn around to see who it was, they suddenly hear a voice coming from the door.

"It seems that streak has come to an end." The voice said. "If you catch that kind of clear understanding."

Hoyt and Billy turn around, seeing Preston standing in the doorway. Hoyt looked and started smirking. Billy started to shiver as if he's afraid of Preston, due to him being a US Marshal and a homicide detective.

"Of all the people who are involved with law enforcement, there would be only one of them that could possibly find me. It's been a long time hasn't it, Preston? How come you didn't show up at the airport for my arrival or should I say, my comeback to the city?"

"Didn't know you were returning to New Haven. Could care less if you didn't."

"Funny sense of humor. You should've checked your calendar, my dear friend if you really wanted to know when it was taking place. I assumed someone like you should've had the knowledge that I would return to the city that made me famous. Due to my past experiences."

"I knew you would. Just didn't think you'll be back this soon." Preston said. "So, why is it that they let you out of prison so early? Good behavior? Good assistance with the mop up crew?"

"I did my time and they released me in the right manner." Hoyt said. "Though, it did influence me of what to do with my life once I returned to the rightful place that I call home."

"The rightful place you call home? Interesting question I have and will love to ask at this peculiar time. How did your time behind bars influence you to be more of a smart-ass rather than a dumb-ass? I figured that someone who was locked up for quite a long time would have better thinking skills rather that going back into your history to what sent you into your rightful home called a prison."

Hoyt laughed as he continued the conversation by saying, "A smart-ass. Though, that's what I am, but, I thought that I could help out with the double homicide that occurred in that neighborhood last night."

"Who told you about that?" Preston asked. "I take it you've already been around the city."

"Oh, Billy here, told me about the situation."

Preston looked over to Billy and pointed at him and looked back to Hoyt. Preston turned back to Billy. Preston smiled as Billy continued to be in fear of him.

"Billy? As in Billy Bronson? Of the Bronson Brothers?"

"Yes sir, fellow Marshal detective or whatever you're supposed to be in the law enforcement. That is who I am." Billy said with a tremble in his voice.

Preston turned back to Hoyt, who said, "He told me about it while we were having a drink at the bar earlier."

"So, that explains the smell of vodka on your breath." Preston said. "I knew you were up to something. You and alcohol don't mix very well, Hoyt."

"Neither, do you and I." Hoyt said. "Though, we were friends long ago, that is until you went off to college and I just stayed here and became a crime lord."

"And after that you were caught and sent to prison in D.C." Preston said. "Yeah, we all get the back-story here."

"Yeah, we all do." Hoyt said. "But, it would seem you're here only because you have me as a suspect involving the murder case. Otherwise, why would you be here."

"I'll put it to you this way, Hoyt." Preston said. "If I find out that you had anything to do with the double homicides or you have any information regarding them, you my friend, will be in some deep shit."

Hoyt laughed and said, "Wow, still using those same old lines from high school, I see."

"Yeah, they still come in use." Preston said.

Hoyt walked back into the kitchen, going back to the closet. He looked back at Preston.

"Now, if you'll excuse us, we have some business to conduct. So, if you please leave."

Preston smiled as he walked toward the door. He opened the door and put one foot out before telling Hoyt it was nice seeing him. Hoyt said the same to Preston as he left the home. Hoyt pulled out the key once again and finally opened the closet. Billy stands behind him, watching as Hoyt pulls out a large black leather box, roughly thirty-six to forty inches.

"Whoa. What's in that box, Hoyt?"

"The solution to our new cause. Wait till you see what's in here."

Hoyt opened the box and he sees what's inside. He began to smile as Billy walked over and looked at what's lying inside of the box. Billy turned to Hoyt in shock as he asked him, "Hey, Hoyt. Is that what I think it is?"

Hoyt pulled out the object that's laying inside the box and holds it up in his hands. Billy starts backing up to avoid being hit by the object.

"Billy, it's time that we blow some shit up." Hoyt said as he looked down at his hands, revealing a grenade launcher. Hoyt looked up toward Billy and released a great smile.

CHAPTER 7

It is now within the evening across New Haven as Preston headed out to eat at a seafood restaurant. He walked in and went up to the counter, where a waitress was waiting. He scouted the restaurant himself to find a perfect table for himself. He smiled at the waitress.

"How many, sir?" the Waitress said.

"Just one, ma'am." Preston said.

The waitress walked Preston to his table, and he gets a glass of water and orders a Shrimp Alfredo Pasta with a salad. The waitress left the table and Preston looked around the restaurant. Seeing lots of people eating in the restaurant and talking with each other, he spotted someone in the distance. He sees a woman that looks highly familiar to him and he realized that it's his ex-wife, Karen Rogers. She turned and saw him, to which he waved at her and she done the same. Preston turned again and saw his ex-wife coming toward him.

"Karen?" Preston said.

"Hi, Preston." Karen said. "It's good to see you once again."

"Same here." Preston said. "Good to see you as well."

"So, how's life been treating you?" Karen said.

"You know, good days and bad days always come and go." Preston said. "How about you and your life so far?"

"Things have been going quite well for me and my husband."

"Hopefully its going well."

Preston looked behind Karen and saw a man approaching them, wearing a smooth grey suit with black tie. He rubbed his hand over his head as he walked toward them and looked as if he knew one of them. Karen turned and noticed him. She called him over to the table. He stopped at the table, smiling as he placed his arm around Karen's shoulders. Preston looked at him.

"From the arm trick, I take it you're the husband that she just mentioned?"

"I'm Richard, Richard Rogers." he said. "You look a little familiar. Have we met at some place?"

"Not that I can think of at the top of a hat."

"This is my husband, Preston." Karen said. "Just wanted you two to finally meet one another."

"I understand. It truly is an honor to finally meet you, honestly. So, what is your occupation exactly. If you don't mind me asking. Just curious is all."

"I run a car dealership. It keeps me in the excitement mood. One day I'll own my own dealership and potentially a car manufacturing business."

"He just loves cars. He's told me how he wants to start a vintage car collection, but, doesn't have enough of the money to afford it. Though, he's getting there. Hopefully, he'll have his collection and be proud of what he's done."

"Well, hopefully, it finds a way to get there and collect all the vehicles he wishes for."

Preston looked at Richard and introduced himself to him and they shook hands. Richard tells Karen that they have to go, to which Karen said bye to Preston, he does the same as he watched them leave the restaurant.

At a 7-Eleven, Emily stopped at a gas station, refilling the gas in her white Lincoln. Once she finished pumping the gas, she walked into the station and paid the cashier. The cashier noticed Emily's badge on the side of her hip. He glanced at her before she turned toward him.

"Something wrong?" She said.

"No ma'am. I was just looking at your badge right there. So, I take it you're a cop or something?"

"US Marshal and a homicide detective."

"Two occupations with different circumstances and outcomes. Marshals are in the big leagues compared to homicide detectives."

"I suppose you could say it that way."

She paid off the gas, nodded to the cashier and walked out of the station. As she walked back to her car, she noticed a black van parked in a shadowed area across from the gas station. She entered the car and sat for a few seconds. Trying to see if anyone will come out of the van. Though, no one did as the van stayed still and she drove off the station grounds.

During the night, Coover and Rusty arrived at a warehouse in the outskirts of New Haven. They walked inside and see four sets of steel tables merged into one with over a dozen men in suits inside.

The men sitting down at the tables are crime lords and the men standing behind them are their thugs, carrying AKs and shotguns. Rusty looked around the warehouse.

"Have any of you seen Colby around here?"

"I'm right here." said Colby walking toward them from the back entrance of the warehouse.

"Colby, we need to speak with you." Rusty said.

"About what?" Colby said. "Is it something involving the money?"

"Yes sir." Coover said. "We just need to have a word with you."

Colby walked toward the end of the table and sits. He told Coover and Rusty to sit as well. They find their sets of chairs and sit as well. The other crime lords stared at them, as if why should they be here. Rusty glared at each of them and turned his attention toward Colby.

"Me and my brother here, boss, are just wondering about our extra share with your upcoming event." Rusty said. "We're just curious about the situation is all."

"The upcoming event will be announced soon." Colby said. "As for now, you two should be concerning yourselves with the Marshals. Since, they'll discover it was the two of you, who committed those murders."

Coover stood up, staring at Colby, "What do you mean the Marshals?! They've already got some suspects in line and we aren't any of them."

"Sure, you aren't, Coover." Colby said. "But, I do believe that you will be soon enough. Just make one mistake and they'll find you."

"I'm sure you heard that Hoyt Bennett is back in town." Rusty said.

"Hoyt Bennett has finally returned, so you say." Colby said. "Well, this is great. He can be a major asset in my event. That is unless he backs out somehow."

"What do you want us to do?" Rusty asked. "Find him and bring him in for you?"

"Or we could just kill him for you." Coover said. "Which ever one you prefer, boss."

"No need for that in this situation. Just concern yourselves about your own business this time around." Colby said. "I'll deal with Hoyt Bennett."

Coover and Rusty left the warehouse as Colby began speaking with the other crime lords in the room. His assistant closed the main door into the office area, other assistants closed the entire warehouse.

Preston headed back to his apartment during the late night. He gets there and realized that the door is unlocked. From his point of view, someone unlocked the door and went in. He pulled out his handgun and kicked in the door. He looked to his left and saw a woman sitting at his table. She is Italian, has beautiful black hair and seductive green eyes. She slowly drinks from a glass of wine from Preston's pantry.

"Carla." Preston said. "What the hell are you doing in my apartment?"

"Hello, Preston." Carla said. "It's been a very long time."

"Yes, it has." Preston said. "Again, what are you doing in my apartment? I don't recall handing you a key."

"Sit down and I will tell you how I came into entering your apartment."

Preston sat at the table and stared at Carla Garcia, his ex-girlfriend of six years. She stared at him as she continued drinking the wine. Preston only stared at her as she drank. Thinning to himself of why she's currently in his apartment.

"I told the complex owner that I lived in this apartment and forgot the key. So, he gave me one and that's how I ended up in your apartment. Funny stuff, huh."

"I don't find anything funny about someone receiving a key to an apartment that they don't live in or pay the bill for."

"You seem surprised, Preston." Carla said. "I kind of figured you would be. Seeing me here and all."

"What exactly did you think how I would react seeing you here." Preston said. "I wasn't expecting you, at all. Especially inside my apartment to which were you do not reside."

"You know I've always done unexpected things." Carla said. "You should remember all those times."

"I do remember those times." Preston said. "But, you would've learned not to do those things after the times. One of these days, it will get you killed."

"I'm sure I would survive it, if you were still by my side." Carla said. "Are you still on my side?"

Preston leaned in. "What exactly are you doing here, Carla?"

"Excuse me, is that the way to say hello, I'm only here to surprise you." Carla said. "Figured you would love this surprise."

Carla took out another glass and poured wine inside. She passed it to Preston, who took a sip out of the glass. As if a glass of wine would pull him out of concentration.

"How would you coming here, not surprise me." Preston said smiling. "As I told you, I don't recall you living here."

"Oh, I almost forgot. I did hear about the incident that occurred between you and Jonny Cartel and the double homicide." Carla said. "It's flowing all around the city. You're not too far from being considered a fugitive with all this on your record."

"I did what needed to be done." Preston said. "I gave him a warning and he didn't take it. So, I had to put him down. Besides, Cartel was a fugitive in his own right of action."

"Now, that's something I wouldn't expect from you, Preston." Carla said. "One day, it will come to pass that you'll be on the other side of the chase."

"I take it you never got to understand me very well, Carla." Preston said. "As a matter of fact, you've never known me very well."

"Oh, is that so." Carla said smiling. "Let me remind you of how you taught me some of your detective skills and some of your tricks. That was really our relationship. You're giving me free lessons on how to do the things of the law."

Preston smiled, "So, you're going to try to use my tricks against me? Is that the real reason why you're here? Some sort of information, you're trying to gain from me?"

"Not exactly, baby." Carla said. "Though, I can tell you that I plan to use them to my advantage when the right situation arises."

"Really." Preston said as he put his glass down on the table. "Because, I remember you always having to use your looks to your advantage to gain whatever you wanted."

"Which is why you're going to teach me the rest of your techniques." Carla said. "I believe I'll need them for whatever comes my way in the near future."

Preston stared at Carla as she does the same. Preston smiled and said, "I don't think so."

Carla put down her glass and gets up from the chair. Preston looked her, as she's wearing all red. She walked behind him and started massaging his shoulders. Preston doesn't do anything, though he's facial expressions shows that he's not liking it. She started rubbing him on his chest. He turned and looked at her.

"You know this isn't going to work." Preston said. "Don't even think it will in your little warped mind."

"Aw, it worked before remember." Carla said. "It worked all the time to be exact."

Carla sat on Preston's lap and begins kissing him. He starts kissing her back and he holds her in his arms tightly and lays her onto his bed. They continue kissing and go to the point of taking each other's clothes off. Now, they are only in their underwear as they continue kissing and she moans as Preston rubs his hand up Carla's thigh. They are both enjoying this moment as they continue to do so. Then, they go under the bed sheets.

Driving a small pickup truck is Hoyt with Billy in the passenger's seat. They drove toward a small building, appeared to be made of brick. it's a jailhouse. Hoyt stopped the truck and looked around the area. Billy stayed inside and began to worry. He looked over at Hoyt and said, "Why here? Why this place?"

"Billy, this is a small jailhouse, where only the minors are concerned to go." Hoyt said. "I figure its best just to put them out of their misery."

Hoyt gets out of the truck and walked toward the back. Hoyt opened the black box from the back and pulled out the grenade launcher. He walked in front of the truck and pointed the launcher towards the jailhouse. Billy noticed a small group of guards at the front door.

"Hoyt, you can't be serious about this!" Billy said. "Hoyt?!"

"These are the moments that create legends, Billy." Hoyt said. "Now, we will become the legends ourselves."

One of the guards noticed Hoyt and pointed at him. Hoyt aimed the launcher and yelled, "INCOMING CALL!" and fired the launcher. The grenade flew into a window and exploded the entire jailhouse. The guards inside are killed by falling debris and the building is up in flames, instantly killing anyone who was inside. Hoyt smiled.

"Hoyt, let's go!" Billy yelled. "Come on, Hoyt!"

"Step one, accomplished." Hoyt said.

Hoyt placed the launcher in the back of the truck and drove away from the scene as the jailhouse is consumed in flames. Hoyt laughed and smiled as he drove away from the area.

CHAPTER 8

Preston woke up from the night he didn't expect. He looked around and noticed that Carla is gone. He put on his clothes and searched the room and found his notes stolen. He knew that Carla took the notes from his room. The notes contained most of Preston's skills and tricks that he's used and currently using in his field of work.

"Shit." Preston said. "Goddamn. Shit."

He grabbed his keys and left for the office.

At another location, inside a mobile home, Billy sat still until he heard a knock at the door. He opened the door and its Hoyt. Hoyt walked in to discuss the recent attack on the jailhouse. Billy is still shaken up by the event and Hoyt tries to discuss the reason for blowing up the jailhouse.

"Hoyt, I just don't understand why that location." Billy said. "Of all locations that could've been chosen."

"Look, I know that it must've freaked you out from the start." Hoyt said. But, from watching that, just imagine what else we can accomplish together. By doing this, we can set boundaries across New Haven and later beyond Connecticut itself."

"I see your point there, but, I don't think I can continue going on like this." Billy said. "Who knows what could happen next. I could be arrested or even shot at."

Hoyt looked at him, "What do you mean, Billy? You're in the business of a lifetime. For God's sake, in this line of work, you get arrested, you get shot, you get stabbed. Hell, in some occasions, you get raped, molested and mutilated. Now, we don't need to deal with your feelings and emotions on this line of work."

"I'm just saying that it's difficult for me to do these things when the Marshal guy knows who I am, and I can't imagine what could happen next." Billy said. "I could go to jail or worse."

"You shouldn't worry about my old friend, Preston." Hoyt said. "That's his instinct to search and find, from all angles. It's in his blood, but, he will never get the opportunity to catch you. That is if you're on my side."

"I'm always on your side, Hoyt." Billy said. "Always."

Hoyt smiled, "That's good to know, because I'll need you for our next task at hand."

"Which is what?" Billy asked.

"I hear from a few anonymous sources that Colby and his crime lord buddies of New Haven gather together at a warehouse on the outskirts of town."

"So, how do we find the warehouse?" Billy asked. "If that's where they are exactly?"

"I already know the warehouse's location. I used to work in there." Hoyt said. "It was once used for a trucking company, until the company closed it down and moved over to China. Now, it's the place where all drug lords hang out and talk amongst each other. The perfect opportunity to get rid of the garbage that fills this city with disgust and hatred amongst its people."

"So, when do we strike and are we using the grenade launcher again?" Billy asked.

"We will be using a launcher alright." Hoyt said smiling. "We strike within the next two days. When the building is packed."

Preston walked into the office and sees Eldon, Emily, and Cody inside of his office. He walked toward the door and went inside.

"Preston, good to see you here up and early." Eldon said. "From the look of your face and body language, you look like you have a rough night."

"Kind of." Preston said. "It was a little rough and edgy for me. What's the situation today?"

"A city bank was robbed and blown to shit yesterday." Eldon said. "Later that night, a jailhouse was blown up. So, we will be going to these two locations today to get evidence and information. We'll go ahead and start with the bank first."

"Alright. Are there any suspects involved with these cases?" Preston asked. "Or am I jumping the front gun here."

"You're jumping the gun here. Though we have no ideas right now." Eldon said. "But, there is a banker who's waiting for us at the bank scene. He could give us answers."

Preston looked. "Great, I'll meet you guys there and we'll discuss everything on the sites."

They left the office and head to their cars. Preston noticed Emily's white Lincoln. She looked at him and he smiled. Cody gets into the jeep with Eldon. They all drove down the street, making a left turn towards the City Bank. Few minutes later, they arrived at the bank scene, looked at the building covered with a black charcoal appearance. They get out of their vehicles and started walking toward the bank. Eldon looked around for Preston, yet, he's nowhere to be seen.

"Where's Preston?" Eldon said.

"He's probably running late to the sites as usual." Emily said. "As always from what I hear in the office."

Cody looked to his left and saw Preston's car heading their direction. He pointed him out.

"Preston's right there." Cody said. "I think so. That's his car isn't it."

Preston arrived at the scene and noticed Eldon and Emily staring at him. He smiled at both of them as he exited out of his car. He looked again at Emily's white Lincoln. She turned to him.

"A white Lincoln, nice." Preston said. "Surprised you had the profit to purchase one."

"It gets me around." Emily said. "And I save my money unlike others who spend it on things they don't need."

"Still, it's a very nice car." Preston said. "Though, it isn't black like mine."

Eldon turned to Preston. Shook his head as Preston only grinned slightly.

"Preston. Don't start any of this bullshit while we're here on business, please. Now let's get this going on this job."

Eldon walked around the bank's locations. Cody and Emily followed him. Preston stood and smirked before he started looking around the area. They noticed all the damage caused from the explosion. Burnt brick walls, windows blown out with huge holes on circling the entire bank. Preston continued looking around the bank for clues. They were not allowed to enter the bank, due to being cleaned out by other officials across New Haven. Cody recognized the damage and approached Eldon.

"From the look of the building, only a high-powered weapon could've caused this much damage." Cody said.

"What are you getting at, Cody?" Eldon asked. "You believe that a larger weapon was used on this place?"

"Some kind of launcher, perhaps." Cody said. "From what I can tell."

Emily walked over to Eldon. "A grenade launcher? Are you sure?"

"No, he's not sure." Preston said. "It was a rocket launcher."

Eldon walked over to Preston, who's standing next to a strap on the ground with a cap. Eldon smiled and turned to Preston.

"Excellent work, Preston." Eldon said. "I have to say I'm impressed by just little work you did finding this."

"Well, you know, I just try my best." Preston said. "Besides, it was just lying there. So, it was in my inclination to point it out for you."

Eldon walked over to Cody and he followed. Eldon told Cody to put the strap into the evidence bag for further investigation and fingerprint analysis. Cody took the strap and placed it inside the bag and walked toward the jeep. Preston turned to Emily.

"I believe it's your turn now."

"Chief, what's that over there?" Emily asked.

"Well, what is it." Eldon said. "I need some description of what's your seeing."

Emily walked over to the area and discovered a wallet. She opened the wallet and noticed it belonged to a banker who worked at the bank who possibly ran out with the civilians during the robbery. Emily waved her hand toward Cody, signaling him to come over to her.

"It's a wallet." Emily said. "Appears it belonged to one of the bankers who worked here. We could check his address and phone to see if he's still alive or dead."

"Let me have a look at it." Eldon said.

Preston walked over to them, "A wallet? You sure it isn't just a notepad or something less important?"

Eldon opened the wallet and finds the information on its owner. He smiled and turned to Emily.

"Great work, Emily." Eldon said. "Impressive work you guys are doing. It must be my lucky day."

He handed the wallet to Cody, who put it inside a plastic bag and walked to the jeep with Eldon. Emily smiled and turned to Preston, who glared at her.

"What?" Preston asked. "You've come to gloat now?"

"No." Emily said. "I'm just telling you to try a little harder if you want to impress me."

Eldon and Cody get back into the jeep as Eldon told Preston and Emily that they're heading toward the jailhouse next. They left as Emily and Preston leave.

Across the street, in a neighborhood, a burgundy Nissan. Inside are two men, one Caucasian and the other of African descent. They are wearing nice suits and ties. They sit inside the Nissan as they watched Preston and Emily leave the bank scene. The Caucasian looked at the African.

"So, what are we waiting for?" The Caucasian said. "Let's just go over there and blow them all to smithereens and be done with the job."

"As much as I would love to, we can't do that. We have to wait on Ray's word."

"I don't know about you, man. But, I'm starting to wonder if Ray has no idea what he's putting his men through. Just think about it, while we're here, watching the area, the Detective Agency have those two

Marshals snooping around."

"What's your point, man?" The African asked. "You don't like what Ray has planned for them?"

"What he has planned seems to be just good and dandy. But, just think about it for a second. One of those marshals is the female from Jersey. You've heard what the guys have said about her. Telling us she's very skilled in marksmanship." the Caucasian said. "The other is that "Instincts" guy who shot Jonny Cartel not too long ago and has already cost us a lot of profit."

"You're speaking of Emily Weston and Preston Maddox. What about them makes it important for us to kill them right now?"

"I just think that Ray should look closer into this." the Caucasian said. "Just to keep a heads up on it before they come busting down his doors and taking us all to prison."

"I'll have a talk with Ray about it and see what he says." the African said. "I'll also ask him about the two marshals. From my time working with him, I know for a fact if he knows the female Marshal."

"Really. Never knew that."

"They have a long history with one another. They were the two most known people in the law area. Whenever someone talked about the law, they were both mentioned."

"That's what I'm talking about. Seems like we should be the ones to end that long feud."

"We'll wait on Ray's word to see if that will be the case."

Coover and Rusty sit inside a diner where they are having a meeting with Ray. He walked in and they sit at the table. Ray is accompanied with two bodyguards, one on his left and another on his right. He sat at the table as the bodyguards stood, guarding the area. Ray looked at Coover and Rusty.

"Glad you could make it, boys." Ray said. "It's nice to see you. So, how's everyone in your neck of the woods?"

"They're doing fine." Coover said. "Everyone's minding their own business. They have no clue to what's going on."

"No problems there, boss." Rusty said. "So, what's the situation you have for us at hand?"

"I heard about the jailhouse that was blown to pieces last night and I also heard from a reliable source that your brother, Billy was there with Hoyt Bennett."

"Seriously." Coover said. "Little young' Billy's teaming up with Hoyt now?"

"According to my knowledge, seems so." Ray said. "So, I'll let the two of you speak with your brother and find a way to tell him that he's on the wrong side of this chess board."

"We'll talk with him, boss." Rusty said. "We will. You have no worries there."

"I hope so, Rusty." Ray said. "Because, I don't want to have to kill him and later have your mother on my trails. I know for a fact what she would do if any of her sons were killed."

"You don't have to worry about our mother." Rusty said. "Once we speak with Billy and tell him about the means, he'll join our side and leave Hoyt to die alone."

"That's great to hear." Ray said. "Well, nice meeting you here."

Ray commanded his guards to leave behind him as Coover and Rusty sat at the table, plotting an idea to pull Billy away from Hoyt. They watch as Ray leaves the diner and they leave as well. Coover leaves with a mug of coffee for some odd reason.

Preston, Emily, Eldon, and Cody arrived at the jailhouse scene and see that's it much more damaged than the bank. Half of the building had completely been turned to rubble with debris covering the ground around it. Other officials are at the scene as well, including United States Marshal Darius Conway, an African-American man. Eldon walked over to him and they shake hands.

"It's good to see you again, Conway." Eldon said. "It's been a long time since you've come across the office."

"Yes sir. It has." Darius said. "Been on some business across the country and now I'm back to work here."

"So, what's the incident here?" Eldon asked. "Any leads you've gathered?"

"Well, according to one witness, they saw a truck drive up and stop in the street." Darius said. "Two men were inside, one of them got out of the truck and went to the back and pulled out a grenade launcher. He pointed it toward the building and blew the jailhouse up, killing everyone inside and the guards up front."

"Any suspects so far?" Eldon asked. "Anyone who seen the shooter and his companion?"

"None have come up yet." Darius said. "But, according to the witness I spoke with, the shooter yelled out, "Incoming Call" before he fired the launcher. So, I hope we'll receive some news very soon."

Preston looked around the area and walked over toward Eldon and Darius. Preston told Darius to excuse him and Eldon, so he could ask him about the scene.

"So, what did Darius tell you about the incident?" Preston asked.

"It seems that a grenade launcher was the cause of this." Eldon said.

"A grenade launcher?" Preston asked. "You can tell what was used on this place just by looking at it?"

"It appears so due to the amount of debris that's here." Eldon said. "First, the bank gets blown up by a rocket launcher. Now, a jailhouse is blown up by a grenade launcher. It seems that this is being done by the same individuals."

"No, not the same." Preston said. "Two different groups of individuals."

"Also, according to the witness, the shooter yelled out "*Incoming Call*" before firing." Eldon said. "You know anyone who's ever heard anyone yell that phrase out before?"

"I have." Preston said. "I have an idea who could've done this. The bank is another story."

Preston walked toward his car. Eldon looked at him and asked him where's he going. Preston told him that he's going to visit and old friend. Preston gets into his car and drove off. Emily and Cody walked toward Eldon and asked him where Preston's going. Eldon told them that's he going on break.

CHAPTER 9

Coover and Rusty drove to Billy's mobile home. They walked to the front door and knocked. The door opened and its Billy. He is surprised to see his two older brothers. He welcomed them inside. As they are inside, they notice that Hoyt is in there as well. Rusty turned to Billy.

"Billy, what's this dick doing in here?!" Rusty asked.

"I have a dick, but I'm not one." Hoyt said. "Rusty, you should ask yourself that same question. Before someone throws it back to you"

"Shut your damn mouth, Bennett." Coover said. "We already know about your deals with our brother here and we're here to tell him to turn a new leaf. Get him away from your crazy ass."

"Calling people names doesn't get you into any places anymore, Coover. So, how would the two of you have a way of taking Billy from my what I had offered him?" Hoyt asked. "You have something better in mind that what I'm offering at the moment?"

"We work for Ray Colby." Rusty said. "You remember him, don't you? The man that put you out of business after you were sent to DC."

"I surely do." Hoyt said. "The big, tall black son of a bitch that took over most of the work in this city."

"Well, how does it feel to have the knowledge of all your former employees working for him now?" Coover asked. "They left your ass high and dry and now they're working for the big man now in the big leagues."

"Overall, it feels quite refreshing, actually." Hoyt said. "Takes weight off of my shoulders from those lazy bums."

"Well, you'll have to release our brother here, since, he's coming with us to join Ray's alliance." Rusty said. "If you don't mind."

Hoyt stood up and looked in the eyes of both Coover and Rusty.

Billy sat at the counter and just watched. Coover and Rusty stared a hole through Hoyt as he just gave them a grin.

"Billy, you're leaving with us." Rusty said. "So, get off your ass and come with us."

"You heard him, Billy." Hoyt said. "Go ahead and follow your worthless brothers out of the door and ruined your chance at a better life."

Billy's jaw dropped. He didn't make a move. Not even a flinch as he was stuck between a hard place at the wrong time.

"What! Are you serious, Hoyt?!"

"Indeed I am." Hoyt said. "Go on, now."

Billy stood up from behind the counter and started walking toward his brothers. But, Hoyt held him back and pulled out a magnum. Coover and Rusty begin to back off as they watch Hoyt's hand on the gun. Billy turned to Hoyt and back to his brothers.

"You really believed I would let your brother ruin his life for the sake of tagging along with his shitty brothers. I don't think so. Billy's got a bright future with me on his side."

"Billy, if you don't leave with us, you're on your own." Rusty said. "You hear me. You're on your own if you stay with this piece of trailer park shit."

"Are you coming with us, brother?" Coover asked. "Be with your family and live big."

Billy stayed quiet and finally spoke his answer., "I'm staying on Hoyt's side. We'll take over this city with or without your help."

"Goddamn it. Fine." Rusty yelled. "But, when mother finds out about your death in the paper, you'll realize what big of a mistake you've just made."

They leave the mobile home and Billy turned to Hoyt, who's still grinning, looked at Billy and said that this city will be theirs, but, they must get rid of Ray first.

Preston drove back to the hideout, continuing his constant search for Hoyt, a moment passed by that he realized Hoyt couldn't be inside. Once Preston pushed the door opened, Hoyt and Billy were nowhere in the hideout. Preston rubbed his head as he glanced around the front.

"Damn it." Preston said. "Where would you be right now, Hoyt?"

He gets into his car and headed for another location. One he believes Hoyt could surely be. Preston decided that it's getting late and he drove back toward his apartment. Preston's cell phone ringed. He answered it.

"Hello."

"It's Eldon. We just got something on our plate and I'll like you to do the job."

"What's the job if I may ask you?"

"We need to deliver around twenty-five thousand dollars to a man named Joel Green. He lives in the suburb area."

"I'll come over to the office after I pay a visit to Hoyt's apartment."

"Very well, Preston. Just make it quick."

"I will. No need to worry there."

Preston hanged up the phone and sat it down in the cup holder as he continued to drive.

Ray and his gang walked into a fancy nightclub, which Ray owns. They walked in and spot lots of women, barely wearing clothes, dancing around the club. Ray allowed his men to enjoy themselves as he walked toward the back office. He entered the office and sees Hoyt waiting for him inside.

"What the hell are you doing here?!" Ray yelled.

"Firstly, tone down your voice and I'll explain why I'm here." Hoyt said.

Hoyt asked Ray to sit and he does. They sit right in front of one another, staring each other down. Ray started balling his fist as Hoyt smirked at him.

"What are you doing here, Hoyt?" Ray asked. "You've playing a big risk standing in my presence right now."

"Be that as it may, Colby. I'm only here to speak to you about Billy, the youngest of the Bronson brothers. I'm sure you know of him."

"Yeah, I know of him. I've already spoken to his two older

brothers to track him down for me and tell him to leave your sorry ass, so he could join my alliance and have a better chance of living."

"Well, that's why I'm here. His brothers had arrived at his home earlier and so I pushed them out. Told them that Billy is on my side and not yours. Figured it would grind your gears a little bit."

"I hope you realize the dangers you are putting that boy in with your narcissistic personality and you are most certainly bound to have him killed the second either of you make a mistake."

"Me narcissistic? Old Ray. Let's both face the facts here at this moment, we both know you're the only dickhead I see here who would be considered a narcissist. But, I am highly impressed that you're using big words. Truly a good job done there on your part."

Ray grinned. Staring into Hoyt's eyes. Piercing them with his anger. Hoyt stared back, showing a slight grin.

"I'll say this last word and you can get off your ass and leave my airspace."

Hoyt leaned in and smirked.

"Go ahead, friend. Say what you must speak so I can get out of your so-called airspace."

"The next time I see you, it doesn't matter where we are or who's around. When the day comes around, I will kill you on the spot. It might be tomorrow, it might be next week. But, it doesn't matter, because, soon you will be dead. Thanks to me."

Hoyt stood up and walked toward the door, he turned his head looking at Ray, Hoyt smiled.

"I can't wait for the day to arrive, friend. Because when it comes along, maybe the two of us will meet our end by our own hands."

Hoyt left the office as Ray sat at the desk, looking down at his pistol that was in his pocket to begin with. Ray thinks to himself that possibly, he could've just killed Hoyt right there on the spot. He later took his hand off his pistol and showed a slight smirk. To which he decided to wait for a better time and a better place to finally execute Hoyt.

Following the day after, Eldon and Cody are at the office,

discussing the wallet that was found at the bank scene. Eldon looked at all the information regarding the wallet's owner. Cody walked into the boardroom as Eldon turned toward him.

"Chief, the owner of the wallet has been found." Cody said.

"That's some great news. So, where is the fellowman?"

"He's here waiting downstairs."

"Good. Bring him in so we can get this all set and done."

"Sure thing, sir." Cody said as he leaves the office.

Eldon put down the information sheet onto the desk and sat in the corner, awaiting the presence of the wallet's owner. Preston and Emily arrived in the office and Eldon told them about the wallet as Cody walked back in.

"While I'm here, I also have the results of the strap cap from the bank scene."

"Well, any leads?" Preston asked.

"There were no traces of DNA on the strap or the cap. I take it that whoever was utilizing it had enough intelligence to know what they were doing and how to keep their fingerprints off it."

"That's a damn shame." Preston said.

Emily turned to Preston and he does the same. She gave him a smirk. He didn't appreciate it.

"What is it this time, Emily? What's the smirk for?"

"It's a damn shame, huh."

"What else could it possibly be. No trace at all. Very clever the shooter."

Emily turned to Eldon.

"What about the wallet? Have you found anything in there that could lead to some information?"

"The wallet belongs to a Richard Ward." Cody said. "He was one of the bankers who escaped the bank before it exploded. According to his documents, he is highly intelligent in physics."

"Wow. That's something." Preston said.

"So, he must've dropped the wallet as he was escaping the area." Emily said.

"Exactly." Cody said.

Eldon walked toward Cody and said, "Is he coming up here yet?"

"He's on his way, sir." Cody said. "He should actually be up here any minute now."

Preston turned to Emily and said, "Well done, Weston. Well done."

"I appreciate your answer, but, I don't really give a shit what you say." Emily said.

Eldon and Cody left the office and only Preston and Emily are inside. Preston turned to Emily and said, "Watch your mouth when you're speaking to me. You're still a rookie in this town."

"What's that supposed to mean?" Emily asked. "I'm been a US Marshal for over seven years now. So, the reality is that I'm not a rookie. No matter where I go."

Emily left the office as Preston stood at the table, watching her leave. He looked down at the information sheets and started grinning.

"She needs some work done." Preston said.

Eldon approached him with an envelope containing the twenty-five thousand dollars. Preston took it and placed it in his jacket pocket.

"You mind if I go ahead and deliver this now?"

"I suggest you do it after we have a chat with the banker. That way it's less on your plate."

"Figured you would say something of that nature."

At the warehouse, Ray is having another meeting with the crime lords of the city. He talked about how they should take out Hoyt and how many ways there are in controlling the city for their own purposes. As Ray continues speaking, one thug told him that a woman is here to see him. Ray told him to let her in and she walked in.

The room is quiet and astounded by the woman's appearance. The woman is Carla. She welcomed herself into the warehouse and Ray stood up and walked over to her.

"From your appearance, you must be Carla Garcia." Ray said. "The ex-girlfriend of the Instinct Marshal."

"You could say that." Carla said. "I'm only here to give you an offer."

"Which is?" Ray asked.

She took out a sheet and showed it to Ray. It is all of Preston's tricks and ideas regarding his position as a Marshal. Ray looked at it.

"How would this help me out?"

"Let me borrow one of your men and you'll see how it will help you in your plan." Carla said.

Ray nodded, "Very well."

He pointed toward one of his men and told him to go with Carla to work on the plans. He agreed and left the warehouse with Carla. One of the crime lords looked over at Ray, who sat back down at his seat.

"She's a fine woman, don't you think?" he asked.

"Indeed, she is." Ray said. "Hopefully, she won't let us down."

CHAPTER 10

Preston, Emily, Eldon, and Cody sit at a table inside the boardroom waiting for the banker to arrive. The banker, Richard Ward walked into the room. He sat at the table, in front of Eldon. Eldon shook his hand and began asking questions regarding the robbery incident at the bank.

"Mr. Ward, if I may ask, what did you see at the bank during the incident?" Eldon asked.

"Well, I saw what appeared to be a male, who was dressed in all black. Wearing a ski mask." Ward said. "He was also carrying a brown bag to put the money in and he also carried a gun also."

"What else did you witness?" Emily asked.

"Well, I also witnessed when he walked up to the counter and slammed the back onto it." Ward said. "He, later, began to point the gun towards the banker, while yelling at him to place the money inside the bag."

Eldon looked at him.

"Is that all you saw during the event?"

"Well, not exactly." Ward said.

Cody leaned in.

"Can you please give us more information on the case. If you can."

"Well, as the banker was filling up the bag, the guy made everyone crouched to the ground, threatening to shoot them on the spot." Ward said. "As he was doing that, another banker reached under another counter and pulled out a shotgun. He raised it up and started blasting it towards the guy. He ducked the shots and killed the banker by shooting him directly in the forehead."

"So, you're telling us that while all this was transpiring, the individual killed a banker inside?" Eldon asked.

"Well, yes. He did" Ward said.

Preston looked over to Eldon and to Cody. He later looked over at Emily, who's listening to Ward. Preston leaned in and looked at Ward.

"Excuse me, Mr. Ward." Preston said. "But, can you do all of us a favor and stop using the word, "well". You're toning it out."

"Well, I apologize, but that's the way I speak." Ward said calmly.

"Preston, don't worry about his vocabulary right now." Eldon said. "Focus on the important things here at the moment."

"It's not the mission at hand. Is that all the information you have for us, Mr. Ward?"

"Well, yes sir it is." Ward said.

"Thank you for your cooperation and you may now leave." Eldon said.

Ward stood up from the chair and Cody handed him his wallet. He thanked them and left the office. Preston looked over at Eldon.

"You can't tell me the guy wasn't annoying."

"He was annoying." Cody said. "Very much, so."

"True, he was annoying." Eldon said. "But, he did give us information that we can use to find out who exactly pulled this stunt off."

"Of course." Cody said. "But, I have to agree with Preston on one particular thing. I just don't understand why Mr. Ward kept saying "well" before every sentence."

Preston smiled, "Tell me about it. Sounds like it's his favorite word to begin every sentence with."

"Enough about Ward's way of speech." Eldon said.

Eldon looked over at his clock and saw it was noon. He told them that they can go on break. Preston said he'll go ahead and deliver the money and afterwards he's going to visit a bar to search for Hoyt. Emily decided to go with him. Eldon allowed it as Cody decided to stay at the office and continued finishing up some research.

Carla and Ray's henchman arrive at a small diner across town and they speak about the plan.

"First off, tell me your name." Carla said. "Since, Ray didn't tell me while we were at the warehouse."

"My name's John." He said. "John Elroy."

"Well, John, are you sure you're qualified to do this task for me and for your boss?" Carla asked.

"Lady, I'm Ray's most valuable asset in his alliance." John said. "Anything that he can do, I can do. So, show me the plan."

"Sure." Carla said.

She pulled out the sheet and showed it to John. He looked at the sheet. Glancing and plotting out the sheet's plan. He squinted his eyes and looked at Carla. Carla looked at him and noticed he was slightly confused by what he saw on the sheet.

"Correct me if I'm making a mistake here. These skills and techniques look like they belong to a United States Marshal or something?" John asked.

"Indeed, they do. That's because I took them from Preston Maddox. I'm sure you heard of him in different discussions."

"This sheet belongs to the Instinct Marshal? Wait a minute, you sure you want to bring him into this? I mean, come on, Carla. You've stolen a very important item from one of the most targeted marshals in all of Connecticut."

"No need to worry of him." Carla said. "Me and him have a long history."

"How long a history?" John asked.

"Our history is long enough that we've shared a bed for years." Carla said. "So, no worries when it comes to Maddox or any of his ways of persuasion. Neither should you worry about his marshal friends."

"Oh." John said. "I need not ask any more questions regarding your history with the Marshal."

Carla goes over the plans with John as they discuss the pros and cons of the situations and begin plotting points to start with.

Arriving at a car dealership, Karen visited her husband, Richard. She walked in and sees him speaking with a customer that is screaming about wanting a eight-powered Mustang. She walked over to him and tapped him on the shoulder. He turned and smiled as he saw her. They hugged, as he commanded one of his employees to handle to loud-mouth customer.

"What are you doing here, Karen?" Richard asked. "I thought you were at work at this time of the day."

"An early lunch break brought me here. I was just curious about what's been going on around here." Karen said. "I just wanted to see how things worked is all."

"Curious about what?" Richard asked. "What have you been hearing?"

"Nothing." Karen said. "I just wanted to see you, that's all."

Richard smiled and hugged Karen. He told her to go back to her workplace and everything is fine. She agreed and left the building. Richard continued his work at the dealership.

Preston and Emily arrived at the home of Joel Green. They approached the front door and Preston knocked. The door opened, and a young man stood on the other side.

"Hello. What do I offer this pleasure?"

"I'm Preston Maddox and this is Emily Weston. We're United States Marshals and homicide detectives. We're here to meet a Mr. Joel Green. Is he here at the moment?"

"Um. No sir, he isn't. I'm watching the house for him while he's out of state. Is there something you're supposed to deliver to him? I could take it off your hands until he comes back."

"That won't be necessary, sir." Emily said. "We'll just return when Mr. Green makes it back in town."

"Are you sure about that, ma'am. Please, I can do a good service here."

Preston turned to Emily and shook his head. Emily only stared.

"This man is not Joel Green."

"Exactly. So, we'll return when he gets back."

"Point taken."

Preston turned to the man at the door.

"We'll just take it back to the office and await Mr. Green's return."

"The hell you will."

The man pulled out a Glock and pointed it toward Preston. Emily went to reach for her Glock and the man spotted her hand inching down to her side.

"I hope you placing your hand on your side to make a pose instead of reaching for that weapon of yours."

Preston held his hands up as Emily slowly raised hers above her head. She glanced over at Preston. He shook his head in confusion.

"Now, the two of you, inside now."

"Excuse me." Preston said. "We don't know what's in there."

"Just get in the goddamn house Right now!"

Preston and Emily slowly walked into the home. Seeing its neatly designed features. Preston turned his head toward the man.

"I hope we don't have to destroy this fine place all for the sake of a delivery."

"Give me whatever it is that you've come over to deliver."

"I don't think that will be necessary, sir."

"Give me the goddamn delivery. Before I shoot one of you in the forehead and leave you here to rot."

Preston reached into his jacket pocket and pulled out the envelope. The man extended his hand for the envelope. Preston handed it to him as Emily turned toward Preston with a confused look on her face as if she's about to yell.

"Preston. What the hell are you doing?" Emily said.

"Just shut your damn mouth, whore. This is between the men in the house. Women aren't allowed to speak until they are given the proper say so."

"So, are we all on the same page or what?" Preston said. "Just being the curious fellow here."

"Yeah, we are. Turn around and face the front door while I check this out."

Preston and Emily turned and faced the front door as the man opened the envelope and seen the amount of dollars that were stacked inside. He pulled them out and held them. He sniffed them and rubbed them on his face.

"I forgot how great new dollar bills smelled. They smell like the new season of a new year. This is amazing to me and you guys just don't get it."

"That's great and all. But, can we go now?" Preston said.

"No, you can't. Not until I've counted all of this. Damn this is a lot of bills. So, how much was this supposed to be anyway, Marshals?"

"Twenty-five thousand." Emily said. "I believe."

"You're shitting me right now. Twenty-five thousand dollars this is? Wow, what a load."

As the man screamed and hollered about the money, Preston and Emily looked at each other. Both conjuring up a plan of their own.

"I can't deal with this." Preston said. "How about yourself?"

"Let's just get this over with so we can continue our previous work."

The man began to kiss the pack of dollar bills when Preston turned around and reached for his gun. He raised it up and fired a shot to the man's heart. The man paused and held his chest as he fell to the ground. Preston and Emily walked over toward him and looked down at him on the floor. He began coughing as he tried to catch his breath.

"The least you could've done is let me keep the cash."

"I don't believe the dead use cash I'm afraid." Preston said.

Preston gathered up the money and placed it back into the envelope. Placing it into his jacket pocket. He and Emily leave the house as the man laid on the floor bleeding to death.

CHAPTER 11

Preston and Emily arrive at the bar and they sit down at the bar itself. They both order a glass of water. They start having a conversation regarding New Haven and each other's lives. The bar was halfway full of customers going in and out.

"I have a quick question." Preston said. "Why did you want to come along with me? Thought, you didn't want to even speak with me. Let alone work alongside me."

Emily smiled and said, "I know I'm new to this town and that you're a pain in the ass. But, since Eldon paired us together. We are partners and we must work together on any case that comes along our way."

"You're right about that." Preston said. "Solving cases to save many lives as we possibly can."

"All of us at least try to accomplish that from time to time. Some succeed and some fail. Depends on how the job was done."

"If they were assigned the correct case to solve instead of picking and choosing what kind of case favored them."

"There's truth in that. I've worked with some who've done that before and it didn't turn out well for the victim nor the detective. But, not getting too much into your personal life. From the information that travels through the agency, I heard that you were once married."

Preston smirked and drank from his glass. He looked at Emily and then smiled.

"Eldon told you, didn't he?" Preston asked. "Can't keep that to himself."

"Yeah." Emily said smiling. "He told me that she filed for divorce and left you. Because of your anger."

"My anger they say? I can believe that to a certain extent, since, everyone believes that I have anger issues. Which I don't. I try to be as nice and polite as I can with everyone. Some take it and some don't. That's one reason why I put my job first in my life. I would guess the anger comes from whatever case I may be on or what fugitive I'm chasing during the time frame."

"That makes sense to me." Emily said as she drank her glass of water. "I've had similar ways back in Newark."

"Similar ways as in being angry most of the time."

"You could say that. There was one time where I was pursuing a sexual abuser and it came to the point that we found him raping an innocent woman. The image drove me insane and I pummeled the guy."

"You pummeled a guy? With those soft bare hands?"

"I'm sure you know how much strength you can gain with you're in a complete rage."

Preston puts his glass down and asked, "Enough about our anger and rage. Back to what you brought up about my previous marriage. What about you? Your little life story?"

"Basically, I'm not the relationship-type of woman." Emily said. "I had one boyfriend while I was in college and that went straight to shit in a heartbeat."

"By your independent attitude, I take it was you." Preston said.

"Not really." Emily said. "I discovered that was cheating on me with my roommate. Something, huh."

"I've heard that kind of story numerous amounts in my day." Preston said. "I've had friends with the same issue and never understood what they did or what they caused."

"Haven't we all been friends with people like that." Emily said smiling. "So, what's this "Instinct" thing that people say about you. I've been hearing it a lot lately and every time someone mentions it, they get uncomfortable."

"I don't know what the hell it is myself." Preston said. "I'm guessing that they mean how I react to my instincts and I follow them. Without hesitation. I just believe it's something the agency created to cause a stir in the field and to scare the fugitives and such."

"So, you just go in with your first instinct?" Emily asked.

"Pretty much." Preston said smiling. "The funny thing about it is my first instinct is always the right one. Never been wrong before and probably never will."

The sound of the bar door opening alarmed the entire establishment. Hoyt an Billy entered the bar and see Preston and Emily talking further down on the counter.

"Billy, look who's here."

"Shit. Why don't we go to another bar. There's one further down the street and it's probably not crowded."

"We're staying and we're sitting over there with them. Just for the sake of fun."

They're approaching both Preston and Emily. Preston had finally found Hoyt. Hoyt walked over to Preston and Billy has entered the bar.

"We meet again, eh' Preston." Hoyt said.

"I could say the same thing." Preston said. "Though, you've already said it. So, no point in saying it."

Hoyt smiled, "Funny. Still with the jokes I see."

"I have to add a little humor every now and then." Preston said. "I've been looking for you by the way."

"Really? You have? So, what is it that I have done this time to bring you onto my coat tails?"

"You heard about the jailhouse incident that took place. From what we received from the witness is that the shooter yelled out, "Incoming Call" and took the shot. Reason being, I only know one man in New Haven who would yell that phrase out before exploding something and the man I'm referring to is you."

"Alright. I'll come out with this one and I know Billy won't be too pleased about this. It was me. Me and Billy to be exact. It was our first task in changing the foundation of this city. Something you don't have the balls to do."

Billy jumped up from the stool and his jaw dropped as he looked at Hoyt. Billy shrugged his shoulders and shook his head.

"What the hell is your problem, Hoyt. You're giving away plot information and details."

"You want to test it out?" Preston said. "Go ahead and try it."

Hoyt looked over Preston's shoulder and sees Emily. He walked toward her and leaned on the bar to the right, staring straight into her face.

"So, who is this beautiful young lady, Preston?" Hoyt asked. "Because, she surely isn't Karen or Carla. From my perspective, she looks better than the two of them combined. If that was possible, we would have ourselves a Old West-style stand-off."

"She is Emily Weston, my new partner on the job." Preston said. "I wouldn't take her too kindly."

"It's a pleasure to meet someone of your stature, Ms. Weston." Hoyt said. "I'm sure you've done your homework and now know who I am and what I've done in this city's history. Plus, what I'm capable of doing if I'm pushed to the proper stage of behavior."

"I know as much about you that I need to know. The infamous, Hoyt Bennett. The man who caused trouble across this city and throughout the state. The one who just got released from prison in D.C. Ready to go back in your little cell over there?"

"I'll tell you one thing, sweetheart. Hoyt Bennett will never go back to DC's super max prison. The reason is simple, I'm not doing anything that's against the law." Hoyt said.

"Number one, if we're going to be speaking with each other. Don't call me sweetheart." Emily said. "You shouldn't test your luck with me."

"Oh my. You don't want me to call you sweetheart? May I ask why you prefer not? Does it make you feel good or bad about yourself in a physical mindset? Not that I care anyways about your mindset."

Preston tapped Hoyt on the shoulder and he turned toward him. Preston wasn't playing around as his face became serious as it was when he shot Cartel. Hoyt knew Preston was serious and decided to play along with him. Testing his buttons, it would seem.

"Why are you here at this time?" Preston asked. "Specifically, I might add."

"Me and Billy would always come to this place for a drink. It relaxes and sooths our bodies of what the world has done to us. In simple terms, it places us from the world and the world from us."

"It's only twelve twenty-five. Past noon." Preston said. "I knew you were a crazy man, but I don't recall you drinking alcohol at this hour."

"The timeframe doesn't matter, Preston. Funny how you said that about me but left yourself out of the picture frame. Try to remember the way you used to drink, you know that more well than us. I look at it this way and see if you can understand where I'm coming from. As long as we can drink and be separate from the world, we're doing just fine."

Hoyt turned to Billy and asked him what drink would he like. Billy, in a problematic mood said he wanted a glass of water. Hoyt looked at him and told him to order a beer and Billy decided on doing so. Billy started to shiver because he's about to drink a beer in the presence of two marshals. Hoyt sat in the seat next to Emily. He glazed at her and smiled.

"Don't mind me of where I sit. So, since you're new to this city? How has it treated you? If you don't mind me getting into that part of your life."

"Just to shut you up, I'll tell you a slight of detail. The city has treated me well. Just came in a few days ago and no problems have I had to deal with that arose from this place. Until, you popped up of course."

"Well, let me ask you this since we're on your traveling and living subject. Where do you live previously before you arrived here?"

"Excuse me, well-established fugitive and pyrotechnic. I'm not telling you where I once stayed. If you want to talk, we'll focus on the here and now. Nothing to do with the past or what happened in the past."

Hoyt leaned in toward Emily's face, getting into her personal space, causing Emily to feel highly uncomfortable and to back away from him.

"You will." Hoyt said with a straight face.

Preston stepped behind Hoyt. He looked over his left shoulder, smiling.

"I see you're watching her back." Hoyt said.

"Of course. She's my partner. Though, she can handle herself." Preston said. "But, when it comes to someone I know, a man especially, they should have some respect for women. Hoyt, last time I checked, you were already heading into some trouble with a certain group of women. May I say, prostitutes, or do you prefer hoes. Your choice."

"Preston, why have only one when you can have them all." Hoyt said. "That's the grand prize."

Billy started laughing and Preston turned to him. Once, Billy saw Preston looking at him, he placed his head down and was quiet. Preston turned back to Hoyt.

"That sounds like me when I was twenty-two." Preston said. "I'll just say this right now, Hoyt. Originally, when the double homicide occurred, I thought you had a hand in it."

"How would I have had a hand in it when I was in D.C. at the time?" Hoyt said. "Answer that for me, Preston."

"Because the murders were so unusual and strange that, since, everything unusual in this town always has a track record that somehow reverts toward you." Preston said. "Though, you were in D.C. before the incident, I thought that some of your drug lords that stayed behind might have heard from your word to cause those two murders."

"Preston, I'm afraid that my men have all gone to work for Ray Colby." Hoyt said. "I would assume a man of your stature would've had the knowledge of knowing that."

"Ray Colby, the elite crime lord?" Emily asked. "I know of Colby. We go way back during my days in Jersey. He's here?"

"Yeah, he's been in town for a few months now." Preston said. "Planning and plotting as he comes. He hasn't started anything yet that we know of."

"Speaking of Colby, Billy and I have a master plan that will soon come to light." Hoyt said.

"What are you talking about?" Preston asked.

"Soon, you will begin hearing about certain events that are occurring around the city and when the time's right, you'll see the demise of Ray Colby." Hoyt said. "It's just around the horizon."

"Hoyt!" Billy said. "You have to stop telling people about the plans! It will only make the operations worse to go by!"

"You're not doing anything, Hoyt." Preston said. "Don't even try to do anything."

"Or what?" Hoyt said. "Or what, Preston? It seems that someone's lost in shadows as to what's about to happen. Before me and Billy leave, I'll give you this only warning."

"Go ahead." Preston said. "Warn me. Give me the warning."

Hoyt smiled, "If I catch you, your sexy partner, or any of your friends from the agency, I will kill them all and that's a promise."

Hoyt told Billy that they're leaving and they leave. Preston stared him down as he leaves. Emily turned to Preston.

"What are we going to do about him?"

"Nothing." Preston said. "He'll lead us to the events."

Preston and Emily left the bar, but, on the outside are Ray's two henchman.

They are waiting in their burgundy car on a street corner. They are watching them going to their cars. The Caucasian looked and pointed.

"That's him!" the Caucasian said. "That's the "Instinct" guy."

"I see." the African said. "I'll call Ray and see what he wants us to do."

The African pulled out his cell phone and called Ray. Ray's assistant answers on the other end.

"Hey, is Ray there? Put him on for me."

"That's the female Marshal too." the Caucasian said. "She looks good as they say."

"Yes, Ray." the African said on the phone. "Sorry to bother you, but, do you remember that "Instinct" Marshal? Well, he's here at the bar. I don't know, he must be tracking Hoyt too. That's exactly what I was thinking, sir. Alright."

He ended the call as the Caucasian looked over. Waiting for an answer.

"Well?" the Caucasian asked. "What did he say?"

"Once we take out Hoyt, we'll take out the Marshal as well."

"What about the cute female Marshal?" "We go ahead and kill her too? Just wanted to bring these things up before we had to do the tasks ourselves. Imagine what would happen if we killed them and we go back to the boss and he wanted them alive. We would be in deep trouble."

"Which is why you're not in charge nor in my position."

The African turned with an emotionless look on his face away from the Caucasian. The Caucasian kept his gaze on him.

"So, back to the previous question. Do we kill the female Marshal, or do we leave her alone?"

"What do you think. Of course, we'll kill her too."

CHAPTER 12

Carla and John returned to Ray's warehouse to speak with him, regarding the plans. Ray is already inside, sitting in the same seat. Carla sat in front of Ray as John stood behind her.

"So, how did the talk go about?" Ray asked.

"Your man, John here, will be a very good asset in this plan." Carla said. "So, when do you want to start?"

"We can start as soon as you see fit." Ray said. "It's all on you, Ms. Garcia."

Carla smiled, "Well, it's good to get this going and don't worry, everything will go as smoothly as possible."

She left the warehouse when Ray spoke with John concerning her.

"How was she during the conversations?" Ray asked. "What did she bring up?"

"She's highly intelligent, boss." John said. "She knows what she's doing. Exactly what she's doing."

"That's great." Ray said. "That's very great. At least we know she's on our side for this battle and not that piece of shit fuck head, Hoyt Bennett."

Coover and Rusty returned to Billy's mobile home to give him one more chance to join Ray's alliance. They knocked on the door and Billy opened. Rusty is upset as he tried to convince his younger brother to join the alliance. Billy declined and said he's sticking with Hoyt and that they will rule over the city. Rusty walked away as Coover tried to be the oldest and convince his brother to join. Billy declined again and Coover wished him luck on his choice and walked away with Rusty. Billy closed the door and from behind, Hoyt is sitting on his couch.

"I see you declined both your brothers, Billy." Hoyt said. "Impressive skill. you're finally learning."

"I'm trying to stand on my own and make my own choices." Billy said. "I've always followed my brothers since we were kids. I never was granted attention or had any appreciation for the things I've done. Now, it seems with me on your team, I can make something of myself."

"You will make something of yourself on my side." Hoyt said. "If you were to join Ray, you'll only be his pawn. Just like your two older brothers. Apparently, they like to be sheep because they only follow, since they can't lead."

Preston and Emily come back to the office, where they told Eldon about Hoyt's upcoming events that will lead to a breath-shaking disaster across the city. Eldon decided to put the entire agency on high alert for any of these events.

"What took you two so long to return?" Eldon asked Preston and Emily.

"We had a long conversation." Preston said. "Nothing much really."

Cody walked over and said, "You guys were gone for quite a while. I was starting to wonder."

Preston turned to Eldon and said, "We saw Hoyt at the bar."

"What did he say?" Eldon asked. "Did he mention anything related to the murders or to the jailhouse attack?"

"He did say that the jailhouse attack was him." Preston said. "Him and Billy Bronson."

"Billy Bronson?" Eldon said. "Never would expect him to do something like that. His brothers though, you can definitely expect that from them."

Preston later said, "He also said that he has something planned for the city and I'm here to tell you that we must do something about it."

Afterwards, Darius arrived inside the area to speak with Eldon, regarding the double homicide. Eldon turned and walked toward him.

"Sorry to disturb you, Chief." Darius said. "But, we've finally found out who was the culprit in the double homicide."

"Who is it?" Eldon asked.

"From what we've covered up. The DNA matches both Coover and Rusty Bronson." Darius said. "We found both of their fingerprints on the kitchen stove and the dryer handle."

"Finally, we know who to look for." Eldon said. "I'll tell my two marshals to go on the search for them."

Eldon walked over to Preston and Emily and told them to search for Coover and Rusty. Preston said he knew exactly who they were, saying they all went to the same high school. Eldon told them that he and Cody are going on a search for Hoyt's plans as they look for the Bronson brothers.

"So, where do we find these Bronson brothers?" Emily asked.

"We'll head to their mother's home." Preston said. "She might know exactly where they'll be."

"You know her?" Emily asked.

"Just like her sons, we have a long history." Preston said.

Preston and Emily headed out to speak with the Bronson brothers' mother. Eldon and Cody left the office, going out to search for clues of Hoyt's plans. Eldon and Cody talked with each other about possible clues that they could find around the city.

"What are we looking for exactly?" Cody asked.

"Any areas that may have significant clues regarding Hoyt."

"So, where are we headed?"

"We'll head to the Westside. Search the areas around those spots." Eldon said. "It might give us some ideas."

Carla and John parked in front of the Marshal Agency, sitting inside a red corvette. John sits in the driver's seat as Carla sat in the passenger's seat. John is starting to become impatient for waiting and turned to Carla.

"May I ask why we're just waiting here, Carla?"

"Just be patient, John." Carla said. "This is only a part of the plan.

Just relax. For my sake."

"Alright now." John said. "So, what are we doing here? You just saw the Marshal and his partner leave, so why are we here when we should be following them?"

"Because, eventually, he'll have to come back." Carla said. "Then, once he does, you'll take him out. For your alliance and for your own good."

Preston and Emily entered the New Haven County on the south-central side of Connecticut. They turned corners and Preston recognized a house on the right corner. He drove towards that direction. Emily looked around at the homes and noticed Preston heading towards a specific house.

"Do you see the house?" Emily asked.

"I do." Preston said. "It's right here. Still looks the same too."

Preston drove into the driveway and parked the car. They exit the car and walked towards the front door. Before, they get to the door, it opened and it's the Bronson brothers' mother. Barbette Bronson. She walked out and looked at both Preston and Emily.

"Oh my." Barbette said. "Is that who I think it is standing before me today."

"Yes, ma'am. It's me in the flesh."

"The well-known Preston Maddox." Barbette said. "It's been a long time since we've seen you in this neck of the woods. Around ten to fifteen years at least."

"You're correct, Ms. Bronson." Preston said. "It's been a long time indeed for most of us."

Emily walked over and shook Barbette's hand as she looked at her.

"Preston, who is this lovely young lady?" Barbette asked. "You never spread the word about you having a lady on your arm again."

"This is Emily Weston." Preston said. "She is my partner in the Marshal and Detective Service."

"Great." Barbette said. "It's nice to see there's a woman in a man's position and doing the job even better too."

"Don't start on that, please." Preston said.

"Thank you, ma'am." Emily said. "I do what I can to help."

Barbette allowed them inside the house and they walk in. Preston sees that the house hasn't changed a bit from when he was just a small child. The inside is still the same with an old couch and wooden walls.

"This place really hasn't changed." Preston said. "You must've loved the way it looked."

"I'm not going to change anything here, just to fit in with this new society we have." Barbette said. "I'm old school and I intend on staying that way."

"However you feel, Ms. Barbette." Preston said.

"You could just call me, Barb, Preston." Barbette said. "You've known me since you were a child. So, don't bother with calling me Ms. Barbette or Ms. Bronson."

Preston smiled.

"So, Barb. We're here on business to ask of your sons. The two older ones exactly, Coover and Rusty."

"What about Coover and Rusty?" Barbette said. "What kind of trouble have they caused this time?"

"They're the suspects of a double homicide." Preston said. "I'm sure you've seen it on the news. CNN had it on not too long ago. MSNBC on the other hand tried to make a joke out of it."

"I heard about the murders that transpired in that neighborhood." Barbette said. "It's very sad. Though, I wouldn't expect my sons to be the culprits. They wouldn't do such a thing."

"I believe The President made a speech about it not too long ago." Preston said. "Not really sure, but, I'll check and see once I get back to the office."

"Well, for one I didn't vote for him." Barbette said. "Do you know where they are right now?"

"No ma'am, we don't." Emily said. "That's why we're here in your presence to ask you if you've seen or heard from them since."

"Last I heard, Rusty said, that he and Coover were headed over to Billy's home to convince him of teaming with that Ray Colby fellow."

"So, your two older sons, they're working with Colby?" Emily asked.

"It would appear so I guess." Barbette said. "They wouldn't be speaking of him unless they were."

"We saw Billy earlier at the bar with Hoyt Bennett." Preston said.

"Hoyt?" Barbette said. "Hoyt Bennett you say? That no-good son of a bitch who nearly drove this county and the city into hell with his actions. Billy should know better. That's probably the reason why Coover and Rusty went to visit him. Though, he always wanted to go on his own, but, he would never listen to anyone."

"It seems he's listening to Hoyt." Preston said. "So, what do you want us to do about your boys?"

"Do what you will with Coover and Rusty." Barbette said. "I'll take care of Billy. Show him the right way of living his life. Instead of working with that no-good bastard."

"Do what you have to do Ms. Barb." Preston said. "Well, it's time that we leave and head back to the office."

Preston and Emily left the house, returning to the office. Barbette went back into the house. She looked toward the back of the home and the back door creaked open Coover and Rusty walked in from the back and notice their mother's expression on her face. Coover whispered to Rusty, saying their mother looked pissed. Rusty looked and shrugged his shoulders. They began staggering as she stared deeply at them.

"When the hell were you going to tell me that you murdered two people?" Barbette asked. "When were you two going to tell me?!"

"Mama, we were going to tell you about it." Coover said. "But, we didn't know the right time to tell you is all."

"When?! When the fuck were you were going to tell me about it?!" Barbette yelled. "I need an answer right this minute!"

"We were going to, but, we wanted to have Billy on our side before going along with it." Rusty said. "That's all, mama."

Barbette stared and said, "It seems that the two of you are being hunted down by the marshals and since I saved your asses this time, you better give me something in return."

"Like what?" Coover asked.

"Either you speak with Billy one more time or I will." Barbette said.

She walked toward the back of the house as Coover and Rusty leave through the front. She murmured to herself about his sons as they glanced back. Rusty tugged Coover's sleeve as the left the home.

Carla and John continue to wait outside. The two are still awaiting Preston's return to the office and now John is out of patience. He gets upset and leaves the car. Carla followed him and said to him that plans have changed. He looked at her as she tells him to go inside and wait for Preston to return on the upper floor and that she'll go in with him to distract the other officials. He agreed, and they walked in. As soon as they go inside, Eldon and Cody returned. They have no clues or information regarding Hoyt's upcoming plans.

"We couldn't find a damn thing." Eldon said. "Not one trace whatsoever at all."

"Something will come up eventually." Cody said. "I'm sure of it."

"Yeah." Eldon said. "Hopefully, Preston and Emily have something for us to follow."

They walked inside and have no idea what's about to happen in the office. Inside the office, Carla is distracting the officials as John headed to the elevator. He held the door opened as he signaled Carla to join him. She told him that she'll find her own way. He stayed inside as the door closed on the elevator, as he's heading toward the third floor. He arrived on the third floor and no one pays any attention toward him. He reached his side for his handgun, not pulling it out, but, his hand in position to do so.

Hoyt arrived at a location across town and walked into the small building nearby. He opened the door and turned on the lights. The building, he could tell it was used as a former pawn shop before it went out of business. The building is now for sale and Hoyt is highly looking into it. Someone else comes through the door and it's the owner of the building.

"Who in the hell are you and What the hell are you doing here?" The owner asked.

"I apologize for entering without calling, even though I don't have a number to this place. But, I'm here to discuss a business proposition with the owner the price on this building." Hoyt said. "You wouldn't happen to be the owner, would you?"

"That would be who you're currently eyeballing, boy. I am the owner of this place." He said. "So, what kind of interest do you have in a building like this and why should I even bother to listen to your offer?"

"Well, my good sir, my interest in your building is quite a simple answer." Hoyt said. "I need a small place for my stash of items."

"My I know what these items are?" The owner said. "If you want to have this building, I must know some details."

"The stash is really just my items that I have back at the house." Hoyt said. "It just some things that should be kept in storage."

"I don't know about that, Mr.?" The owner asked.

"Hoyt, Hoyt Bennett." Hoyt said smiling.

"Oh, so you're the guy who caused the whole mess of things a while back and went to prison for it." The owner said. "I knew I recognized you from somewhere."

"Yes, I am he." Hoyt said. "So, do we have an agreement on this building of yours? I can take it off your hands."

"I'll think it over and speak with you tomorrow about it." The owner said. "Do we have a deal?"

Hoyt shook the owner's hand and said, "Yes, we do have a deal."

CHAPTER 13

Hoyt left the building with the mindset of intending on having the building, by any means necessary. He drove down the streets and passed by a group that he noticed. He turned around and passed by the area again. He looked closely and noticed that the men standing in that spot used to work for him. He smirked as he drives away.

Preston and Emily returned to the office and walk in. But, they realize that everyone is armed and searching the building. Preston walked over to one official as Emily glanced around the entire location before approaching the officer.

"Officer, what's the hell is happening here?" Preston asked. "What is going on?"

"Some pissed off guy came in with a gun and started threatening everyone near him." The officer said. "They're saying he's up on the third floor. No one's gone up there so far. They're awaiting backup."

"No shit, pal, we're the backup." Preston said. "Emily, we have to go up there."

"I'm aware of that, smart guy. How do we get up there without being noticed by sound or anyone in general?"

"Just follow my lead and we'll get up there in a hurry."

Preston and Emily ran toward the stairs, heading to the third floor. On the third floor, the majority of everyone is either hiding or sneaking up on John, who's standing in the middle of the room, pointing the gun at all the locations around him. Carla is standing by his side, smiling and laughing at the officials.

"I'll ask again god damn it." John said. "Where's Preston Maddox?! Where's the Instinct Marshal?!"

No one responded to his question and he fired the gun to the ceiling. Sounds of harsh screaming are heard around the room as he repeated the question. But, this time Eldon stepped out of the office and Cody stood with him.

"You aren't Preston. Neither of you." John said. "So, who the fuck are you, then to stand up in front of a gun?"

"I'm Eldon Ross, the Chief Commander of this agency." Eldon said. "I'm also Preston's boss and you're trespassing on my territory and threatening my people."

Carla smiled and said, "Preston's boss. Wow, I wouldn't expect him to have a boss. I always assumed that he would go into work for himself. Not someone else."

"Listen here, woman. Either the two of you go ahead and leave this building or it's a slight possibility that the both of you might just have to die here and leave in a coroner van."

"Die here?" John said. "Really? Let me tell you something, old boy. The only motherfucker that might possibly die in this place today is either you and your little bitch standing next to you. How's that sound for a threat."

Eldon pulled out his gun and fired at John. He moved out of the way and started shooting the surroundings. Eldon and Cody hid behind the office walls as John continued to fire toward them. Preston and Emily arrived on the floor and crouched down by the entrance wall.

"Who is this guy?" Emily asked.

"Must be one of Ray's men." Preston said. 'They're probably here for us I assume."

"Didn't expect us to be on a hit list this soon."

John stopped firing the gun and looked at Carla.

"When is he coming, Carla?" John asked. "We can't wait this long for him to show up."

"Don't worry. He'll be here soon enough." Carla said. "He can't resist making a save for innocent people."

Preston and Emily ran into the room as John pointed the gun

toward them. Preston spotted Carla standing by John and he's confused, yet remembers his plans were stolen back at his apartment.

"We meet again, Preston." Carla said. "So, who's your friend, there?"

"Carla. What are you doing here?" Preston asked. "What are you doing with this man?"

"We're here on a mission assigned by Ray Colby." Carla said. "We're here to kill you basically."

Preston smirked and looked at John.

"So, you're one of Ray's men." Preston said. "I knew it would have to be. Neither the Bronson brothers or Hoyt would do something like this. They would just shoot everyone they see."

"I do this shit different, Marshal." John said. "Now, since people are always saying that you have the "Instinct". Whatever that's supposed to be. I was wondering, do you know exactly when I'll decide to shoot your head off."

"If you really want to know. Just try me." Preston said. "See, where we go from there."

John laughed and glanced toward Carla.

"You sound like you aren't afraid of being killed on the spot." John said. "A man without any fear of a gun."

"No one's ever had the chance of doing it." Preston said. "I've always been the one doing the shooting and putting people down. So, what makes it different if you're on the other side of the gun this time and I'm in the same position as always."

"Alright. Let's just see how good you really are." John said.

"Oh, I like the way this is going." Carla said. "Exciting stuff we're seeing here."

Emily looked at Carla and said, "Just keep your mouth closed, alright. Before, I become the one to put a bullet through your head."

Carla laughed and said, "You have a feisty partner, Preston. I wonder what else she can do beside talking."

"You'll probably find that out sooner than you think." Preston said. "She's not one you'll like to piss off. Believe me, I know for a fact."

Eldon and Cody peeped out of the office, seeing Preston and

Emily standing in front of John and Carla. Cody turned to Eldon.

"What should we do, boss?" Cody asked. "We need to help them in some way at least."

"We could create some form of a diversion for them." Eldon said. "Make it a little easier for them."

"Like shoot the guy in the leg?" Cody asked.

"We could try." Eldon said.

Just as Eldon pointed the gun, Darius snuck into the office and pointed his gun toward John. Eldon looked at him.

"How'd you get in here?" Eldon asked.

"I was already in here. Just was waiting for you, that's all." Darius said. "What should we do? Let Preston and Emily handle it, or shall we just cause a minor disturbance?"

"I have one suggestion. Why don't we just try shooting the guy in the leg." Eldon said. "Will open up some kind of chance."

"Alright, it makes sense to me." Darius said. "Let's do it."

Darius fired his gun and the bullet went through John's leg. He stumbled as Carla pulled out her pistol and pointed toward both Preston and Emily. They stood still as Carla smiled.

"Who the fuck did that?!" John said in tremendous pain. "Where the fuck did that come from?! Shit!"

"Just be lucky it wasn't aimed for your head." Preston said. "That wouldn't have been so pretty to see your brain splattered."

"You're making jokes, boy. You know something, I'm getting a little tired of being in this damn marshal joint place anyway, so I'll just put your ass down right now."

John had set up his gun stance and prepared to aim, before he can fire the gun, he is shot in the back of the head and fell to the ground. As John fell, Carla stood behind him, with the pistol up and smoke coming from the muzzle. Preston is appalled by Carla's decision and so is everyone else in the office.

"The hell just happen here?!" Eldon said.

"Why did you do that, Carla?" Preston asked. "I don't really understand what that was for?"

"You've never understood me, babe. I'm the only person that's allowed to kill you. The *ONLY* one."

Carla smiled and looked down at John's dead body. Blood slowly begins forming a puddle around his head.

"I'll explain the news to Ray." Carla said. "Just tell him it was a accident. He'll be fine with it."

"Speaking of him. Where is Ray?" Emily asked. "Since you know where he's located?"

"You really think I'll tell you? After the threat you gave me." Carla said, "You really have a lot to learn about New Haven, sweetheart."

Carla walked toward the front door, Preston stood in front of her.

Preston stared and said, "Either you tell us where Colby is or I'm personally taking you to prison for murder. We have eye witnesses to attest to it"

"Wow. I like your options. It turns me on." Carla said. "OK. He operates at a warehouse on the outskirts of town. It was a former trucking company building. Now, may I leave?"

Carla left the office as Emily turned to Preston.

"Let me ask a question here. Why did you let her leave?" Emily asked.

"Because she'll lead us to Colby himself." Preston said. "Simple solution right in front of us."

CHAPTER 14

Hoyt arrived at Billy's home. But, once he opened the door, he discovered that Billy isn't there. He walked in and searched the home.

"Billy, where the hell are you?" Hoyt said to himself.

As he prepared to leave, he turned around and was hit directly in the head with a wooden baseball bat. Hoyt fell to the ground. Being knocked out from the bat. He was completely unconscious and unaware of what had happened. The holder of the bat was Rusty. He laughed as he looked down at Hoyt. Coover walked in behind him and looked down.

"He went down quick, bro." Coover said. "The bastard couldn't take a beating. No shit, he couldn't take a swing of a bat."

"It was easy." Rusty said. "Easier than I expected it to be. Let's drag him to the truck and take him to Ray. See what he wants us to do with him."

Coover looked around the home. Searching around the area for someone or something. He walked back outside toward Rusty.

"Rusty, where's Billy?" Coover asked.

"Billy's over at mama's house." Rusty said. "She'll convince him to join us with Ray. You'll see. Mama has it all under control."

They drag Hoyt's unconscious body to their truck. They tossed him in the back and covered him up with some sheets that were lying in the back. They drove off the premises, returning to Ray's hideout.

Back at the office, officials are cleaning up the amount of blood left on the floor from John's head after being shot by Carla. Preston, Emily, Eldon, Cody, and Darius are inside the boardroom, talking about the recent event.

"Why did you let her leave, Preston?" Eldon asked. "You saw what she did. She shot another human being right there. Right outside this room."

"I let her leave, so she could lead us to Colby." Preston said. "It's a very simple plan."

"How is it simple?" Darius asked. "She killed him, but, she could've easily killed you and Emily. As well as the rest of us on this floor if it had come to that."

"I see that I somehow placed everyone in danger." Preston said. "But, me and her have a long history with one another."

"Please, don't tell me that she's an old flame?" Eldon asked. "We don't need any more of your personal details falling into business again."

"She was." Preston said. "Kind of. We met when we were very young, and I also taught her some techniques. So, that could explain how she knew how to use the gun in the first place."

"So, her with the gun is really your fault." Emily said. "Should've seen that from the start."

"Everyone just relax." Cody said. "We must have a plan to go by in case she comes back with others."

"Ok, so what's the plan, guys?" Emily asked. "If any of you have one."

Preston looked around and said, "I say that we follow Carla's trail, so that we know for sure where Colby is and how to stop him."

Darius nodded.

"I'll have to go with Preston on this one. The plan sounds good. Good enough to start from."

"Alright then." Eldon said. "We'll track down your old flame and hopefully, that leads us to Ray Colby."

As they prepared to leave the room, Cody thought and brought up Hoyt's plans. Preston looked and decided that he'll go search for Hoyt as soon as he leaves. Emily agreed to join him in doing so. They leave the boardroom.

Carla went to another one of Ray's hideouts. This time a cabin in the woods. A cabin larger than the average cabins. She walked in and Ray is sitting behind a desk. He looked up and saw Carla. But, he doesn't see John.

"Where's John?" Ray asked. "What happened out there, Carla?"

"John didn't survive the initials of the plan." Carla said. "He was shot."

Ray stood up, as he's angry about what happened with John. But, he's still concerned if the plan went the way it was supposed to go.

"Did the plan go as followed?" Ray asked.

"No." Carla said. "As soon as John was shot, I left the building and that brings me to you at this moment, standing before you and telling you this terrible news."

"You said you could get the job done." Ray said. "Apparently, you couldn't. I find out that a lost one of my soldiers and I also find out that Preston is still alive and that's gonna cause problems for me, my lady. Lots of problems. How am I supposed to explain this news to the head chief? How do I explain this?"

"I'm sure you'll find a way to do so." Carla said. "That is, if you want me to explain it to him. I could do that, if you like."

"Very well." Ray said. "Since all you seem to be used for is bringing news, go ahead and tell the chief this. I'm sure he'll love to hear it from you. Right from your mouth."

Carla left the cabin as Ray looked down at the table and slams his fists.

Preston and Emily traveled down the interstate in search of Hoyt. Emily asked him about his history with Carla and why he let her leave. He told her that because Carla looked innocent and nice, she isn't. He also told her that Carla is highly skilled with armed weapons, thanks to him training her during their past relationship. Emily wonders if Preston can stand up against her, instead of falling prey to her seductive ways.

"When was the last time you actually saw Carla in person?" Emily asked. "And I'm not talking about in the office."

"A few days ago, she was inside my apartment." Preston said.

"She must've picked the lock or something, because she doesn't have a key to it. I didn't even live here during our relationship."

"That must have been a surprise." Emily said.

"It was shocking to say the least." Preston said. "But, enough about me. What's the history between you and Ray Colby?"

"Ray was one of New Jersey's top crime lords." Emily said. "Him and I always had confrontations with one another. Later, I find out that he fled from the state and went somewhere else to hide. Now, I find out that this is the city of which he flocked to."

"It seems our past lives are coming back to us." Preston said.

"Looks that way." Emily said. "Strongly, too."

Emily then asked, "Also, at the bar, what was that phase Hoyt had said to you?"

"Which one?" Preston said. "Because, I can't fully remember what that jackass said to me. To make it even stranger, I was drinking water."

"He said something about being lost in the shadows. Something of that nature. Though, I believed it was like that or maybe it was lost shadows. Something around that I know."

"It was lost in shadows." Preston said. "It's basically a phrase used to tell people when they have no idea what's either going on around them or they have no knowledge of what's about to happen around them. To put it short, Hoyt is about to do something around this city and that's what he meant when he told me that I was lost in the shadows."

"I was just asking about it." Emily said. "In a sort of way, I kind of like it. Sounds interesting."

"I'll tell you what's interesting." Preston said. "The term *Pteronophobia*."

"*Pteronophobia*? Never heard of it. Why is it supposed to be interesting?"

"It means fear of feathers."

"That is interesting. Never knew something like that existed." Emily said.

Preston said, "I didn't either, until my cousin ran from some chickens on his parents' farm in Arkansas."

"You learn something new every day, don't you?" Emily said.

"Pretty much." Preston said smiling.

Right back at the cabin in the woods, Coover and Rusty arrived with Hoyt in the back of the truck, still unconscious, blood slowly flowing from a cut on the back of his head. They dragged his body to the front door and headed inside. Ray sat at the desk reading some files as he noticed Rusty and Coover entering and dragging Hoyt's body across the wooden floor.

"Boys, for the love of the Heavenly Father, just pick the son of a bitch up. I don't want any of his blood on my wooden floor. Especially, blood from a Bennett."

"We brought him here." Rusty said. "Just like you asked, boss."

"I should thank you, boys." Ray said. "You're doing a much better job than that slut I hired. What about your little brother? Has he decided to join my alliance?"

"We should be receiving an answer soon." Coover said. "Mama's currently speaking with him about it."

"I'm sure she'll convince him to join." Ray said. "She has that strong presence amongst us. Especially, among her sons."

They place Hoyt onto a metal table, a table that belongs to Quarles Funeral Home. Hoyt is completely unconscious.

"What do you need us to do with him?" Rusty asked.

"Leave him here and I'll send him to the funeral home." Ray said. "Since, I'm good friends with the owner, they'll know exactly what to do with Hoyt."

Preston and Emily arrived at Hoyt's hideout location and they realized that he isn't there, not seeing his truck parked at that spot. Preston decided to visit Billy's mobile home, believing that Hoyt could possibly be there.

"Are you sure he could be there?" Emily said.

"It's worth a shot to check out."

CHAPTER 15

Billy is at his mother's home as she continued to convince him to join Ray's alliance. Billy disagreed with his mother and said that he feels better being on Hoyt's side, saying that he has full control over himself and that he's not following. Barbette continued to try and get through her son, she knew she's not getting anywhere by speaking to him.

Billy jumped up from the couch and decided to leave the home. He turned around and looked at his mother. His mother could see the sadness in his eyes for disobeying her. So, could Billy see the sadness in his mother's eye for not joining Ray and herself.

"I'm truly sorry, mom. But, whatever happens to me in this line of work, it just happens."

As Billy leaves his mother's home, she walked out the front door and watched him drive off. As he drove off, she contacted Ray and told him to do what he must, since Billy didn't listen to her.

Funeral assistants from Quarles Funeral Home arrive at Ray's cabin and they take Hoyt's unconscious body and place it in the back of one of their white hearses. The assistants thank Ray and tell him that the owner is quite pleased. They left and Ray smiled as something finally was accomplished.

At the office, Darius told Eldon and Cody that there was a fugitive on the loose in town and that they've been assign the task of capturing him. Eldon had agreed and sent Darius and Cody on the job. Cody became very excited to work on another mission as Darius turned toward him.

"Please tell me, you've done this before?" Darius asked.

"They've never sent me out to search for a fugitive." Cody said. "I've only visited case sightings, like the bank and the jailhouse."

"Hopefully, you do a great job on this one." Darius said. "Since the guy we're looking for is on the government's top ten list of fugitives."

"This is going to be fun." Cody said smiling.

Darius and Cody left the office, heading towards Darius' black Kia Forte. Cody liked the car and said, "This is a nice ride. Can I drive it once we head back?"

"You're not driving this car." Darius said. "The only thing you're driving is that head of yours on this mission. Got it?"

"Yeah." Cody said. "Sure, I do."

Preston and Emily made it to Billy's mobile home. They notice Hoyt's truck parked, but no sign of him. Preston gets out of the car and walked to the front door. He knocked. Receiving no response. He knocked again with no response. He decided to open the door and once his hand touched the doorknob, the door opened with no one inside. Preston walked back to the car.

"Find anything?" Emily asked.

"No sign of Hoyt or Billy." Preston said. "There must be a place."

Hoyt had awoken and regained a little consciousness as he saw himself lying on the table in an embalming room. He looked around and saw no one inside. He gets up from the table and walked to the back door. He opened the door as he bumped into one of the funeral assistants.

"What are you doing up?" The assistant asked.

"What am I doing here?" Hoyt asked. "That's the real question."

The funeral assistant begins to back up from Hoyt as he walked closer to him. Hoyt stared at the assistant and said, "I'll ask again. Why am I here? What is this place?"

"You're at Quarles Funeral Home." The assistant said. "You were brought here on Ray Colby's command."

"Ray Colby's command you say?" Hoyt said. "So, you're telling me that, Ray had someone to knock me out. Then, they brought me here. For what? I'm not dead."

"They probably brought you here to take your organs." The assistant said. "Possibly your kidneys or something else."

"My organs." Hoyt said. "You're telling me that this funeral home also takes organs from unsuspected people. This is a new thing."

Hoyt reached in towards his back for his gun, but, realized it isn't there. The assistant smiled and pulled out a gun from his back. Hoyt looked up and noticed that the gun the assistant was holding was his.

"Why do you have my gun?" Hoyt asked.

"I might be a dull kind of guy, but, I'm not stupid." The assistant said. "Start backing up, Bennett."

"You know my name as well, I see." Hoyt said. "Interesting. You know how to fool someone don't you. Just like how you're fooling yourself right now."

"What are you talking about?" The assistant asked.

Slowly slipping from Hoyt's right sleeve, appeared another gun. Hoyt clenched it and shot the assistant in the forehead, blowing his head and killing him. Hoyt walked over to his body and started smiling. He also took back his gun.

"I'll take that, thank you." Hoyt said, taking the gun back. "I surely appreciate you holding on to it for me."

Hoyt heard someone coming towards the front door and he exits out through the back. He sneaked around to the front and steals one of their hearses and drives off with it. As Hoyt drives away, he looks at the interior of the hearse and smiled.

"Never knew it looked so good in these things."

Hoyt reached in his pocket and found his cell phone. He contacted Billy and told him to meet up at a local Convenience store on the outskirts of town. Billy agreed with a stumble in his voice as he headed toward the location.

Darius and Cody arrive at a small loan office. They walk in and speak with the lady in the front. They speak to her about a fugitive named Douglas Greene. According to the information given to Darius and Cody, Douglas used to work at the loan office, before his quit and went into a life of crime.

"We're only here to ask if you have any information regarding Mr. Greene." Darius said.

"I'm sorry, gentlemen. But, we have no information on him around here." The lady said. "All we know is that he decided to quit. We never seen him again."

Cody leaned in and said, "Do you know anyone who was good friends with Mr. Greene? Someone that used to work here?"

"There is a guy named Richard Dillon." The lady said. "He goes by the name, RJ Dillon. He lives in Hartford. If you find him, he might have the information that you're searching for."

"Thank you, Ms." Darius said. "Have a good day."

Darius and Cody leave the loan office and walked toward the vehicle. Cody looked over to Darius with a small grin on his face

"So, looks like we're heading to Hartford." Cody said. "This is starting to become one great trip."

"Keep in mind that we're here on business, Cody." Darius said. "Nothing more and nothing else."

Preston and Emily returned to Barbette's home to find any information on Hoyt and to see of Billy is there with her. They knock on the door and she opens it with mid pull, blowing a small gust from the inside of her home toward Preston and Emily.

"You've returned I see." Barbette said. "Something I never would've expected in my short wilds."

"I am truly sorry to bother you again, Ms. Bronson." Preston said. "But, we are looking for your son, Billy. Have you seen him?"

"He was here about an hour ago." Barbette said. "He left to head back to his place. He should be there at this moment."

"We've just come from his home, ma'am." Emily said. "So, we

thought that he would've came here."

"Well, he did." Barbette said. "He just left before you arrived."

"Did he mention where he was heading off to? Any particular place?" Preston said. "Just a question that I thought I could ask."

Barbette looked with a frown and said, "No. But, I believe that he was going out to meet with Hoyt Bennett someplace in town."

"That's a problem." Emily said. "Because we can't find Hoyt either."

"Hmm." Barbette said. "That's none of my concern. If you do find my Billy and that prick of a human being, you let them know for sure that Barb told you where they would be."

"We'll pass on that message. We sure will." Preston said. "Have a good day, Ms. Bronson."

Preston and Emily left Barbette's home. She watched them drive off and returned into her home and shut the door, murmuring to herself.

Hoyt is parked in a Convenience store parking lot, which is surrounded by cars and people. He's sitting in the hearse waiting for Billy to arrive. He looked to his right and saw Billy's truck. Billy pulled up next to him and Hoyt tells him about the events and this is the first place of where they will start. Billy walked slowly with a look of confusion.

"What the Sam hell are you doing driving a hearse?" Billy asked. You're an undertaker now suddenly?"

"The hearse? It's a long story and I'll explain to you the details at another time." Hoyt said. "Though, I am undertaking this line of work for a short while."

"Speaking of time, what do you mean about the events starting here?" Billy said. "I'm not getting the big picture here."

"Just watch the shopping center, Billy." Hoyt said. "Just watch and watch very closely."

Billy looked and watched for about a couple of minutes. As nothing is happening. Billy turned to Hoyt with a midst of disbelief.

"Watch what, Hoyt?" Billy asked. "What's going on?"

"Billy, look inside your glove box." Hoyt said.

Billy looked inside the glove box and finds a detonator. He pulled it out and looked toward Hoyt. Billy, he starts to shiver in fear.

"Hoyt, what is this?" Billy asked in fear.

"That is a detonator, my friend." Hoyt said. "When you press the button, we will all witness an explosion that will be seen across the land and later, on the nightly news."

"I.... I can't do it, Hoyt." Billy said. "I'm sorry, but, I can't do something like this."

"Just hand it to me, my good friend." Hoyt said. "I'll take care of it."

Billy handed the detonator to Hoyt and he grabbed it. Hoyt flipped up the detonator's top and looked at Billy, smiling with intense energy running through his body. Billy shivered.

"Ladies and gentlemen. Also, you too, Billy. The events have officially begun." It's time to finally blow some shit up!"

"Oh my God!" Billy yelled. "HOYT!!!"

"*INCOMING CALL!!!!*" Hoyt yelled loudly.

Hoyt pressed the button, detonating the bomb and caused an explosion to the entire Convenience store store. Flames fly up into the air as they begin to engulf the entire building with people running from the doors on every corner, screaming in fear and terror. Billy is terrified completely as he looked over at Hoyt, smiling and laughing insanely.

"Let's go!" Billy yelled. "Hoyt, let's get the hell out of this place!"

"What's that, Billy?" Hoyt asked. "I can't hear you through the screams coming from the sheep running from the barn."

"Let's go!" Billy yelled again. "Right now! Let's go!"

"Right now?!" Hoyt asked. "Right now?! You mean right now?!"

"Come on, Hoyt! Damn it!"

Hoyt puts the hearse in drive and exited the parking lot, passing by people who are scattered across the lot. Hoyt stuck his head out of the window and started hollering toward them. Screaming various words and famous quotes. They drive off the lot and head back on the main street.

CHAPTER 16

At the office, Eldon tells Preston and Emily that a Convenience store has been blown to smithereens. Preston asked how it happened and Eldon has no answer to give him. Emily tells them they should head there to ask any questions about the incident. They leave the office, going to the Convenience store. Once in the jeep, Eldon calls Darius and Cody to tell them about the incident.

"Hello, Darius." Eldon said.

"Darius here." Darius said. "Eldon, what's the situation?"

"We just received a call that a Convenience store was blown up." Eldon said. "So, I, Preston, and Emily are heading there now to figure this all out."

"Ok. Do you need us to come along?" Darius asked.

"No, just continue what's your doing on your case and we'll deal with this one." Eldon said.

He hanged up the phone, while he drove down the street, heading to the decimated Convenience store building.

Ray learned of the Convenience store incident and he knows Hoyt is behind it. He commands his men to track down Hoyt and kill him. By any means of force. His men leave the warehouse, entering their SUVs and driving out of sight. Inside the warehouse is Barbette, who Ray didn't realize was inside with him. She sits in front of him.

"Ms. Bronson. I wasn't expecting to see you here." Ray said. "A place such as this of all the ones we have."

"I'm here to ask you about my sons. Mainly I'm here to ask about my Billy." Barbette said. "Do you have any information on him of where he is or anything in particular?"

"All I am aware of is your son being partners with Hoyt." Ray said. "I sent Coover and Rusty to speak with him, but they didn't receive an answer."

"So, you have any information on where Hoyt's whereabouts are right now?" Barbette asked. "Any information?"

"He was at Quarles Funeral Home." Ray said. "But, it seems that he escaped and blew up a Convenience store downtown."

"He blew up a Convenience store?" Barbette asked. "That's the best he's got to offer? I could give two shits on a paper plate about some goddamn Convenience store being blown to smithereens."

"You believe that you can do better?" Ray asked. "That's what your voice is telling me."

"Of course, I can do better!" Barbette said. "I can do a hell of a lot worse than what he's just done. I could cause panic across the entire city. Hell, I can cause panic across this entire state."

"I believe you there, Ms. Bronson." Ray said. "So, what's the plan concerning your baby boy?"

"Do what you will with him." Barbette said. "I tried speaking with him, he wouldn't listen. Coover and Rusty tried, so just do what you must to keep the alliance going."

"To keep the alliance going, we must kill Hoyt." Ray said. "I've already sent some of my men to take him out as we speak. They'll do a fine job."

"Let's hope they do." Barbette said. "Bring us a bundle of good joy and good fortune to our tables."

They shook hands and she left the warehouse. Ray gets up from the seat and leaves through the back door rubbing his head.

Hoyt and Billy are at the hideout and Hoyt is happier than a little boy during the holidays. Billy is still shaking with fear as Hoyt tried to calm him down.

"Billy, just relax, my friend. The first event is over. So, now we celebrate it."

"How can I celebrate when thousands of people were killed right in front of my eyes. How can I live with that in my mind, just popping up continually?"

"You can get through it, friend. You just have to relax your mind and prepare for the second event."

"Ok. So, I'll ask this right now. What this second event you have planned?"

Hoyt turned and smiled.

"It's time that we take our skills to a bigger location." Hoyt said. "We'll head up to New Haven City Hall eventually and just blow that place up too. Blow it to complete shit."

"Wait and excuse me. But, City Hall." Billy said. "That's a pretty big spot to do this, Hoyt and you're going to need some heavy artillery and explosives to complete something of that status."

"That is why you call it an event. Because it's a huge location for our city and it's the only location where the entire city will actually pay attention to our needs. Once City Hall blows to shit, we will have complete control over New Haven."

"If that's how you feel, Hoyt. If you say so."

Hoyt picked up a glass of vodka and hit Billy's glass and drank it. Hoyt smiled as he believes his events are finally coming into play. Billy continues to join in, even though he's scared.

Preston, Emily, and Eldon arrive at the decimated Convenience store. Still with charcoal-like smoke arriving from the building. Fire trucks, ambulances, and police cars are surrounding the location. They walk toward one of the officials. He is checking each person that arrives at the scene with a clipboard.

"What's the clipboard for, officer?" Eldon asked. "Don't think we'll need one on this investigation."

"It's to check if anyone inside is either injured or dead." The officer replied. "So, I see you got the call."

"Yeah we did and while I have you in front of me. Maybe you could tell me if there are any witnesses that seen anything unusual before the explosion took place?"

"We only have one witness so far. He's over there at the ambulance. He's being checked for injuries."

"Thanks." Eldon said.

They walk over to the ambulance and see the witness being searched for any signs of injury. He is not injured, and they release him. Before he walks away, Preston stands in front of him.

"I'm sorry, but, who the hell are you?" The witness asked.

"I'm Preston Maddox. United States Marshal and Homicide Detective. Me and my partners here just want to ask you some questions regarding the incident."

"All I saw was the explosion and nothing else after that but people running for their lives."

"What else did you see?" Eldon asked.

"Smoke, debris." The witness said. "What did you think I saw? UFOs beaming down at us?"

Preston and Eldon smiled. Emily walked toward the witness.

"Please, just tell us what else you saw and we'll be out of your way." Emily said.

"Since you put it that way, lady. There was one thing I did see."

"Well, by all means, please tell us, then." Eldon said. "For your sake I suppose."

The witness paused for a moment and uttered, "I saw these two guys, both white. They were both in trucks, parked next to each other. They stayed in there until the explosion and once that happened, they were the first ones gone."

"Did one of them yell out anything?" Preston asked. "Anything that may seem familiar to you or to this place?"

"One of them did yell out the words. Some of them I couldn't understand. But, I noticed he yelled out the phrase, *"Incoming Call"*. Don't know if that will help you or not."

"Shit!" Preston said. "It was Hoyt. It was him."

"How can you be so sure about that, Preston?" Eldon asked.

"He's the only son of a bitch that would yell out that phrase before an explosion would take place. I'll go ahead and look for him."

"We're coming with you." Eldon said. "You hear me, Preston."

Preston leaves the scene as Eldon and Emily get into the jeep and follow him. Preston stops at a red light and on the side of him arrives Eldon and Emily in the jeep. Eldon rolled down the window.

"Where are you headed?" Eldon asked.

"Going over to Hoyt's hideout in the outskirts. From my understanding, that's where he'll be currently."

CHAPTER 17

Darius and Cody arrive at a small home in the suburbs of Hartford. They find a large brick home with a mailbox on the front lawn. The initials on the mailbox are, "RJ" Cody looked at it and turned to the house.

"Appears to be his place, Mr. D." Cody said. "What do you think?"

"Looks like it could be." Darius said. "Also, don't call me, Mr. D. Wherever you thought up that name."

"Sure, no problem." Cody said.

They walked to the front door and Darius knocked. He knocked again, no response. Cody looked over at him, believing that he's not at the house. Darius knocked one more time and the door opens. An African American male is standing on the other side.

"Excuse us, sir." Darius said. "But, we're United States Marshals from New Haven on a case concerning a man named Richard Dillon. Also known to some people as, RJ Dillon."

"Never heard of the guy." The man said.

"What's with the RJ initials on the mailbox, sir?" Cody asked. "According to that and my knowledge, it makes you appear as the guy who we're looking for."

"What has this guy done to have some marshals on his trail?" The man asked. "If I am able to know."

"RJ Dillon is a fugitive of the United States government." Darius said. "To put it in a short sentence for you, the guy's a con artist."

"A con artist you say." The man said. "From what you're saying is the guy's been giving lots of people trouble in a lot of various ways."

"A little too much trouble." Cody said. "We were given information from a loan office and the information states that RJ lives in this very house. In the end, that's why we're here and the initials on the mailbox plainly give it away for us."

"Well, I'll say this and you two can be on your way off this property. I don't know any RJ Dillon." The man said. "So, if you please leave my home, we will have no trouble."

"We can't leave this property until we receive concrete information regarding RJ Dillon and this location." Cody said. "So, if you don't mind, we'll wait here until he arrives or comes back from wherever he's currently placed."

"You'll just wait for him? Ok. If you say so." The man said as he shut the door in their faces.

Cody turned to Darius, curious.

"Did he just slam the door in our faces?" Cody asked. "Because, its looks that way."

"Yeah." Darius replied. "By that means of action, he knows something we don't know."

Darius knocked on the door again. No answer as he knocked twice as hard on the door. The door opened, and RJ Dillon walked out, facing Darius and Cody. Wearing his expensive white suit with nice black shades.

"Didn't my assistant just tell you two dickheads to leave this property." RJ said. "So, why in the blue hell are the two of you still here?"

"So, you're RJ Dillon I see." Darius said. "If you're not aware, me and my partner here are on your property to take you into custody for your con artistry."

"My ass you aren't. I'm not going anywhere in any shape or form."

He reached behind him and pulled out an RPK machine gun. Darius and Cody backed up a couple of feet with their hands in the air. Their faces show a slight fear within them. Though, they stand their guard.

"Wow, an RPK. OK. That's a nice firearm you have there, RJ."

"Thank you, boy." RJ said. "I won it in a poker game a few months back. Thanks to the great ace."

"Did you shoot the loser after the game was over?" Darius asked. "Just seems obvious that you would do something like that and since you're a con man, you've probably did more than just that with anyone."

"How about I just shoot the two of you, right here on the spot." RJ said. "That way I can be rid of you easily. Since you won't leave my property."

"You don't have to do that, Mr. RJ." Cody said. "We'll just leave right now if you like."

Darius and Cody start walking towards the car slowly as RJ has the machine gun pointed toward them. They get to their car and RJ commands them to get inside. They get inside and once RJ puts down the machine gun, Cody fires a gun at his knee. RJ yelled and dropped the RPK. His assistant runs out of the house, with an AK. Darius pulled out his pistol and shot the assistant in the chest. Cody runs out of the car and drags RJ with him. They place RJ in the back of the car and Darius looked at Cody.

"Didn't think you had it in you." Darius said. "Very good skill set."

"I might be a rookie Marshal in training, but I'm highly skilled in the presence of marksmanship." Cody said.

Handcuffing RJ's hands and legs, they left the area, heading to the interstate, returning to New Haven. Darius looked in the back toward RJ and glanced over to Cody, who's driving the vehicle.

"You're sure he'll be comfortable back there all cuffed up?" Darius said.

"Who gives a damn if he feels comfortable. I say he deserves it for what he's done to many innocent people."

Ray's men arrive at a small location, where they meet with Coover and Rusty about assassinating Hoyt. Coover tells the group that they must be silent on this mission and Rusty tells them that their primary target is Hoyt, but, by Ray's order and Barbette's answers, if Billy pops up on the scene, that they must shoot him as well. Rusty decides to also tell the group about the marshals. Rusty said that if any of the marshals arrive on the scene, they must take them out as well.

"We must do what we can to keep this all quiet." Rusty said. "If the marshals arrive on scene, we take them out. Completely."

"Every single one of them." Coover said. "Whether its Hoyt, our dear brother, Billy, or the marshals, we have to put them down."

"Basically, men." Rusty said. "No witnesses. No casualties. That way there won't be any traces that will lead to us, Ray, or mother."

"You're sure about all of this?"

"I'm damn sure about it."

They begin to march out with their guns and weapons. They head toward their vehicles and leave, driving to Hoyt's hideout.

Preston, Emily, and Eldon arrive at Hoyt's hideout. Eldon looked around the deserted area of grass. Emily looked around as well. Though, they spot both Hoyt's and Billy's trucks, confirming that the two of them are currently inside the hideout. Preston walked toward the front door. He knocked, and Billy opened it.

"Marshal!" Billy yelled. "Marshals!"

Preston shoved Billy out of the way, letting Eldon and Emily walk in. Hoyt arrives from the kitchen area, smiling. Preston doesn't smile, not an inch. Neither does Eldon and Emily. Preston delivered a right-hook punch to Hoyt, which knocked him to the ground. He picked him up and shoved him against the wall, knocking down one of the mounted deer heads.

"You no good son of a bitch!" Preston said. "You no good piece of shit!"

"Preston, what have I done to cause such anger from you?" Hoyt asked. "Killed someone you loved in the process or something worse than that?"

"I know, we know. Hell, everyone now knows." Preston said. "The Convenience store that exploded, that was you. It's all on you, Hoyt. The witness gave you out with your "Incoming Call" battle cry."

"Preston, just relax for a minute." Eldon said. "Let the man get a breather."

"No!" Preston yelled. "There is no relaxing right now, damn it. He's killed thousands of people today and I'm not going to stand by and let him kill a thousand more! To hell with his breather!"

Preston punched Hoyt again and threw him across the counter to the kitchen. Eldon tries to calm Preston down, but, it isn't working. Billy crouches in the corner to avoid Preston. Preston continues pummeling Hoyt and Emily stopped him from doing any more damage to Hoyt as he's bleeding from nose to mouth.

"Preston, enough is enough now." Emily said. "Just calm down, please. So, we can settle this like civilized people."

Preston responded to Emily and stopped attacking Hoyt.

"I'm starting to like her even more so now." Hoyt said.

"Don't push your luck." Emily said. "Or I'll just let him continue to beat your ass to a pulp."

"Come on, Emily. There's no need for that right now." Eldon said.

Preston looked over at the corner, where Billy is and he pointed toward him, saying he's next if he tries anything that Hoyt has done. As they prepare to take Hoyt to their car, they notice headlights coming towards the house. They ducked down to avoid being seen.

"Who's that outside?" Emily asked.

"Probably someone that's come to kill Hoyt." Preston said. "For all the shit he's caused so far.'

Eldon took a peep outside the window and saw what appeared to be seven cars, all having dozens of men walk out, with weapons in their hands. Eldon ducked down and told the rest of them what's going on outside.

On the outside, Coover and Rusty are leading the pack of Ray's men toward the hideout. Coover recognizes Billy's truck and points it out to Rusty. Rusty looked at the hideout.

"Billy!" Rusty yelled. "Billy, we know you're in there, little brother. We know your good buddy, Hoyt is in there too. So, why don't the two of you do use a favor and just walk on out here nice and calm, so we can finish our business here."

"Come on little brother." Coover said. 'We're only here to talk with you. But, Hoyt, we're here to kill that no-good bastard."

Inside the house, everyone is crouched down, preparing their firearms. Hoyt looked over at Preston, still in pain from Preston's attack.

"You have to help me, just this once." Hoyt said. "Please."

"Why?" Preston said. "So, you can kill more innocent people. You've done enough. I should just let you die here."

"But, you won't." Hoyt said. "Because, we were once friends."

"We were friends a long time ago, Hoyt." Preston said. "That time has come and gone and its over for you."

The pack of men are closer to the house as they start banging on the windows and the front door. One man decides to kick the door down. But, he couldn't do it, since he hurt himself in the process. Coover and Rusty pull out their handguns and fire at the windows, knocking them out. Preston looked over to Hoyt and asked him of a back door. Hoyt pointed toward the kitchen and they all head out the back. Just as they left, Coover knocked down the door and they entered the hideout. They didn't find anyone around the area.

Just as they searched the hideout, they heard engines sound. Coover and Rusty looked at one another and walked to the outside. To which, they see Preston, Emily, Eldon, Billy, and Hoyt leaving in their vehicles. Rusty now upset, turned toward his brother. Pointing at them running off in the distance.

"Shit! They're running away, fellas!" Rusty yelled. "Grab your gear and get in your vehicles!"

They jumped into their vehicles and proceed to chase them all down. Now, on the highway, there's a chase between the two groups. Coover drives behind Hoyt's truck and Rusty begins firing at him. Hoyt ducked down as the shots came in inches closer toward his head.

"Did you hit him, bro?" Coover asked. "Did you hit him?"

"What's it look like to you, no I didn't." Rusty said. "Just keep your eyes on the damn road and just drive."

Now, Emily started to fire a couple of shots toward the pack around them. She popped out the tires on some of the men's vehicles, stopping them from the chase. She fired more shots toward Coover and Rusty, knocking out their back window. Coover started to yell as he's in a fury.

"She just knocked out our damn window, bro!" Coover said. "That isn't going by easy with me, man."

"Don't worry, mama doesn't like the bitch anyway." Rusty said. "So, we'll kill her for mama's sake."

Rusty begins firing toward the jeep as Eldon and Emily both ducked. Eldon covers his head, while continuing to drive.

"I didn't think it would be like this down here." Emily said. "I thought it would be more subtle and a little quieter."

"This is New Haven, Ms. Weston.' Eldon said. 'Not your kind of New Jersey feel of the day.'

Emily continued to fire at the pack. The intersection turns into a two-way street. Now, Coover and Rusty are driving on the side of Hoyt. Rusty fires toward Hoyt, he ducked his head and reached for his gun.

Once Rusty stopped firing, Hoyt rose up from the door and shot Rusty in the chest and also shot Coover in the right arm. Coover screams in pain, losing control of the truck. The truck drives off the interstate and dives down into a ditch on the side. The truck started flipping over around three times. Hoyt cheerfully yelled out the window.

"That's right my people!" Hoyt yelled. "That's how you handle these bastards around here!"

Coover and Rusty dragged themselves from the damaged truck. Coover helped Rusty walk his way up toward the road. Staggering and stumbling in pain, the two of them try to gain more strength as they inch closer to the road.

"Come on bro." Coover said. "I got you, don't worry."

Another one of Ray's men drive on the left lane, directly next to Preston. He looked over at them as they threat him by screaming out words. He pulled out his gun and shot their tire, causing them to turn and flip across the interstate.

"These assholes never learn." Preston said.

Emily looked over at Preston's car and he's pointing in front of them, telling them to go forward. They pass him and so does Billy and Hoyt. But, Hoyt slows down a bit next to Preston. Hoyt looked over at Preston.

"Preston." Hoyt yelled. "The next time you come into my place of business and proceed to beat me down, you won't be so lucky."

"I'll take my chances." Preston yelled. "You best be careful on this road."

"I'll be just fine and dandy. See you next time, Preston." Hoyt yelled as he drove away.

"That son of a bitch." Preston said. "He'll never get it straight through his head."

Ray, Barbette, and Carla meet at his nightclub, inside his office. Ray is pleased to see Barbette there, but he isn't pleased at all, seeing Carla.

"I have to thank you, Ms. Bronson." Ray said. "I never would expect to see you in this type of place."

"Wherever business must be settled, Colby, I'll be there." Barbette said. "So, what's the reason for us being here at such time?"

"I received a call from the chief and he's not too pleased with what's going on." Ray said. "He heard about the Convenience store incident and has told me take out Hoyt."

"We're all trying to take out Hoyt, Mr. Colby." Barbette said. 'The real question is how are we supposed to do that with the marshals on his trail?"

"You can leave the marshals to me." Carla said. "I can deal with them easily. Instead of killing them, I'll just use my persuasion on them."

"How can you convince me to trust you this time, Carla?" Ray asked. "You've already had one of my most allied men killed at the agency."

Barbette looked over at Carla. She took another glance before keeping her glaze locked on Carla. He raised her finger and pointed toward her.

"Wait a god damn minute now. You're the lady who lead John into that building?" Barbette asked. "You lead him in there, armed and not in the state of mind to do so?"

"He seemed like he was ready to me, Ms. Bronson." Carla said. "I just didn't know he had it in him to proceed with the mission at hand. He was a strong-minded guy."

"What happened to John isn't our main priority of the matter now." Ray said. "What currently matters to all of us is we find a way of taking out Hoyt, getting rid of these marshals, and ruling over this city."

"May that be done in a hurry." Barbette said. "Very quickly, before more shit comes into play and ruins what we already have here ongoing."

She shook Ray's hand and left the office. Ray leaned over to Carla and told her that she cannot fail him one more time or he might have to put her down himself. She laughed as she left the office.

CHAPTER 18

Darius and Cody returned to the office. They've taken RJ to the downtown jailhouse and left him there, until the morning. They walk into the office and placed all of their equipment back into their locations. Cody leaves the office, heading home. Darius is doing the same. As they both head downstairs, Cody turned to Darius.

"We did a good job today." Cody said.

"I could say, yeah we did do a good job." Darius said. "A great job, really."

They walk towards their cars and they leave, heading to their homes.

Preston returns to his apartment and realizes that its unlocked again. He decides not to pull out his gun and walked in. Once he was inside, he turned on the switch and he's standing toe-to-toe with Ray Colby. Preston grunted as he saw Ray standing in front of him with a pistol pointed directly towards him.

"It seems that everyone has a key to my place." Preston said. "So, Carla gave you the heads up on my resting spot or did you just bully the owner into giving you an extra key?"

"It's the best thing Carla's done for me so far in her line of work." Ray said. "You have no need to worry if I try to kill you here. I'm only here to tell you about Hoyt's current situation and how it concerns me and my elite group."

"I could give a shit about your elite group. What's this situation have to do with Hoyt and your pals?" Preston said. "Is it about his patterned explosion attacks over the past few days or is it something that he's done to you in a way that I have no knowledge of? I assume it's something more personal going on here?"

"I'm going to say this once and only once in a way that you can understand, Marshal. Either you leave Hoyt to me and I'll spare your entire agency from a total disaster. You and your marshals are invading my business. My property, you guys even ran some of my men off the road during that chase you guys had."

"Well, I'll say this, Ray." Preston said. "I'm not going to leave Hoyt alone because he is my task to accomplish. As of right now, I'm going to give you a ten-second count to leave this place, before I put a bullet through you and tell your elite friends that another one has been brought down."

Ray smiled. He nodded as he stared at Preston.

"Ten seconds, you say?" Ray said. "Sounds like a threat towards me. How should I take it from you when your weapon isn't even in your hand and mine is? Explain that to me? I can put a, what you say, bullet through you, before you even pull out your weapon."

"You'll pay to find that out." Preston said. "Just like your old buddy Cartel did. He played this game as well and you know how it ended for him don't you."

"Smooth. Ray said. "So, before I go I would want to say."

"Ten." Preston said. "And counting."

Ray laughed. He shook his finger toward Preston, who continued to stand still. Ray nodded his head.

"Funny and clever." Ray said. "You really know how to intimidate your enemies, Marshal. In ways that other marshals or detectives wouldn't even give a mere thought towards."

"Nine." Preston said. "The countdown is still on going, Colby."

Preston slowly moved his right hand to his side, almost ready to pull out his weapon. Ray doesn't even notice it. Ray placed his gun back into his back and slowly moved inches closer to the door.

"Ok." Ray said. "Alright. I'll leave. But, take my advice under serious conditions, Marshal or there will be consequences on your head."

Ray left the apartment and Preston turned around and made sure that Ray left the area.

The next morning, Coover and Rusty are visiting the hospital to search for any injuries on their bodies due to the crazed speeding chase. They find bruised ribs on Coover, but a broken rib and a dislocated shoulder on Rusty. Barbette arrived and seen her sons in the hospital room.

"What happened?" Barbette asked. "What happened to my two babies?"

"Mama, we were ran off the road by those marshals." Coover said. "We were just trying to do the job."

"Don't talk about it in here, Coover." Rusty said with pain in his voice. "We don't need anyone hearing about our business. They might try to pull something against us, so we would have to pay more."

Leaving the hospital, walking towards their mother's partially clean brown Durango. They helped Rusty walk to the car and help him into the passenger's seat.

Coover inched closer to Barbette so he could whisper the information to her. In order to avoid confrontation with people in the hospital.

"Mama, we tried to take out Hoyt." Coover said. "But, those marshals invaded the plans. If they didn't we would've had him."

"Was Billy there as well?" Barbette asked. "Was he with Hoyt when this was taking place?"

"Yes ma'am." Coover said. "We tried to have spoken conversations with him, but, he didn't respond to us. Nor, did he come to visit us here."

"It's alright, my sons." Barbette said. "Billy has decided to leave the family that raised him. There's nothing we can do to save him now. He's on his own at this point."

At the office, Eldon speaks with Darius and Cody about their case in Hartford. Darius tells Eldon that the case when nice and they've placed

RJ in custody. Eldon is impressed and thanks them both for their help in finding RJ. Preston and Emily walk into the office and Preston told Eldon that Ray was inside his apartment last night, giving him a warning not to have any marshal or law enforcement officers involved with Hoyt. Eldon tells Preston that he should take Ray's words and shove them up Ray's ass. Preston laughed.

"So, if I may ask you of this. Your anger craze, yesterday." Eldon said. "What the hell was that all about?"

"Throughout most of his adult life, Hoyt has killed thousands of people across this city and state, Eldon." Preston said. "It's about time that someone gave him a beat down and to be honest, I wasn't even quite finished with him."

"He deserved a lot more, I believe." Eldon said. "Though, you can't let your anger take control over yourself. It could cost you dearly."

"He deserved a lot more." Preston said. "A thousand times more. Since, he's killed that number of people, some innocent and some not. He deserves it."

"If Emily didn't calm you down, you've would have possibly killed the guy." Eldon said. "Imagine how that would look upon you."

"Me and Hoyt were once good friends, long ago." Preston said. "Times have changed and so have the friendships and trust."

Eldon later told Preston to head out toward the courthouse, so they can discuss RJ's case. Preston looked over at Eldon, asking if Darius and Cody should be there, since they picked the guy up in the first place. Eldon said that they will be there and so should him and Preston.

At the courthouse, the judge is sentencing RJ to four years in prison for his previous crimes such as being a con artist, he's also convicted of burglary, kidnapping, and a case of three homicides. The security handcuffed RJ and took him out of the courtroom through the back doors and towards a police car, that's parked in the front of the building.

They open the front doors and it is crowded with reporters and journalists, asking RJ questions concerning what he's done over the years.

He gives them no responses as he gets into the back of the police car and it drives off. Eldon and Preston walk over to Darius and Cody and congratulate them on solving RJ's case.

"You guys did great." Eldon said. "I should tell the head office to give you guys some higher power of authority."

"I don't think you should do that, Eldon." Preston said. "Might cause their egos to take over and when the ball drops their careers would be over in a nutshell."

"I don't have that much of an ego, Preston." Darius said. "Though, I think we all know that Cody does to a certain extent."

"Not really, guys." Cody said. "When it comes to egos, you won't have to look toward him for being some kind of a narcissist."

At the warehouse, Ray finds out about what happened with the chase and that he lost a few of his men during the event. Coover and Rusty walk in with Barbette on their side.

"Coover, Rusty. Are you alright?" Ray asked.

"We're fine, boss." Rusty said. "Just some minor injuries, that's all."

"Hoyt and those damn marshal folks hurt my two sons, Colby." Barbette said. "They ran them off the road and into that foul ditch. Now their means of transportation is completely damaged."

"You shouldn't have to worry, Ms. Bronson. I'll go ahead and purchase your boys another truck. Though, we seriously need to consider the process of finding Hoyt and your youngest son." Ray said.

"It would be best if you could lead both Hoyt and that Instinct Marshal into some kind of a trap." Coover said. "You know, lead them both there, simultaneously, so that way, we can kill them both at the same time. Good plan, huh."

"The two birds and one stone play. It could work. But, how would we lead them to the same location?" Ray said.

"You let me handle that large obstacle, Ray." A female voice said from the front.

Ray looked and its Carla once again. Ray's had enough of her and commands his security to take her out. She tells Ray that she knows exactly how to lure both Preston and Hoyt into the same location to be killed. Ray asked her how and she said that she'll handle it, since she doesn't want them involved with it. Ray stood up and decided to allow Carla to go forward with the plan and that he has to leave for a trip to Newark, New Jersey.

Barbette stood up and thanks Ray for her son's new vehicle and said that they must take them all out soon. They leave and Carla leaves behind them, telling Ray not to worry. One of Ray's men walked up to him with a photo from the Caucasian and African-American men who were waiting inside the car.

"Sir, the two watchers told me to bring this picture to you." The thug said. "They suspected it would be highly useful to you."

Ray looked at the photo and it's a picture of Emily. Ray thought back to his New Jersey days and remembered who Emily was and knew she's also from Newark. He only focused on the picture as he decided to place a hit on her by hiring one hit man. He even exceeded the plan as to let the marshals know where he's headed, saying to his group that it would just to fool them and lure them into the trap.

"By doing this, they will never know what's going to hit them." Ray said. "Won't even have a clue what will be coming up on their front steps."

"You got it boss." The thug said.

The thug left the warehouse as Ray continued to read some unknown documents that were stacked on his desk.

At the office, Eldon contacts Preston and Emily to tell them that Ray has made an announcement that Ray is traveling to Newark for a business trip. Emily suggested that she'll go ahead and search around the city for Colby, since she's a native of the area. She left the office. Preston looked and turned to Eldon.

"So, as of now, I'm on my own?" Preston asked. "Due to Emily running off on her own merry goose chase."

"That appears to be the case." Eldon said. "Also, since Cody is currently partnered up with Darius, that does leave you on your own."

"Alright." Preston said. "I'll take only small portions of this to savor in."

"I almost forgot about this because of your savoring. Something did come up that I personally believe you'll be happy to solve on your own." Eldon said.

"Which is what?" Preston asked. "Picking up lunch for the agency. Or the fugitives in questioning."

Eldon leaned over his desk and pulled out a document from underneath a small pile of paper notes. He handed the document over to Preston, in which he opened it and found it containing a picture of Carla meeting with Ray at the warehouse in the outskirts of New Haven

"You have got to me shitting me. This is what you wanted to give me to do. Go around town to search for an ex and an elite crime thug."

"I figured it would do you some good. Get some of that steam off your chest at least."

"I'll manage my stream progress. So, who exactly am I searching for on this case? Can't be Colby because Emily's already on the chase."

"There have been reports of seeing your old flame circling around town. Talking and making deals with a many of people that seem to be getting paid under the radar by Colby and his elite crime friends. So, you're on this case. Since you know her very well."

"I'll go ahead and do it. But, once I am finished with this one, I'm going ahead to look for Hoyt. Some of those events haven't happened yet and we need to stop them."

"Go ahead and do that. I won't stop you there."

In the outskirts of New Haven, just around a small field near a steep hill, Hoyt and Billy are sitting in a truck, over viewing Ray's warehouse. Billy looked around at the area, searching for any of Colby's henchmen around the location.

"So, far I don't see any of Ray's guys out here." Billy said. "What are we going to do when everything is in complete order, Hoyt?"

"Good of you to ask. The last plan will involve his warehouse in a huge way. It will be an epic event for us. But, so far two of the events have happened and we can't look too far into the near future."

"Wait, I thought only one of the events had took place." Billy asked. "The two have actually happened?"

"Listen very closely. The jailhouse was the first event in the long process. The Convenience store explosion was only the second one and that went somewhat how I expected it to go. As of this moment, we have just two more events to go before the main course, being the warehouse here, takes its place atop the other four."

"If I may ask you, what are the next two events? I take it you're going to blow up Target next or a mall? Because, personally I don't like Target, Hoyt. They're just cheapskates over there. Don't do shit about their customers."

"Convenience store didn't either. I would expect you to hate nearly all of the retail stores."

"That was a good point. I never thought of it in that way."

"One thing's for sure, Billy. I'm not blowing up another shopping place. That already took its course. This time, it has to be something quieter than the last two places. Something to get people off their asses when it culminates."

"Could you give me some kind of a hint as to what place would be like that? Because, I don't know any quiet, quiet places that you could actually blow up without causing a problem."

"Believe me when I say, there's a place, Billy. There's a place around this land that's point-blank right up our noses and around the corner. But, I'm starting to think that we need more members, just to have a full overview of the entire city."

It's nightfall in New Jersey as Ray arrived in Newark. After exiting his private plane, he's escorted out of the airport approaching his vehicle. He's heavily guarded with security as they lead him towards his black SUV waiting for him out front. They walk out of the airport as Ray entered the SUV and it pulled away with three of his henchmen already inside the back of the SUV. Ray nodded at them as he reached into his jacket and pulled out his phone and started dialing a number.

"Hello, chief. This is Colby. Yeah, I'm in Newark. Everything will go as planned as we discussed. The female Marshal? She shouldn't be too far gone behind us. We'll have her in place as soon as she's in our sights. Don't worry, chief, it's all in good hands."

Ray hung up the phone and started smiling to himself.

CHAPTER 19

Carla sat in a room as she was having a meeting with six of Ray's thugs and she discusses the plan to lure both Preston and Hoyt into the same location, only for them to be killed by the six thugs. As the thugs sat at a round table, looking at Carla standing up in front of them. One of the thugs stood up. He gained the attention of the other five thugs and Carla herself as he began questioning Carla's proposed plan of attack in the woods.

"So, what's your position in this plan, sweetheart?" One thug asked. "If you don't mind a man like me asking such a question."

"My plan is to be the backup." Carla said.

"Backup?" The thug said. "What kind of backup are you talking about? More guys like us or some highly trained folks that are in this for the sake of execution and a little extra profit."

"You'll just have to wait and see who they are." Carla said. "The backup will do us some good in this task."

Another thug stood up and said that she's responsible for John's death and why should they trust her on this mission. Carla said that she can be trusted, since what happened with John wasn't her fault. The six thugs look at one another and turned to Carla.

"We'll help you out on this one, Carla." The thug said. "But, don't think for a second to turn on us. By any means."

"You won't have to worry about that." Carla said. "You're all in good hands being with me."

The thugs nod as Carla left the room. Though, the first two thugs are a little uncertain about Carla's motives in the process.

Eldon contacts Darius and Cody to come to his office. They enter his office and sit at the desk. Eldon turned to them with documents in his hand.

"What's going on now, chief?" Darius asked.

"We've just received a new case that concerns a hit man." Eldon said.

"Hit man? Cool." Cody said. "Sounds like it should be great case to work on."

"Who's this hit man and what's his case of being the cause?" Darius asked.

"The hit man's name is currently unknown at this moment." Eldon said. "But, for some odd reason, his only targets are female prostitutes."

"Prostitutes? He has some obsession with prostitutes." Darius said. "I wonder why he would have that type of agenda. For whatever reason, sure doesn't sound like fun."

"That's what I'm trying to figure out." Eldon said. "Since Preston is busy with a case and Emily's out of state, I'm going to join the two of you on this one. Just to have some time out of the office."

"Where's the first place that we should look?" Darius asked.

"We'll head to a local street in the low side of town." Eldon said. "That's where most of the prostitution business takes place. If its crowded with women by tonight, we should find out hit man."

"Hopefully." Darius said.

Hoyt and Billy enter small building. Inside is a group of people playing poker. Hoyt looked at the guys and yelled to get their attention. They turned in fear and started walking towards him, pulling out their guns and knives.

"From my perspective it sure looks like a nice game of poker is being played here in the centerfolds." Hoyt said. "Mind if me and my friend here join in on the game and try to win some prizes of our own."

"Who the hell are you two boys?" One man said. "What the hell you're doing here in our place?"

"Gentlemen, gentlemen, please. No trouble has entered into your doorstep." Hoyt said. "Now just calm down and relax yourselves. I'm only here to present you fellow gentlemen an offer that you cannot possibly refuse according to how you're behaving as of this moment."

"Oh yeah. What type of offer?" The man said.

"An offer that will bring in a lot of money." Hoyt said. "As well as some control over the city."

The man looked over at his friends as they start to nod their heads in acceptance. The man turned his attention back to Hoyt. Staring him into his eyes.

"Money and control, you say? Alright." The man said. "I'll say we're all in. What do you need us to do?"

"If you and your group just follow me to my new safe haven and everything will be explained there." Hoyt said. "Please follow quickly and quietly, so we don't cause a disturbance."

Emily arrives through the interstate, entering Newark, New Jersey. Once inside the city she's already determined and going on the hunt for Ray. She drives down and travels through the downtown area to search for any evidence that will lead to him. Though, she doesn't find anything, she drives past an office building, she notices a man who looked similar to Ray physically. She slowly entered the parking lot to have a closer look. The man she was looking at wasn't Ray.

"Damn it." Emily said. "No sign of Ray here. Where could he have gone? I could check the agency. They should remember who I am."

Preston is visiting a small diner. The diner is quiet, as there aren't many people inside. He walked toward the counter, where he speaks with one of the waitresses about Carla, since that's the diner where she was located.

"Excuse me, Ms." Preston said. "I'm here to asks some questions regarding a woman who was in here a few days ago."

"Sir, you are?" The waitress asked.

"Oh, I'm Preston Maddox." Preston said smiling. "United States Marshal and Homicide Detective. I'm here to ask about a woman that was seen in this very place not too long ago."

"Marshal, huh. You can ask me anything you want, baby." The waitress said. "And I mean anything that's on your mind."

"Ok. I'm just here to ask about this certain particular woman." Preston said. "That's all there is."

"Well, do you have a picture of the woman?" The waitress said. "That way it would be easier for me to help you out, sir."

"As a matter of fact, I do." Preston said. "Here it is right here."

He showed her a picture and she looked at the photo and glanced toward Preston and back to the photo. She recognized Carla in the photo.

"I remember her and the guy she's with." The waitress said. "They sat right over in that corner, towards the window."

"Ok. You're getting somewhere now. While they were here, did you over hear their conversation or anything related?" Preston asked.

"They were talking about a plan that they were trying to do." The waitress said. "It involved something with officials and such. But, I didn't hear anything else."

"Did they mention a location of any kind?" Preston asked. "Or anything related to that matter?"

"They spoke about a warehouse across town." The waitress said. "They were saying that after they finish their plan, they'll head back there. But, they didn't mention any other locations, sir. But, you can visit an antique store across town. There's a gentleman there named Tanner. They spoke about him, so he could possibly give you some information."

"If that's the case and it seems that it is. I thank you for your honesty, sweetheart." Preston said. "I really appreciate all of the help you've given me on this task."

"You're welcome and here's my phone number." The waitress said. "You can call me if you want to know more. Whether it involves your case or just a personal call."

Preston smiled, "I'll keep the personal call in mind. Have a good day, ma'am."

Preston left the diner drove away as he continued to search around other possible locations for more information.

CHAPTER 20

Hoyt and Billy arrived at the old pawn shop building along with the group of poker guys. They walk in and see all of the weapons that are laid out through the building. The place is also painted white and it's all clean. Billy turned to Hoyt.

"Whoa, whoa! Wait a second now?" Billy said. "Please tell me that you bought the place before you start talking with these fellows?"

"I sure did." Hoyt said. "It wasn't much. Just negotiating, really."

"Nice place, Hoyt." The man said. "We agreed to your offer. So, what you need us to do?"

"I need you and a few of your guys to head out towards the downtown area and cause a scene." Hoyt said. "A big scene."

"A big scene? What kind of big scene? A riot? A shootout? Rob drivers and steal their cars kind of big?"

"A shootout will do just fine." Hoyt said. "Though, I like the riot idea a lot, that can wait another time and you never told us your name?"

"Sorry about that, my newly found friend." The man said. "My name is Russell. Although, my guys call me Leader."

"They call you Leader, huh." Hoyt said. "Sounds good. But, you know that I'm the leader of this organization and you're the leader of your groups. So, they'll call you Leader and I'll just call you Russell. Alright."

"You got it, Hoyt." Russell said. "Whatever you say from this point on end."

Hoyt smiled and shook Russell's hand. After shaking his hand, Hoyt and Billy leave the pawn shop, letting Russell sit with his men. Thinking about Hoyt's offer.

Coover and Rusty are at a car lot with Barbette as they pick out their new vehicle. They are looking at the trucks. Coover spotted one and pointed it out.

"How about this one, Rusty." Coover said. "This one could help us out at least."

"It could work." Rusty said. "But, I don't like green. Green doesn't suit me well. As long as it's an F-250 and not a bright color, I'll be fine with it."

"How about the silver one over there?" Coover said. "That one suits you well enough. Come on, brother. It's only a vehicle we need to use."

Rusty walked over to the truck and looked at the interior. He started smiling and turned toward his mother slowly.

"Rusty, do you like this one?" Barbette asked. "You look like you do."

"Yes ma'am, I do." Rusty said. "Brother, how about you? You like this one, here?"

"I do." Coover said. "I really do."

"Let's go inside and speak with the dealer." Barbette said. "After this, the both of you should thank Mr. Colby for doing this. This is his money we're dealing with after all."

Preston had arrived at the antique store across town. He walks in and sees tons of priceless antique glasses and statues. Preston looks around toward the counter for the cashier or any employees.

"Excuse me! Anybody here?!" Preston yelled. "Hello?!"

The clerk walks from the back and looks at Preston. Preston stood still as he stared at the clerk. Who walked slowly toward the counter near Preston. The clerk took a big swallow before speaking to Preston.

"What do you want?" The clerk said. "Sir. Good sir."

The clerk had noticed Preston's badge and gun on each side of his belt. He becomes startled as he took one step back from the counter."

"Oh. A badge and a gun." The clerk said. "I take it you're a policeman, huh."

"What? No. I'm not a cop, I'm a Deputy United States Marshal and Homicide Detective." Preston said. "Since you know what I am, what's your name, slick?"

"My name's Tanner." The clerk said. "Tanner Powell."

"Well, Tanner Powell. I was told by a waitress at the diner across the block from here that you could have some possible information regarding this woman and this man."

Preston showed Tanner the photo of Carla and the thug. Tanner looked at the photo and turned back to Preston.

"No, man." Tanner said. "I have no idea who those two are. Sorry, I can't help you there, sir."

"You said your name was Tanner, huh?" Preston said. "Almost forgot after hearing you speak like that in such manner. By the look of you, I would've though your name would've been something like Troy or Steven. Hell, maybe even Freddy."

"I have some relatives named Troy and Steven." Tanner said. "Cousins on my father's side. No Freddy in my family, though I believe not to be. I really don't know everyone in my family, so I couldn't really tell you exactly."

"Yeah, great. I'm sure you'll find out sooner or later." Preston said. "And what's going on with both of your eyes? You've been smoking dope or something?"

"It's a rare form of pink eye, sir." Tanner said. "It very, very contagious, so, I would recommend that you don't touch me, sir. If you do touch me, you could get infected too and wake up the next morning with one of these or maybe something worse."

"I don't think I'll end up turning into a Dead of any sort. Though, you have no need to worry. I'm not going to touch you by any means." Preston said. "No worries there. I'm just looking for the woman on the photo. Her name is Carla Garcia by the way. The waitress told me that they spoke about you. Saying that they came by this location."

"Never heard of her in my entire life." Tanner said. "Don't recall seeing her in this place."

"From what I understand, according to my knowledge is she operates at a warehouse not far from here." Preston said. "With that warehouse nearby this area, you're sure you didn't see her?"

"Sorry, I can't help you." Tanner said. "Truly can't."

"Ok, then." Preston said. "If that's the way you want to go on this day."

Preston walked over to the shelf and tampered with the antique glasses on the shelf. He started saying a rhyme before he tapped on one and knocked down one of the antique glasses. The glass smashed on the floor in pieces. Tanner freaked out and Preston looked at him.

"Oh shit." Preston said. "I thought it was plastic. My bad."

"Come on, man." Tanner said. "Please don't do this. Don't break anything else. I'll get in trouble over this."

Preston knocked down another glass as Tanner continues freaking out, rubbing his head and grinding his teeth. Preston picked up one of the statues from the bottom shelf. He walked toward the counter with it.

"Oh, goddamn it, man!" Tanner said. "Please!"

"Listen, Tanner Boy. All I'm trying to do is incarcerate a very bad man and the woman on the photo, Carla Garcia, may help me in completing this task. So, unless you want me to continue being a clumsy asshole in your store, why don't you tell me if she came in here. And if so, where was she headed?"

"Alright. She came in here one day with the guy on the picture. She was buying an antique to take to Quarles Funeral Home." Tanner said. "She also spoke of a hair salon. That's all I know."

"A hair salon." Preston said. "You're sure about that?

"Yes sir."

"You're positive about it?"

"Yes sir."

Preston placed down the statue and took out of his jacket pocket a one-hundred-dollar bill and laid it on the counter. Tanner looked at it while glancing at Preston.

"There you go, Tanner. I broke it, I bought it. Make sure you take care of those eyes will you."

Hoyt, Billy, Russell, and his group of men arrive in the downtown area during rush hour. Hoyt pulled Russell aside as he commanded him to bring him men towards the eastern side of the area as he and Billy decide to watch over the western side. Russell commands his men to stand still by the wall on the building next to them, which is New Haven City Hall. Billy pointed it out to Hoyt that they're standing right in front of City Hall. Hoyt's eyes lit up as he smiled.

"Oh my. This plan is proceeding excellently."

"How do you figure that, Hoyt?"

"Just watch, my good friend. Prepare to see something truly amazing in this area. City Hall is just icing on the cake for us."

Hoyt pointed toward Russell, who later commands his men to set up their gear and prepare themselves. His men reached toward the pair of duffle bags that sat in front of them, pulling out their assault weapons such as RPKs and AKs. A few of Russell's men appeared to have carried shotguns on their shoulders. The traffic later stopped, as to the light turned red. Hoyt turned to Russell and gave him the signal. Russell signaled to his men as they run out in the middle of the open road and start firing shots all around the street. Hoyt and Billy ducked behind a wall, as Hoyt laughs while watching Russell's men. Billy stared at Hoyt as he laughed.

"This isn't funny, Hoyt! What the hell is this?!" Billy said. "What have you placed them under?!"

"All of this was only a test for Russell and his men, my friend." Hoyt said. "I just wanted to see if they had the loyalty to go along with it. Besides, it was Russell's idea for this shootout. They also picked this spot and Russell gave them the signal to fire."

"Why couldn't you have just chosen the riot. It would've been so much safer compared to what we're watching. We wouldn't have to duck our heads for Christ's sake if they were just hijacking people from their cars and beating them down on the street. We could've stood by and just watched as it was happening."

"True point you have there. Though, he did mention having a riot here instead of gunfire." Hoyt said. "But face it Billy, this is more fun!"

Russell's men continued firing all around the area. They've knocked out windows on the nearby building, even blowing out the windshields of the cars. the stoplight turned green and the cars suddenly started to move without any hesitation. They're drove quickly to avoid the gunshots.

Russell screamed at his men to move, in which only a few had done. The drivers within the cars appear to be pissed and start to run over the remaining men on the road. Hoyt looked up and saw what was happening. Billy turned and looked as well with fear in his eyes.

"Holy fucking shit! They're being ran over! Goddamn it, those people are running them over nonstop!"

"I didn't think today's society would have this sense of mind in them. Shit, Billy, we could recruit more people like these drivers here. A lot more of people like this."

Russell's men are jumping out of the roadway and one turned to Russell.

"Leader, what do we do?" The thug asked.

"Let me ask Hoyt." Russell said. "He'll tell us what we should do."

Russell ran across the road to the other side of the street. He looked over at Hoyt, who's still crouched down beside the stained walls.

"What in the hell shall we do, Hoyt?!"

"Head back to your cars and return to the site. Me and Billy will meet you and your remaining men up there and then we'll regroup there and begin the process."

"Got ya, boss." Russell said. "Let's go men."

He commanded his remaining men to head back to the cars. They get in their vehicles and drive off, heading back to the site. Hoyt and Billy do the same.

"What are we going to do about him and his men?" Billy said. "Are you going to promote them in some kind of way or just get rid of them when the time is right?"

"I won't do anything to Russell or his men. They've done a great job here and have proved their loyalty to us."

Emily had arrived at the Marshal agency in Newark. The building is a five-story structure facility. Its taller and larger than the agency building in New Haven. She walked inside, and she runs into an old partner, an African American woman. She spots Emily and walked over towards her. They both hugged and greeted each other.

"My, my, Emily. What brings you back to Newark?"

"Some serious issues, Gloria. I'm here on a case that concerns Ray Colby. I'm sure you remember him, don't you?"

"Wait, he's back in town? Where the hell has he been all this time because we haven't seen a trace of him or heard about it?"

"He's been in New Haven for quite some time now. He appeared to have moved his occupation of doing some of his dirty work up there. Though, I have yet to run into him yet. I've only had recent encounters with a few of his thugs."

"Are they like any of the guys here would be?"

"Not exactly. They're worse. Much worse. Appeared to have been trained for this particular job."

They head to the fifth floor by use of the elevator. Emily recommended the stairs, but Gloria denied her entry due to the stairs repaired for some damage that occurred prior to Emily's arrival.

Once on the fifth floor, Gloria walked into her office, walking behind her desk, she pulled out a document from the drawer that contained the files of all Ray's previous and reported locations and hideouts throughout the state of New Jersey. Emily looked at the map and took a photo of it with her Samsung phone. She turned to Gloria.

"I have to say I should truly thank you for helping me with this."

"Don't mention it, Emily. Remember when you were stationed here. We were once partners. Whenever you need help, I'll always be there for you anytime you need it. So, who's your partner over at New Haven?"

"Preston Maddox. I'm sure you've heard about the guy."

"The Instinct Marshal!" Gloria said. "The guy who shot Jonny Cartel is your partner!"

"Yeah, the guy who shot Cartel and is known for using his supposed instincts to solve his cases. For those who don't know, the guy is also a huge pain in the ass. A complete narcissist."

"I thought he would be a nice one." Gloria said. "Since, he's a handsome gentleman."

"He is a nice guy." Emily said. "Only whenever he decides he wants to be."

    Emily thanked Gloria again as she leaves the facility. As she enters her car, she took out her phone and looked at the photo of the map. After reading through the map's targeted locations, she decides to go for the first location, which is a construction site. As Emily leaves and drives off, there's a small black corolla sitting across the street not too far from the facility. Inside is a man, wearing a brown fedora. He watches as Emily leaves and proceeds to follow her.

CHAPTER 21

Russell and his men return to Hoyt's site as Hoyt and Billy are already there waiting for them. Russell exited out of his truck and walked toward Hoyt, furious look on his face as he approached him.

"May I ask what in the hell just happened out there?!" Russell asked. "We were nearly hit by those damn cars, Hoyt!"

"I didn't expect that, Russell." Hoyt said. "But, you only lost about what, two, three of your men. They can be replaced very quickly. No hard feelings."

"That's not the case. They were good men." Russell said. "They put their lives on the line doing this kind of shit."

"I still say that you should've gone with the riot plan." Billy said. "Otherwise, your men would still be here."

"You have a point there." Russell said. "But, that's not the case here at the moment."

"The case is over." Hoyt said. "We now focus on what's in the next case. In which, the next one won't be so terrible as the one that's just transpired."

"Why won't it be so terrible, Hoyt?" Russell asked. "Why, is it located in a safer location?"

"Because we're going into the woods for this one." Hoyt said. "Think of it as trying out your stealth movements."

"Great. Great. Right up my alley." Russell said. "Going into the woods for what?"

"You'll find out when I tell you." Hoyt said. "You and your men may return to your homes now. You're done for the day."

Russell and his men left the site. Billy turned to Hoyt, asking him about the woods and why they're heading that direction. Hoyt decided to tell him that there is a secret cabin hidden in the woods and when the time is right, that they will have to blow that cabin into entire pieces.

Eldon, Cody, and Darius are on a street at the lower town. Cody looks around the area and tells Eldon that this is the location where the prostitution takes place. Eldon says that they'll come back later and patrol the area in search of the hit man. Eldon tells Cody to have his sniper ready for use, because he might need it. Darius asks Eldon how they're going to patrol the area. Eldon pointed across the street.

"We'll have to set up a secret location across the street there." Eldon said.

"At that abandoned building?" Darius asked. "It looks like it could help us out."

"Yeah. It could work." Eldon said. "Me and you will be on the inside, as Cody will be on the roof."

"Why the roof?" Cody asked. "I can shoot from the windows, you know."

"The roof is best for your sniper." Eldon said. "Unless it rains, then you can shoot from the windows."

"Well, hopefully it pours." Cody said.

Preston arrives at a hair salon. He walked inside, seeing all the women getting their hair done and the smell of washed hair surrounding the salon. He walked toward the counter, where the cashier was standing.

"I'm sorry to bother you." Preston said. "But, I'm Preston Maddox, United States Marshal and Homicide Detective. I'm here on business and I'll like to ask you something."

"Ok." The cashier said. "And your point?"

"I'm looking for a woman." Preston said. "Carla Garcia. Have you heard of her?"

"Do you have a picture of this Carla?" The cashier said.

"Right here, Ms." Preston said. "I just came from an antique store down the street and the clerk said that she's was headed here. So, I'm just here for some information."

He took out the photo and the cashier quickly denied seeing her.

Which through Preston off for a second before he was able to gather himself.

"Well, Ms., according to some documented information, she came in here a few days ago." Preston said. "Are you sure you didn't see her. She had to be wearing red, that's all she wears."

"Listen, in this line of work, someone like me sees a lot of different women that come into these places who wear different styles of red, sir. I'm afraid that you have the wrong location or maybe you were fooled."

"According to you, it seems I have." Preston said. "Have a good day, ma'am."

Preston leaves the salon and gets into the car. He pulled out the folder containing the documents. On the document, it mentions that Carla might have visited Quarles Funeral Home. Preston reads it and heads over to the location.

Ray sat inside a meeting at a Newark office. The meeting concerned the crime lords with their deals involving the drug shipments. One crime lord gets the attention and started asking about their shipments. Another one asked the exact same thing.

"My question is simple, gentlemen." One crime lord said. "How do we move our shipments around the country and deal with these officials and their marshal service?"

"We must create a strategy that will confuse the officials and certainly those marshals." Ray said. "I've already had to deal with two and I don't need anymore."

"How do we create this strategy?" The crime lord said. "There has to be some form of way that we could create something of that category."

"Gather your men for a meeting and hire yourself a strategist." Ray said. "That's what I've done."

"You hired a strategist?" Another crime lord said. "Never would expect you to do something like that, Mr. Colby. Thought, you plotted out your plans on your own and didn't take hardly anyone's advice. Unless it was handed to you."

"The strategist I've hired for my alliance is a former lover of a marshal." Ray said. "The Marshal that shot one of our associates, Jonny Cartel."

"The Instinct Marshal?!" The crime lord said. "You have him on your case? If he's watching you, he could possibly find the rest of us. That guy never makes a mistake. He uses his instincts for crying out loud."

"Everything will be fine." Ray said. "You won't have to worry about the Instinct Marshal. My strategist has already designed a plan that will take the marshal off the face of the earth."

"I hope so, Mr. Colby. I hope she does." The crime lord said. "If not, we'll have to tell the chief to let you go or better yet. He'll probably have us kill you if the plan doesn't go as followed."

Ray stared at the other crime lord. He grinned toward him before clearing his face of the grin.

"Anything else you'll like to say, Mr. Colby." The crime lord said. "Since, you won't join in on our little part in this situation."

"No one can get rid of me." Ray said. "I'm the best crime lord around these parts. I make things happen and I also end things. The chief will never get rid of someone who's highly intelligent and skilled as I. You can say what you want, but get this straight. You cross a line with me, I'll take the marshal's job and put you down myself."

Emily arrived at the construction site. Seeing that they're in the middle of building a new office building. She walked toward a few of the constructors to ask them about Colby. Some of the constructors look at Emily and check her out.

"Pardon me, gentlemen." Emily said. "Do any of you know the whereabouts of Ray Colby?"

"He's not here at the time." One constructor said. "Though, he frequently visits. Since this is his office that we're building at the moment."

"This is his office?" Emily said.

"Yes ma'am." The constructor said. "We don't know what it's for, but, this is commanded by him. He's paying for it. He usually comes by on Tuesdays and Thursdays just to see how it's all going. Sometimes, he'll pay some surprise visits. We all hate those."

Emily looked around as she thanked the constructors for their help and left the construction site. She looked at the photo again to search for another location. The location that she's looking at now is a shooting gallery.

From behind her is the man in the corolla. He picks up his cell phone and contacts Ray.

"Ray, sorry to bother you right now. This is Desmond. I'm on the female Marshal's trail at this moment." Desmond said. "What do you want me to do once I have her?"

"Do what I'm paying you to do." Ray said. "Kill the bitch and you'll receive your reward."

"Very well, then." Desmond said.

Desmond hung up and drove off down the street, making a left turn into the small traffic.

Eldon, Cody, and Darius returned to the street where the prostitution line takes place. Eldon decided to set up camp inside the abandoned building. The moon shines down on them during the night sky. Thunder started to rumble and the rain proceeded to pour down. Cody looked at Eldon, smiling.

"Fine, you get the window." Eldon said.

"It makes it easier for me." Cody said.

Cody reaches into the back of the SUV and pulled out a Barrett M82. Darius looked over at him, nodding his head.

"That's a nice one, Cody." Darius said.

"It's my favorite one." Cody said. "I've tried a bunch, but, this one stands out the most for me. Plus, its easy for me to handle. The other ones were just bulky and slow on reload in my opinion."

Eldon pulled out an array of weapons from handguns to pistols to rifles. Darius walked over to the table as Eldon set up the gear. He looked through the weapons.

"We're going to need all of these?" Darius said. "Chief, he's just one man, not an entire army."

"We're dealing with a hit man, Darius." Eldon said. "We're going to need as much as we can possibly get our hands on. Besides, we don't know where his location will be. So, just grab whichever weapon you like and mark your place."

Darius grabbed an AK and stood guard at the metallic garage door. Cody went to the upper floor, placing and pointing the sniper rifle out of the window at a minimum. Eldon stood by the windows on the first floor, looking out. On the other side of the street, a limo pulled up slowly. Eldon looked outside and sees the chauffer open the back doors. Coming out are six prostitutes, all carrying umbrellas.

"They look hot don't they, chief?" Darius said.

"They seem to be alright." Eldon said. "But I'm disease-free and I'll like to keep it that way."

The prostitutes stood on the sidewalk as an array of vehicles went back and forth on the road. Few of the cars parked over near the sidewalk, the prostitutes walk toward the cars and some leave. As Cody was looking out the window, he noticed an unusual occurrence to the left side of the building. He pulled out his communicator and contacted Eldon.

"Cody, what's the situation from your point of view?" Eldon said. "Do you have anything in your sights?"

"Something's going on to the left of the building. Appeared to have looked like a man sneaking across. Looked to me as if he was carrying a weapon of some sort."

"Me and Darius will keep watch down here and search the area. Just keep your position and stand your ground until you have a full visual of what's moving around."

Eldon and Darius noticed a few of the prostitutes were already taken by buyers as they see only three are remaining on the sidewalk. Darius shrugged shoulders as Eldon shook his head.

"It looks like they're going fast." Darius said. "They must be good or something. I mean, to go that fast, that's incredible for prostitutes. Especially in today's age."

"I don't know how this business goes and works, Darius. Though, from the way you're talking about it in such a high manner, it seems to me that you know some stuff about this line of work. But, as for me. I'm a married man with three children, so I have no idea how the prostitution business works nor, will I ever get in line at the academy of whoredom."

"I'm currently in a relationship as well." Darius said. "Though, my brother is a pimp. So, that's where I learned a lot about the prostitution business. Growing up with someone like that shows you a lot in your youth years."

Cody looked out of the left window and seen another individual, who's standing on top of the building to the left. Cody spotted a man, wearing a black fedora, black leather jacket and some black jeans, aiming at the prostitutes with a sniper rifle. Cody contacted Eldon and warned him of the hit man being on the roof of the left building. Eldon ran up the stairs and stood by Cody, looking out the window toward the hit man.

"That's him." Cody said. "The appearance, the sniper, and the stance. He's the guy we're looking for."

"Make sure you have a clear go around just in case he decides to move over an inch."

They continued to look out the window at the hit man. Cody turned his rifle and aimed the weapon out the window through a small crack. Pointing it toward the hit man, Cody goes into deep focus as he slowly prepared to fire the immediate shot. Eldon reached to his side and raised his gun, aiming out the window to the hit man.

"Do you have a clear view to gain a clean shot?" Eldon said.

"Yes I do, chief." Cody said. "Ready for the commanding order."

As Cody prepared and placed his finger on the trigger to fire, the hit man turned to the right direction and started firing toward them. Eldon and Cody ducked down as glass began to shatter all around them from the broken windows. The gunfire caused the remaining prostitutes to run away from the sidewalk. Meanwhile, downstairs, Darius began to hear the gunshots coming from the upper floor. He stood up and ran upstairs. The hit man continued firing shots from his rifle as they're still crouched on the ground.

"We now know it's him." Eldon said. "And he knows it's us that's followed him."

"What are we going to do? Are we just going to wait till he runs out of ammo and take the shot?"

"Just wait for the moment where he assumes we're dead and then you take the shot."

Darius burst through the upstairs door and crouched down on the ground to avoid being shot by the hit man. He slid over to where Eldon and Cody were hunkered down.

"Looks like whatever you did gave him some knowledge of our whereabouts. So, you found him and he found you." Darius said.

"Yeah." Eldon said. "Could you see him from downstairs? A clear view at least."

"If he were to move closer to the edge, I could get a shot at him from downstairs. we should be able to see him."

"Alright, I'll go downstairs and attempt to take the shot." Cody said. "I will need you two to cover my back by firing shots toward him for a distraction."

Cody swiftly sprinted downstairs and ran to the left side of the building, looking outside the small pair of broken windows. Once he looked out of the window, seeing only half of the hit man close to the edge of the building.

Cody aimed the rifle out the window toward the hit man and used the scope to have a closer view. He knew from then on that he had a clear shot.

"I have a clear shot, chief. What should I do now?"

"Take the damn shot."

"Yes sir."

Cody stood still and fired the shot. The round went through the hole of the window and flew through the air, inching near the hit man, who continued firing at the upstairs floor. Eldon and Darius were stilled ducked underneath the windows. The round went pass the brick wall and hit the hit man in the chest. Holding his chest, the hit man crouched down as he fell to the ground. Not hearing anymore gun fire, Eldon and Darius took a small look out the window and saw the hit man down on the ground, slowly moving.

"So, we're going to the roof to check if he's still breathing?" Darius said.

"Something like that." Eldon said. "Let's get up there."

Upon reaching the other building and making it to the rooftop, other police officers with many officials had arrived at the scene as well. They make the discovery that the hit man survived the sniper shot from Cody as the officer slowly placed the hit man in the back of the police car. Shutting the back door, they thanked Eldon and his marshals for helping out with the cause and drive off. Eldon turned and told Cody that he was good at keeping his eyes open at his surroundings, otherwise, they probably wouldn't have caught the hit man. Eldon walked over to another officer.

"Did you find the name of the hit man, officer?" Eldon said. "Because, we didn't have any sort of information on the fellow."

"We don't have any knowledge of his real name, sir." The officer said. "From what we've gathered, the name he goes by is The Jackal. Something within that category."

"What's all on his record?" Eldon said."

"According to his criminal records, The Jackal was one of the country's most primary hit men. He primarily completed jobs and tasks for certain companies who were involved with the prostitution business. He also did some small duty in the marijuana business and the crystal meth business."

"So, he was basically killing off prostitutes because he was paid by a competitor to do so." Eldon said. "Never knew a job like that ever existed."

"Though, we hope to question him as soon as he recovers. We should have more information tomorrow at noon, hopefully. We'll contact you when we've gathered enough information."

"Thank you, officer." Eldon said.

Eldon walked over to Darius and Cody, who were discussing the type of rifle The Jackal used for his assassinations. They turned toward Eldon as he approached them in a slow manner.

"What's next on the agenda now, chief?" Darius said. "Any more places we should probably be looking out for."

"I'm going to get a drink." Eldon said. "I would assume that the two of you would be coming along with me? Just to celebrate what we've just accomplished here."

"Sure." Cody said. "I'm up for it."

CHAPTER 22

Inside his hideout, Hoyt and Billy discussed the cabin location with Russell and his men. Hoyt tells them how the cabin is hidden deep within the woods and he discovered there were a trail of tire tracks that lead to the location.

"So, how are we going to be able to head over there on foot?" Russell said. "We're going stealth mode on them or something?"

Hoyt told him that they will have to drive at a closer location, then they'll walk to the cabin on foot. Russell agreed to the decision and they start preparing themselves for the plan. Billy looked at Hoyt and leaned over toward him across the covered table.

"Now, this cabin that we're going to hit, Hoyt. Is there any chance that Colby and my brothers could be inside at the very moment we drop ship?"

"I wouldn't assume they would be, Billy. According to a reliable source of mine, Ray's currently out of state and your two brothers are currently going car shopping for a new truck. So, from adding all of that up, I doubt that they'll be inside the night we invade the place. Don't concern yourself with possible outcomes. I'll take care of those situations."

"I'm just checking, because my mama might cross paths with us and you know how she feels about you." Billy said. "I don't want anything to go down between my mother and you, Hoyt. Things could turn very ugly if that were to happen."

Hoyt smiled and patted Billy on the back.

"I'm sure your mother and I will be just fine if we were to cross paths on this task. I'm well aware that she doesn't like me at all and I'm fine and dandy about her opinion for someone such as myself. But, for right now, let's just concentrate on the plan ahead, alright."

Emily entered a small convenience store and when she glanced around the area, she noticed the same black corolla that's been following her. She walked into the store when Desmond gets out of the corolla and followed her inside. She walked down the small aisle and Desmond continued to follow her. She looked back as Desmond pulled out a magnum and started firing. She ducked and the cashier crouched behind the counter.

"Take the money! Take it!" The cashier yelled. "Please don't kill me!"

"I don't want your money and I'm not here to kill you, fool." Desmond said. "I'm only here for the female Marshal."

Emily peeked around the aisles as she began loading up her gun. She stayed quiet as Desmond walked slowly through the aisles one at a time.

"Emily." Desmond said. "Emily Weston. I know you're in here, baby girl. I suggest you just come on out and take this bullet from your good friend, Colby."

"So, Ray sent you to do his dirty work?" Emily asked. "Not a surprise there? He's always had pawns to do the work, he was afraid to do."

"He sure did." Desmond said. "He's also paying me to do it for him. Since, he's on business at the moment."

"Business, huh?" Emily said. "You sure its business and not murder?"

"I don't give a shit what Ray does with his time." Desmond said. "All that matters to me, is killing you and getting paid. So, just come on out, so we can end this."

"Sure, no problem." Emily said.

Emily slowly took a peek toward her right and saw Desmond walking through the aisle. She turned and fired at Desmond's leg. He fell to the ground as Emily ran over toward him and immediately, she kicked the magnum out of his hand and kicked him in the gut two times.

"You're good aren't you?" Desmond said. "Surprised me there for a bit."

"Better than you think." Emily said. "I'm not your average

officer."

Eldon, Cody, and Darius sat inside a bar, having a share of beers. The door opened and Preston walked in. From his slouchy appearance, it appeared he also had a rough day in searching for Carla. He sat next to Eldon and glanced over toward Cody and Darius.

"Look who else decided to join us." Eldon said. "How's your day of investigating been?"

"It went as fair as it could possibly go." Preston said. "It's been a busy day overall."

"Don't assume that its just you that's had a rough day doing your job." Eldon said. "The three of us just dealt with a hit man who only targets prostitutes and nearly took us out with a sniper."

Preston turned, "Say that again. A hit man whose only occupation was to target prostitutes and you're saying that he nearly had all three of you in his range?"

"Not exactly." Cody said.

"Me, Cody, and Darius just captured the son of a bitch who was targeting prostitutes, while we were there searching for him. Though, apparently from the brief information we had, he was hired by a competitor to take out those prostitutes. Seems like he had an easy job to live by."

"It would seem so." Preston said. "Though, killing prostitutes isn't one on my list of things to do. Nor would I ever assume that there would be such a occupation for one man to take upon himself."

"Maybe he needed to money for some major crisis."

"That is possible."

Darius looked over at Preston.

"Just imagine how that job would be like." Darius said. "Hunting down women and assassinating them."

"Just sounds like a pervert with a sniper to me." Cody said. "Though, I'm not a pervert, by any means."

Eldon took a gulp of his beer and looked at Preston.

"So, how did your search go for Carla?" Eldon said. "Did you find any information on her?"

"Not exactly as I thought it would." Preston said. "I went to the diner and the waitress told me that she was indeed there but didn't know any other information. The next location was an antique store. Freaked out the clerk and he told me to head to a hair salon. The cashier there, acted like a complete bitch, but she didn't give me any information. So, tomorrow, I'll head out to Quarles Funeral Home. Hopefully, I'll find some information there."

"You might." Eldon said. "Because, according to some sources, Ray and the owner of the funeral home are good friends. So, Carla might've visited the place and gave the funeral assistants some information regarding her plans."

"I hope so." Preston said. "Otherwise, I might just have to visit Ray's warehouse myself."

"As long as you have backup when you decide to do that." Eldon said. "We'll have your back on that one, no worries about it."

Preston smiled, "I appreciate that. A lot."

CHAPTER 23

The next morning, Preston headed for Quarles Funeral Home. He arrived at the funeral home, seeing their white limousines and hearses parked in front, each with a license plate saying, "Quarles". Preston walked towards the front door. He opened it and went inside. Preston looked at the interior of the funeral home. Seeing the nice brown colored walls and its burgundy carpet. One of the assistants walked toward Preston.

"Nice place, it really is." Preston said. "They must be having some good business here."

"Welcome to Quarles Funeral Home, sir." The assistant said. "How may I help you here on this particular day?"

"Yes, please. Though, I'm not here to make any arrangements. But, I'm looking for a woman named Carla Garcia." Preston said. "And to be fair I'll show you a picture of her. Maybe it can refresh your memory."

The assistant looked at the picture.

"Do you recognize her?" Preston said. "Because if you do, you can say so."

"No. No sir." The assistant said. "I don't recognize this woman. Perhaps, you have this place mistaken."

"No." Preston said. "There's no mistaken identity here. I have documented proof that she was inside this building. She had spoken with someone inside this building. Whether it's you or one of your other co-workers, she spoke with someone here. Would the owner happen to be here? If he is I would love to speak with him on this matter. So, is he here?"

"He's not here, sir." The assistant said. "But, if you'll like to leave a message, I could tell him."

"I'm not going to leave any kind of message." Preston said. "Look, I'm a United States Marshal. So, you better give me some type of information now or I'll search this entire funeral home, room by room. Hell, I'll even pay a visit to the embalming room if that's what I'll have to do."

"I'm terribly sorry, sir." The assistant said. "But, there's no information here regarding who you're looking for. I can help you out with something else."

Preston squinted his face and pulled out his gun and shot it in the air. The assistant ducked down on the ground in fear, covering his head. Preston leaned down toward the assistant, holding the gun in his hand and smiling.

"I didn't want to do this." Preston said. "But, if doing this completes this case, then I'll do whatever's necessary to get the job done. Now, I'll give you one more chance to tell me what you know. Starting right now. Go."

"There's a cabin." The assistant said. "A cabin in the woods not too far from here. Its right around the interstate, sir. She came in one day and spoke with one of our directors about it. She told the director that the location is one of Ray's hideouts from you people."

"Wait, I'm sorry. Did you just say, you people?" Preston said. "You going racist here, pal? I'm very sure your family raised you to have just a little respect for people and their racial backgrounds. Didn't they?"

"No sir. I didn't mean it in a racial sense." The assistant said. "By you people, I meant the law. That's all I know. The cabin in the woods. That's it. Nothing else."

"Ok then. Thank you for cooperating with me today." Preston said. "Really, you should've told me earlier, otherwise you would've pissed your pants in front of me like a coward."

Preston leaves through the front door as the assistant realizes that he just pissed his pants. He shook his head in shame as he walked down the hall toward the restroom. Outside, Preston gets into the car and contacted Eldon on the phone.

"Eldon, its Preston." Preston said. "I found a location. A cabin in the woods on the outskirts of town. I'm heading there now. I'll contact you if I need backup of any kind."

Preston leaves the funeral home and drives toward the interstate. He passed through the vehicles on the road as he's heading to the New Haven forest.

During the moment in which Preston headed to the forest, Emily arrived at the shooting gallery place. She gets out of her car, but, noticed the place was surrounded by thugs. She believed those men to be associates of Ray. She decided to walk in, but, the men won't allow her.

"Look honey, no one inside without an appointment with Mr. Colby." One thug said. "Not even someone who's sexy as hell such as yourself."

"Well, go inside and tell your boss that Emily Weston is out here waiting to see him." Emily said. "He knows exactly who I am. The supposedly sexy as hell woman."

"Alright." The thug said. "Wait right here, baby. Guys, please watch her."

The thug walked inside approaching Ray. He tells him that Emily is waiting for him. The thug walked back out and allowed Emily entrance to the shooting gallery. She walked in and looked to her left and she finally sees Colby. She walked toward him as he was sitting down in a chair, with a silver revolver in his hand.

"You don't want to try anything stupid, do you Watson?" Ray said. "Seems after a long search, you've come across this way and have finally found me. Though, I am impressed that you did in such short time and not your new partner."

"Preston doesn't fully understand what you're capable of." Emily said. "But, I do. I know what you've done and how you've done them. I've chased you down for years and you're still doing the same damn shit as you were once before."

"So are you, Watson." Ray said. "You're still a marshal. Going around solving cases and capturing fugitives across the country. Sometimes even going across the world to find your criminals to save countless people from trouble. So, don't come to me and tell me that I'm doing the same shit. Because you're doing it as well."

"At least all the shit I do, isn't illegal." Emily said. "Think about that for a change and maybe you'll just realize it for once that you're on the opposite side of the law."

"I realize it very well, indeed I do." Ray said. "You and I have a long history with one another. Right here in this city for exact. Though, tell me something, Watson. How come you were moved over to New Haven in the first place and left New Jersey? You seemed to be well at home over here."

"I'm not here to talk about my business life, Colby." Emily said. "I'm here to tell you that I'm taking you straight to prison. Also, I know about John Elroy, you thug. The thug that was shot by Carla."

"What do you mean, shot by Carla?" Ray said. "Not from what she's told me. She told me he was shot by one of your marshal buddies."

"He was shot in the leg by one of my partners." Emily said. "She's the one who killed him. She shot him in the back of his skull and I'm kind of surprised that you put your trust in her to use a few of your men. Seemly enough that she might kill them as well behind your back and tell you another complete lie. The woman's only trouble, Ray and since you like trouble, you just planted yourself into a lot of trouble."

"I'll tell you this, Watson." Ray said. "You let me go for only this time and this time only, just let me deal with Carla and once that's done, then I'll take my place behind the prison walls. Do we have an agreement on that?"

"No, we don't have an agreement on that." Emily said. "You leave Carla to Preston and I'll deal with you. This is our battle. Carla is Preston's problem to handle, not yours or mine. Now, you're coming with me right now. Let's get moving."

"Very well, then." Ray said. "If that's what you want. You've made your decision and so have I."

Ray looked down and smiled. He then raised up the revolver, Emily looked toward it and Ray fired it. Emily moved out of the way, quickly as she pulled out her handgun and fired a shot at Ray, hitting him in the shoulder.

"Nice try, asshole." Emily said. "You forgot I'm highly skilled in marksmanship. You know that knowledge full well."

The thugs outside could hear the shooting taking place and without hesitation, they ran inside. Emily finds a back-exit door to her left and escapes using it. Once she's outside she headed out and ran toward the front. She got into her car and drove away. The thugs ran back out and start firing at Emily in the car. The thugs helped Ray into his SUV. Where he sat with rage.

"Are you alright, sir?" A thug said.

"I'll be fine." Ray said. "Just track her down quickly."

"Yes sir." Another thug said.

CHAPTER 24

Coover and Rusty test out their new truck, by driving it across town and they're loving it. They even try to impress some women they pass by during a red light. The women aren't impressed by their lack of seriousness. They drive the truck back to their location. They walked towards the house, but, Rusty smelled something that's similar to gasoline.

"What is it, Rusty?" Coover said.

"You don't smell that, Coover?" Rusty said. "It's coming from the house."

"I smell something." Coover said. "You sure it isn't mama cooking us a nice hot meal."

"Hell no it isn't mama's cooking. We need to move from the location." Rusty said. "As soon as we can. Get in the truck and let's get out of here."

They ran back towards the truck and as soon as they pull off, the house exploded and is now engulfed in flames. Coover looked back and is enraged.

"What the hell!" Coover said. "What the hell is going on! Someone just blew our home up, Rusty!"

"I think I know who done it." Rusty said. "Let's go tell mama what just happened and after that, we'll go visit Hoyt and Billy."

After they left, from the other side of the house, rises both Hoyt and Billy. Hoyt is laughing as Billy turned to Hoyt.

"You could've killed them." Billy said. "They're my brothers. My two older brothers."

"They'll be fine, Billy." Hoyt said. "You see they escaped the area.

Besides, they were already going to hand your over to Ray, so you could be killed. I'm basically doing you a favor by causing them to leave. As soon as they track you down and find you, the first thing they'll do is hand you over to Colby. Now, do you want that to happen?"

"No." Billy said. "I don't want that to happen. They wouldn't do that to me. I'm their brother."

"Yes, you are. But, they take the commands and orders from Ray and your mother." Hoyt said. "Whatever your mother commands, they will do it and so will Ray."

"What's the plan now?" Billy asked. "We gather up with Russell and his group and head to the cabin? Or do we wait on something else to happen?"

"We'll gather up with Russell and head straight for that cabin." Hoyt said. "They won't know what will hit them."

Eldon received a call from Emily, stating that she's on her way coming back to New Haven and her job in Newark was done. Cody walked in the office and Eldon tells him that Emily is coming back soon. Cody nodded while implying that the judge wants them both at the courthouse to discuss The Jackal case.

"Why do they need us at the courthouse?" Eldon said.

"We're the guys who brought him into custody." Cody said. "In that sense, they would need to speak with you, me, and Darius about the case. They just want to know what went down that night."

"Oh Goodness." Eldon said. "Let me contact Darius and we'll meet up at the courthouse."

"Sure thing, sir."

Cody walked out of the office as Eldon picked up his cell phone and contacted Darius. Darius answered, Eldon tells him that they must meet up at the courthouse, commanded by the judge to discuss the case of The Jackal. Darius agreed and told Eldon that he'll show up at the courthouse.

Ray is inside of a hospital in Newark as he is being bandaged up on his shoulder. Two of his henchmen are inside the room with him. Ray looked at one and asked him if they found Emily. The thug tells him no, but, they could contact Carla and see if she knows if Emily's returned to New Haven. Ray agreed and sent his henchmen out of the room.

The doctor finished up the bandages and he leaves the room. He walked outside and turned to the left, The SUV was sitting outside, waiting for Ray. Ray gets into the SUV. Inside the SUV, one of his henchmen looked and told him the news that Emily was headed back to New Haven. Ray smiled and said that he must do something that will bring Emily to her knees.

On the outskirts, Russell showed up in the front of the woods, along with his men behind him. One of his men walked over and asked Russell if Hoyt and Billy are nearby the forest. Russell tells the guy that they should be coming soon, since Hoyt's hideout is close to the forest. Russell pulled out a set of binoculars and looked around the interstate for Hoyt and Billy's trucks. As Russell uses binoculars to look around the woods, he sees two trucks coming near them.

"I see something over there." Russell said. "It should be them I would suspect."

The trucks pull up in front of them and stopped on the side of the road. Hoyt and Billy jumped out of them. Hoyt walked in front of Russell and his men. Hoyt stopped and smiled.

"See, my men." Russell said to his men. "They wouldn't let us down."

Russell looked at Hoyt and Billy. Smiling.

"Great to see you. So, what the plan, boss?" Russell said.

"Russell, I know the shootout didn't go correctly as planned, so, I'm apologize to you and your gentlemen, regarding that incident." Hoyt said. "But, this mission right here, will go as planned. No need to worry there. First, we will head out into these woods, find that cabin and once we've done that, blow it to shit."

"Hoyt, what about bears?" Billy said. "You know that bears live in these woods. What should we do if we run into one?"

"I'm sure you've been told what to do when you encounter a bear in the woods." Hoyt said. "Make sure if you encounter a bear. Just llie down and play dead. That whole crock of shit."

"I'm not too sure about that." Billy said. "Not too long ago, some guy said that doesn't work. They can still kill you. you're still breathing."

"Don't worry about the goddamn bears, Billy." Hoyt said. "Fellers, let's head out toward the cabin. We should at least reach the location by nightfall."

"Alright, guys." Russell said to his men. "You heard Hoyt, let's get a moving on."

They start walking through the woods, heading towards the cabin.

Eldon, Darius, and Cody are at the courthouse, where they're sitting inside the courtroom, observing The Jackal case. The judge is demanding that The Jackal be sentenced to eight years in prison. Right after the case is over, the judge calls Eldon, Cody, and Darius over to his office in the back of the courtroom. They walk in and the judge tells them to sit down in the chairs, in front of his desk. They sit in the chairs as the judge sits behind his desk, drinking a cup of coffee.

"You needed to speak with us, your honor." Eldon said. "That's the reason why we came. We didn't come to see the hit man get handcuffed."

"I called you guys here, on this wonderful day, to just ask you about your encounters with The Jackal." The judge said. "So, how was the whole thing? How did it play out?"

"It was all as well, judge." Eldon said. "We were just doing our jobs as officials of the law. That's all and nothing else."

"The whole thing was crazy at the time as well." Cody said. "Though, we got the job done. No worries."

"No worries, huh." The judge said. "Let me ask you gentlemen something. How did those prostitutes look? Were they delicious? Did they look smoking hot? Would any of you try them out just for the sake of pleasure and desire of your own hearts?"

"They looked hot, alright. I can tell you that." Darius said. "But, I wouldn't put money down to see if they're delicious in any way."

"You have a point there, Marshal." The judge said. "They might have some of those STDs out there. Just spreading their sickness across lives and ruining families. Nothing but filthy whores they are."

"You could say that again, judge." Eldon said. "But, all things go to Cody here. He's the one marksman who put the hit man down for the count."

The judge stood up and placed his cup of coffee on his desk. He walked over to Cody and extended and shook his hand.

"You don't know how you've made so many people happy by doing what you did." The judge said smiling. "Congratulations, Marshal on your fine job."

"Oh, I'm not a marshal yet, sir." Cody said. "I'm still in training for that spot. Right now, I'm only considered a Contemporary Marshal."

"Very well. Good job anyway."

The judge turned to Eldon with a smile on his face.

"The Jackal fellow is in the other room. I'm just telling you because if you want to get more information out of him. He's all yours."

"Well, thank you, Your Honor."

Eldon told Cody and Darius about The Jackal. He walked out of The Judge's office and into the room next door. Inside the room were concrete walls and only two windows on the front and back. Two chairs and one table. Sitting in one chair was The Jackal sitting at a table with his hands cuffed. Eldon looked at him through the window.

"He seems calm right now. Thought, he would be highly pissed off."

"He might be pissed when we walk in and have a chat with him." Darius said. "So, shall we piss him off."

They entered the room and The Jackal raised his head up toward them. Giving all three of them a demeaning glare of intent rage. His eyes pierced them and later they subdued. Eldon sat at the table while Cody and Darius stood behind him, on both sides of the table.

"So, we hear you'll be in federal prison for a total of eight years. How do you feel about that?"

"How do I feel about that? It's simple to be honest. Funny, you law enforcement types never understand the truth about people like me."

"Well, explain to the three of us how you're so different about you than the rest of the rotten criminals and fugitives that we've come across in this line of work?"

"I'm one of the best there is in my field and my boss knows that. So, he won't let me stay in a room with three walls and a cot with a pot to piss in. He knows he'll need me when a situation occurs."

"You're saying your boss will bail you out or something? Or will he just find a way for you to escape the cell."

"My boss is a man who has enough Federal Reserve notes to bail me out and to buy me a mansion that I could live in for the rest of my days on this Earth."

Cody leaned in, gaining Eldon's attention as the Jackal looked at him from the chair.

"Chief, you mind if I have a word with Jackal here?"

"By all means. Have a word with him. He's done me wonders today. Your turn, Cody."

Eldon stood up from the chair, allowing Cody to sit down in front of The Jackal. They have a ten second stare down before Cody smiled.

"So, tell us, what is your job exactly? Besides just going around killing innocent women for the sake of money."

"I am a hit man. Which you're already aware of. I hunt down and kill whoever I'm ordered to buy the ones who pay me the greenbacks to do it."

"So, you don't just hunt down prostitutes for the sake of paper. You're telling us that you take operations to hit anyone you're order to by the one who's paying you."

"You're smarter than you look, young one. You sure you're in the right type of fieldwork, pal?"

"I'm nowhere in comparison with you or anyone that's in your line of duty. That's all I needed to know. Thank you for your time, Jackal."

Cody leaned up from the chair. They looked over to Darius, seeing if he wanted to have a word with Jackal. Darius declined as Jackal laughed. They leave the room as Jackal continued to laugh. Eldon was last to leave as he looked back.

"Chief, I just want you to know. When I'm bailed out, I'm sure my boss will have me come for you and your two Marshal boys. Believe you me."

"If and when that day decides to take its course along our lives, me and my Marshal boys will be ready to take your sorry ass down once more, Jackal."

Eldon shut the door as Jackal smirked and looked at his handcuffs.

CHAPTER 25

Preston reached the entrance to the forest. He gets out of his car and he looked to the right and saw a pack of F-150 trucks sitting on the side of the road by the trees. He walked over to the trucks and looked inside. He recognized two of the trucks. Preston showed a faint grin.

"I see Hoyt and Billy's trucks." Preston said. "I wonder what's their business here?"

He walked into the forest as the sun is slowly setting. The forest becomes darker as he goes deeper, he pulled out a flashlight to watch his surroundings. He looked down and noticed some tree branches, scattered across the ground. All of which were broken and smashed, as if something passed through this area. He notices human footprints within the dirt and proceeded to follow them.

While Preston headed deeper into the forest, across the street is Carla and her pack of thugs. The thugs are all armed with automatic weapons. Carla commanded them to cross the interstate to reach the forest. They crossed the interstate by running, neither of them walked across. Carla is the last to cross. She reached the other end as one thug took out a flashlight and they proceed into the forest. Carla pointed out the trail that goes straight to the cabin, which the thugs followed her.

"We should follow this trail, my men." Carla said. "This trail was made by Ray, so it will lead us straight to the cabin."

Hoyt, Billy, and Russell, and his men are now in the middle of the forest as they hear howls from coyotes and wolves. Billy, shaken in fear of being attacked by a bear of some sort of animal, turned to Hoyt.

"How far are we from the cabin, Hoyt?" Billy said. "It's getting very freaky out here."

"We're not too far from the cabin." Hoyt said. "You should see the reflections from the windows. Once you see those, you know we've made it there."

"So, once we've reached the cabin, Hoyt." Russell said. "What do we do at that point? Just blow the place straight to Shit-Ville?"

"Now that's some smart thinking there, Russell." Hoyt said. "But, I would prefer we looked around at the interior, see what we can take and then, we'll blow the place to Shit-Ville. As you like to call it."

Russell turned and saw what Hoyt was carrying over his right shoulder, which was a black metallic box. Russell, now curious, decided to ask Hoyt what's inside the black box. Hoyt stopped in his tracks and turned to Russell, showing his grin toward him.

"You'll find out once we've reached the cabin." Hoyt continues walking as Russell catches up with Billy.

"He sure is secretive about his work isn't he." Russell said.

"Don't say it to him, Russell." Billy said. "You'll only put yourself in much greater danger. Hoyt doesn't like it when people talk about him behind his back. Believe me when I tell you that."

"Why is that?" Russell said. "Something happened to the last guy he was partners with?"

"The last guy who talked about Hoyt behind his back ended up six feet under." Billy said. "That should clear your thought of mind I would assume."

Billy continued walking with Hoyt as Russell showed a worried grin upon his face.

Preston continues walking through the forest and he hears the howls of coyotes and wolves around the area. He heard something moving through the trees toward his right. He reached down for his gun and pulled it out, holding it in his hand, he slowly continued walking and he heard the sounds coming closer. Preston looked to his right and saw a average sized brown fox run past him in a pace.

"Nothing, but a fox." Preston said. "Lucky bastard has me a little freaked out."

Preston later hears something behind him, he turns and its one of

Carla's thugs. He grabbed Preston by the neck, choking him. Preston delivered several elbow shots to the thug's head and punched him. The thug fell to the ground as Preston began kicking the thug and afterwards tossing a pile of leaves onto him.

"Useless asshole." Preston said. "You should never attack a marshal from behind. Doesn't do you any good."

Preston leaned down and snatched the thug by his shirt. The thug bled from his nose and mouth. Preston stared at him, grinning.

"What the hell you are doing out here at the brink of night?" Preston said. "Tell me. Tell me now before I put a bullet through you."

"I was with Carla, until I took a wrong turn and lost the group." The thug said. 'That's it. I haven't done nothing else I swear."

"That's not all I'm looking for, shit kicker." Preston said. "Why is she out here, and why is she leading a pack of Ray's thugs from his pack?"

"I'm not telling you anything else." The thug said. "You no good motherfucker!"

Preston put the gun directly on the thug's head, with his finger inches away from pulling the trigger. The thug began to panic.

"Ok. Ok!" The thug said. "We're here to kill you. That's why she brought us out here. To kill you. That's our purpose."

"Kill me?" Preston said. "Why would you want to do that? I'm only after your boss and that witch from my past. So, I would really like to know something right now and that is who assigned this operation to you?"

"It was all Carla's idea." The thug said. "She told Ray about it and he accepted it and granted her the use of his men. That's all I know, honestly."

"Well, I have to thank you for telling me the truth." Preston said. "While, you're at it, get a real job for Christ's sake. And make sure it's a legal one."

Preston leaves the thug, laying on the ground in a pile of leaves as he continued walking through the forest as he places his gun back into its holster. As he walks, he notices a reflection, coming from in front of him. He started moving faster and he saw that he reached the cabin. Preston walked around the entire cabin with his gun in his hand. He walked toward the front door, grabbing on the knob, he opens the door. He looked around and sees Ray's desk and some of his equipment scattered across the cabin. He notices that the cabin is a two-story house. As he proceeds to walk upstairs, the lights turn on. Preston stops in his tracks and hears people coming in. He turned and saw Hoyt, along with Billy, Russell and his men.

"Hoyt. Billy." Preston said. "Who's your new group of buddies here?"

"Preston, this is Russell." Hoyt said. "Known to his men as Leader."

Preston stared at Russell and smirked before turning toward Hoyt.

"I now can see why they call him 'Leader'." Preston said. "Because they're just like you. Followers. Can't lead for shit, so you decide to just follow whoever you see around you."

Hoyt smiled and said, "You know Preston. What the hell are you doing here? Would you care to tell us that?"

"Unlike you and your pack of shit, I'm here on business." Preston said. "Now, I just ran into one of Ray's thugs and he told me that his men are heading this way to assassinate me."

"Assassinate you?" Hoyt said. "This is a great day after all. I get to see a longtime friend die and I get to see something blow up. This is indeed a great day for Hoyt Bennett."

"No, it isn't, Hoyt." Preston said. "This isn't awesome. What will be awesome though, is throwing you, Billy, and your pack of followers here into prison. Where you can rot."

Russell pulled out his AK and points it at Preston. Preston doesn't move an inch and smirked at Russell.

"You really think you can put one through me?" Preston said. "Be honest here. You think you can, before I put one through you? Just give me your honest answer, *Leader*."

"You are one funny son of a bitch, Marshal." Russell said. "I should do those guys a favor and take you out myself."

Hoyt turned to Russell. Telling him to put down his AK. Russell nodded and lowers the weapon. Preston turned to Hoyt.

"See what I mean." Preston said smiling. "Followers only follow.

Can't make any decisions for themselves. Tell me, Hoyt. Where do you go to find people like this, because I'll never figure that out myself."

A bullet rams through one of the front windows, hitting one of Russell's men. Everyone inside the cabin ducks down behind the walls, the desk, and even the chairs. Hoyt turned to Preston, who's crouched on the ground, reloading his handgun. Hoyt takes out his pistol. Preston looked over at Hoyt and the pistol.

"Nice firearm, Hoyt." Preston said. "Where'd you get it? Or should I say, where'd you steal it from?"

"It was a gift from my dad." Hoyt said. "You remember him, don't you? He and your father were business partners back in the day."

"Yeah, they were." Preston said. "Right now, we need to focus on the guys out in the front and not on our past."

"Let me ask you something, Preston." Hoyt said. "They say you use your instincts to solve your cases. So, tell me, what do your profound instincts tell you about the outcome of this cabin shootout event?"

Preston nodded and smirked.

"My instincts are telling me that we'll live." Preston said. "Though, you'll be heading back to prison. Not so good for you, huh."

Carla and her thugs surround the entire area of the cabin. She walked toward the front door, with two thugs behind her. She looked inside the windows, seeing all the guys inside, all of whom are still scattered and crouched down. She looked to her right and saw Preston. She smiled.

"I'll go through the back door." Carla said. "You gentlemen find a way to get those men out of the cabin. Leave the Marshal for me to handle."

Carla heads toward the back door as he thugs begin shooting out the windows of the cabin. Preston, Hoyt, Billy, Russell, and his men are still crouched behind the walls and desks. One of Russell's men comes up from behind a chair and fires his machine gun out the windows. He kills a few of the thugs, but, one thug comes across and shoots him in the chest, right over the heart, instantly killing him.

More of Russell's men begin to fire, but the thugs begin to take them all out instantly. Russell watches as he sees his men falling dead on the ground.

"No!" Russell yelled. "Goddamn it! Hoyt, we need to try another tactic, now!"

Hoyt raised up his pistol, looking at Russell.

"As you command, Russell." Hoyt said. "As you command."

Hoyt leaned up out the window and started firing at the thugs. He began taking most of them down. The other thugs begin shooting toward him. Hoyt ducked back down behind the wall and moved over toward the desk. Billy is shaking with fear and has no clue or idea of what to do.

"Hoyt!" Billy yelled. "What in the hell do I do!"

"What the hell you think, Billy." Preston said. "Shoot back at the assholes!"

Billy raises up and fires his machine gun out the windows. He ducks as the thugs continue to fire back.

"It's not working!" Billy yelled. "There's too many of them out there!"

"Just keep shooting!" Hoyt yelled. "Just keep firing! You'll take some out. It shouldn't be that many left standing!"

Preston looked out the windows and starts firing. He's taking out the thugs one by one. He ducks as they fire back. Preston moves across the cabin to the left and continues firing out the window as he moves across. The thugs fire back and continue firing. All of the windows are all knocked out. The thugs stop shooting. Preston takes a peek out of the windows. He sees only four thugs remaining, as the others are all dead. Preston looked at Hoyt.

"Hoyt, just take a shot for Christ's sake." Preston said. "There's four of us and there's four of them. Russell, Billy, I suggest you two take some shots, now."

"You heard, Preston, boys." Hoyt said. "Aim and take your shots."

They start taking shots out the windows at the four thugs. Billy shoots one thug in the head and starts jumping up and down in excitement. Another thug fires towards Billy and he crouches down, back against the wall. Hoyt looked down at Billy.

"What the Sam hell are you doing, Billy?!" Hoyt said. "Shoot the worthless pieces of shit kicking assholes, goddamn it! Shoot!"

Preston and Russell are firing at the remaining thugs. Preston kills one and now there's only one more thug remaining. Preston looked at Hoyt.

"You want to take this one or shall I go ahead?" Preston said. "I'm going to need an answer now."

"Let me take the shot, Marshal." Russell said. "I got this motherfucker in a clean spot."

Russell fired a shot and killed the last remaining thug. They lower their weapons and look at one another. Billy stood up from the wall, Hoyt only stares at him. Hoyt turned to Russell.

"I'm truly sorry about your men, Russell." Hoyt said. "I truly am. They served their purpose for you and this group and have done a great service."

"They sacrificed themselves to protect their leaders." Russell said. "They knew what they were going into."

Preston looked and placed his gun back into its holster and looked at Hoyt. Seeing him with the pistol in hand.

"You're not too bad with that pistol." Preston said. "Must've been training for some time."

"Same to you with that Glock of yours." Hoyt said. "You know how to use that weapon."

"I was a former marksman instructor." Preston said. "It helped out a lot."

As they prepare to leave, they hear the back-door opening. Hoyt walked over to the door and sees Carla walk inside with two thugs. They backed up against the windows as Carla stared at them. She turned her attention toward Preston, who's not pleased at all to see her.

"Why are you doing this, Carla?" Preston said.

Hoyt looked and started smiling.

"Carla." Hoyt said. "So, this is Carla? Wow, I didn't recognize you there. How's life been so far?"

"Life's been truly great to me, Hoyt." Carla said. "You didn't think that I would forget about you, huh?"

"There was some doubt in my mind that you would." Hoyt said. "You should've called me. We could've hung out together. Just like we did in the old times."

Preston turned to Hoyt. Showing a faint grin.

"This isn't a social visit, Hoyt." Preston said. "She's here to kill me on Ray's behalf."

"Wait. She's working with Ray?" Hoyt said. "How interesting indeed. More sheep scurrying in the field for me to slaughter."

"Why do you think she's here?" Preston said. "Didn't you see those thugs walking behind her?"

"You shouldn't have to worry, Hoyt." Carla said. "Ray can take care of you. I'm only here for Preston."

Russell raised up his AK and shoots one of the thugs, the other thug pulled out his weapon and Billy shot him in the head. Hoyt and Preston turned toward Billy.

"SHIT! Goddamn it! He shot at me!" Billy yelled.

Carla pulled out a revolver and aimed it toward Preston. He looked at the revolver and stared her in the eyes before scouting the surroundings of the cabin. Looking out for any of Carla's men.

"Meanwhile, I'm only here to kill you, honey." Carla said. "The rest of these guys are Ray's problem, not mime. So, babe, are you ready to go to heaven?"

"Depends on the time their open. Speaking of time, do you have a watch on you? Because, if you do you could tell me the exact time. Because, correct me if I'm wrong. But, I believe that the gates are closed around this time of a day."

"So funny all the time. Yet, you're only as funny as the ones who laugh at your joking and smartass remarks. Now, I suggest you close your eyes, babe. I don't want you to look at what I'm about to do to your pretty face."

"But, I want to see your face before you take the shot. Last sight of my time in the world would be looking upon you. So, I'll just keep my eyes opened if you don't mind me doing so."

"Your choice."

Hoyt ran over and backslapped Carla with his right hand. She fell to the ground as he escaped along with Billy and Russell. Preston knelt down at Carla, as she held her face.

"You shouldn't trust Hoyt. Never" Preston said. "Even in your contorted and disfigured mind, you shouldn't trust a man like him."

"I shouldn't trust anyone, Preston." Carla said. "Not even you."

"I agree with that as well." Preston said smiling. "Only to an extent."

On the outside, Billy and Russell are backing up as Hoyt opens the black box and pulls out a grenade launcher. He aims toward the building as Preston and Carla look toward him. Preston and Carla run toward the back door as Hoyt aims the launcher toward the front room. He gets to the aiming in its position and starts smiling. Hoyt turned to Russell and Billy.

"Billy, Russell, grab your pairs of socks and hold your balls in your vices. For this is it, my friends!" Hoyt yelled. "INCOMING CALL!!!"

Hoyt fires the launcher, blowing up the entire cabin. Russell and Billy duck down to avoid being hit by debris. Hoyt stood and watched at the cabin as it was engulfed into flames. Russell looked at the cabin, so does Billy. Hoyt turned to them.

"That's what I'm talking about, guys!" Hoyt yelled. "That's what we came to see! This is what we want! Now, only one more place remains, and we will have started a new era across New Haven."

They ran off the area, going into the darkness of the forest. From the right side, Preston and Carla walk out of the forest. Preston looked at Carla, both are covered in ash from the explosion and smell like burned wood

"The next time you want to try something with Hoyt being involved in the location, don't try it." Preston said.

Preston leaves the area as Carla walked toward the left of the forest. The cabin is completely engulfed in flames. The cabin now, is falling toward the ground, as its now decimated from top to bottom. The cabin is now just a pile of ashes as the smoke reaches above the trees in the forest, alarming some of the nearby residents of the area.

CHAPTER 26

Emily returned to New Haven and arrived at the airport. She walked outside and sees Preston waiting for her inside his car. She walked over to the car and gets in. She looked at Preston.

"Didn't know you were picking me up." Emily said. "Should've called someone to do it instead."

"You don't worry about me." Preston said. "It's only for Eldon that's all."

"So, how's New Haven been since I was out?" Emily said. "The standard way I presume."

"Extremely crazy as usual." Preston said. "How was New Jersey? Interesting?"

"It was crazy." Emily said. "Not crazy as here. But, just crazy."

"Well, it seems you're heading back to the office." Preston said. "Since, your car is parked there for some reason. You should've parked it here, that way you could've drove yourself to the office without anyone, such as myself picking you up."

"Just drive, Preston." Emily said. "The faster you go, the quicker we'll be on the same page."

"If that's what you really want."

Preston drove off, leaves the airport.

At the office, Eldon and Cody are talking about the stock market as Darius walked inside, telling them that Emily's back in town. Eldon said he's happy and asked where she was. Darius told him that Preston and Emily are heading to the office as they speak.

"It's a good thing she's back in New Haven." Eldon said. "Some great news there. Hopefully, she solved that case of hers, so she can continue her work with us."

"Looking at the time, Chief. Emily and Preston should be here any minute now it appears." Darius said.

From the front door, Preston and Emily arrived. They approached Eldon's office Eldon walked out of his office with a smile on his face as he greeted Emily back from her visit to New Jersey. Preston walked into the office behind her with his arms crossed.

"Good to have you back here in New Haven." Eldon said.

"Just doing my job, chief." Emily said. "That's all. So, what's been going on since my absence?"

"A few things, really. Me, Cody, and Darius had to settle a case involving a hit man who only targets prostitutes." Eldon said. "Cody took the guy down with one shot."

"Wow." Emily said.

"Just doing what I've been taught." Cody said.

"Wish I was on that case." Emily said.

Emily looked at Preston.

"So, I'm sure you had something to do, Preston." Emily said. "What did you go out and do for yourself?"

Preston stared and later smiled toward them.

"Nothing much, really." Preston said. "Just went to certain places to track down Carla and her devious plans."

"Speaking of her, did you find Carla?" Eldon said. "I've been meaning to ask you that? So, from what you've just said, you found her?"

"I did find her." Preston said. "Though, Hoyt and his group of followers intervened. As did some of Ray's men and afterwards, everything went to hell."

"What happened?" Emily said.

"I went into the cabin, at that moment is when I ran into Hoyt and his men." Preston said. "Afterwards, the shooting started and once I and Carla escaped, Hoyt blew the place to shit."

"He blew the cabin to shit?" Eldon said. "He's always blowing things up."

"That's what Hoyt does. That's what he always does. When he

and I were kids, during the Fourth of July, Hoyt would take all the fireworks and place them in a certain location and light them up. Causing a massive explosion wherever he was. I can say he's destroyed at least ten to twenty buildings in his lifetime. It's what he's good at so he continues to do it. That's what he does."

Eldon turned to Emily.

"Did you find Colby?" Eldon said.

"I did." Emily said. "After a long search, I found him at a shooting gallery and managed to shoot him in the shoulder."

"You shot him in the shoulder?" Eldon said. "Did he survive?"

"Yeah, he survived barely." Emily said. "He's probably somewhere plotting his revenge against me."

"If that's the case, Emily. He'll be at the warehouse." Preston said. "Since his cabin has been destroyed."

Hoyt and Billy speak with Russell at his newly designed hideout location, sitting at a round wooden table, speaking about the final event. Russell says that they need more men to back them up on this final event. Hoyt tells him that the three of them will do just fine, since this one will require a bigger weapon, rather than the typical grenade launcher. Billy looked at Hoyt with a questioning look.

"Now, what do you mean when you say a bigger weapon?" Billy said. "How big are we talking here? Because, the grenade launchers will do just fine."

"Of course they do, Billy." Hoyt said. "But, since this is the final event that will change all of New Haven and its people. The event must require an even bigger weapon to do the job and the weapon will be in our hands the day that event comes."

"So, I take it specifically, you already have this weapon in your possession, boss?" Russell said.

"I already have it." Hoyt said. "I'm always prepared before the time is upon us. Keeps me on the complete balance."

Coover and Rusty are at the warehouse, seeing Ray with his shoulder bandaged up under his coat. Rusty's face showed a slight concern for his boss as Coover had no words to conjure up from his mouth.

"What happened to you, boss?" Rusty said. "Was it Hoyt? If so, me and Coover can go now and take him out."

"It wasn't Hoyt, gentlemen." Ray said. "He had nothing to do with it. That I know of at this time. It was Weston."

"I'm sorry, boss. But, who in the blue fuck is Weston?" Rusty said. "If, you could tell us."

"The blonde female Marshal." Ray said. "She came to me and shot me in the shoulder, when I was in Jersey. I had her, but, it seemed that she knew exactly when I was going to shoot her. Like she saw it before."

"You think she also has the "Instinct"?" Coover asked. "Because it's been said it's possible she has it."

"I'm not too sure." Ray said. "During her time in Jersey, the officials, as well as the crime lords would always say that she had some sort of technique, similar to Maddox's Instinct."

"Well, boss, is there anything you need us to do for you?" Rusty said. "Since, we're not busy at the moment."

"No, I'll be just fine." Ray said. "Just contact your mother for me. We're going to have a plan for this task very quickly."

"You got it, boss." Rusty said.

They walk out of the warehouse and in comes Carla, Ray looked up at her and noticed the bruise on the right side of her face.

"What the hell happened to you?" Ray said. "One of my men didn't do it? Did they?"

"No, none of your men are responsible for the bruise on my face." Carla said. "Hoyt. He hit me in the face."

"Hmm. I see" Ray said. "Don't think that I didn't hear about my cabin in the woods. How you allowed it to be destroyed."

Carla's face showed a faint grin as Ray looked up at her with dire disappointment in his face.

"Carla, I give you one primary task to take and looked where your actions have done to my secret location." Ray said. "I know that Hoyt was there, along with his new group of vigilante buddies and the Bronson brothers' youngest blood. I suppose that's how you received that bruise upon your face. When Hoyt bitch slapped you and left you for dead."

"I had them where you wanted." Carla said. "I would've killed them if I saw what Hoyt was about to do."

Ray smirked and said, "From my point of view, you deserved that slap to the face. You were too highly focused on Maddox that you forgot the task at hand, which was to kill him without any hesitation. Only if you didn't let your emotions get in the way, he would be dead, and I would be thanking you right now. But, he's not dead and neither is that bastard, Hoyt Bennett."

"I understand that my emotions got caught in the task." Carla said. "But, I was close to finishing it completely."

"Being close enough doesn't mean shit to me, Carla." Ray said. "You had a job to do and you didn't get the job done. So, how am I supposed to feel about that? Knowing that the men I let you use for the job are now dead, because of your selfish emotional needs. The cabin, my only known secret location is now destroyed because of you. Speaking of which, I don't know what else I can use you for, Carla. I don't know anything else."

"Just give me another chance, Ray." Carla said. "Please, just give me another chance. I know I can do it this time. I can promise you that on this one."

"I have no need of you or your false promises, Carla." Ray said. "Just leave my warehouse at this moment. Leave yourself or I'll have one of my men here make you leave. Leave this earth that is. So, I suggest you make your choice right now."

Carla walked out of the warehouse as Ray's facial expression showed he's highly upset about what happened to his men and his cabin. He slammed his fist to his desk and tossed the sheets of paper to the ground.

CHAPTER 27

Hoyt and Billy head out toward the warehouse. Russell is behind them inside his truck. They stop and get out of their vehicles and Hoyt uses the binoculars, looking in front of him. He sees the warehouse.

"There it is, my wonderful congregation. There's the warehouse, my boys." Hoyt said. "That's where Ray does most of his dirty work. Now, we've got him where we want him."

"You want to go in there right now and take him out?" Russell said. "You know we could do that for you."

"Russell, I appreciate your bravery. But, we'll save the chaos for a later time." Hoyt said. "Right now, we're only scouting the location just to make sure where we'll be once the time comes along."

Billy looked around the area, scouting out the entire area. He turned to Hoyt, thinking.

"So, when the time is accurate, Hoyt." Billy said. "How do we complete the job here? We're going be in this spot or are we going to be a little closer to the place? What if someone catches us while we're out here on this. We're going to be screwed."

"Billy, Billy. I'll say this once and only once directly to you, my friend." Hoyt said. "You focus on the plan and I'll focus on the ones that you're speaking of. Things will come into plan, I'm highly sure of it."

Coover and Rusty walked into their mother's home. She walked out across from the kitchen. She looked at them as Coover smiled. Rusty walked toward his mother.

"What in the hell are you boys doing here?" Barbette said. "You should be helping Ray out right now with his problems. You know that his cabin was destroyed last night. And we all know who did it."

"We know about the cabin, mama, but, he told us that he didn't need anything, mama." Rusty said. "He only wanted us to speak with you."

"Well, what did he say?" Barbette asked. "Not something terrible I hope."

"He said something about planning something fast." Rusty said. "He also wants to speak with you in person. About the situations concerning Hoyt and the marshal people."

"Very well, I see." Barbette said. "I'll pay a visit to Ray and see what he wants to talk about. But, I want to make sure that the both of you stay by his side. As of this moment, he'll need all the help that he can get."

Preston, Emily, and Eldon are sitting at a diner, at noon, eating lunch. Eldon speaks with Emily about her trip in Jersey. Preston turned and looked at Eldon.

"I'm highly surprised that you survived the trip, Emily." Eldon said. "I was a little worried that you wouldn't return. But, you proved me wrong."

"She can take care of herself, Eldon." Preston said. "You heard what she said about Colby. She shot the guy in the shoulder. Not too far from the chest. Good job, Emily."

"I was only doing my job." Emily said. "Though, I don't let my emotions get in the way, like Preston when he's facing Carla."

"It's not that my emotions get in the way of business." Preston said. "Just that I knew her for so long that I wouldn't think that she would be able to do something like this of this caliber."

"Preston, you should know that everyone you've either dated or slept with over the years, will eventually come back into your life one way or another." Eldon said. "You of all people should have that in mind."

"Eldon, I don't know how you conjure up all this kind of shit."

Preston said. "Exactly, where do you find all of this information?"

"The library, Preston." Eldon said. "It's the sort of place that carries all kinds of books. Fiction and non-fiction. They also have books on nature and politics."

"I know what a library is, Eldon." Preston said. "I've been to one before."

"I'm sure you have." Eldon said. "Probably when you were in high school. Was that the last time you saw a library? Or you didn't even attempt to walk in a check out a book."

"Very funny, Eldon." Preston said. "Hilarious."

Emily looked at Eldon and asked him about the plan to take down Ray. Eldon said that they will have to come up with something clever to pull off, so Ray and his alliance don't figure out the marshals have in store for them. Preston said that they need to watch their surroundings. Emily asked why would they, because of Ray's crime partners? Preston nodded and told them that they need to watch out for Hoyt, Billy, and Russell. Since, Hoyt has been trying to kill Ray and take back his place as crime boss of New Haven.

"Well, no shit." Eldon said. "We'll have eyes across the entire location. Ray and his friends won't even see us on the outside"

"How is that, Eldon?" Preston said. "You're going to spread all of us out across the warehouse or have you brought in a group of interns to do the scouting."

"Not exactly, though I decided to contact the CIA and I also called in some SWAT groups to cover our backs." Eldon said. "No big deal about it."

"Did you make sure that they bring grenade launchers?" Preston said. "Because, they could come quite in handy for this one."

"Why do we need grenade launchers, Preston?" Eldon said. "We're not like Hoyt and his group of *let's blow shit up* buddies."

"I'm just saying that we should have some with us." Preston said. "Only to have an even match against them. Who knows what they'll bring with them."

"I see your point on that." Eldon said. "I'll think it over with the CIA. See what answer they'll give me, if I choose to do so."

"Very well." Preston said.

Barbette arrives at Ray's warehouse, where Ray is looking at a map of the entire city. He looked up and asks Barbette to sit. She sits in front of him and he moves the map to the side of the table.

"I'm pleased you could make it, Ms. Bronson." Ray said. "I'm sure you know our times are starting to get rough around here. Mainly on me."

"I can tell." Barbette said. "My boys came to me and told me that you wanted to discuss something you have in mind. Some sort of plan that will change the state of this city."

"I have a plan and I'm asking you to be a part of it." Ray said. "Just to see how you feel about it."

"I would like to hear it, Mr. Colby." Barbette said.

"This plan concerns all of the crime lords that surround this city." Ray said. "I'm going to have a meeting at this warehouse in a few days to speak with them about it publicly. But, I'll tell you about it right now. The plan involves taking out Hoyt and his group of explosive buddies."

"What about my son?" Barbette asked. "Specifically, Billy. What do you have in mind for him?"

"I figured that you would deal with him yourself." Ray said. "I don't want to be the cause of you losing one of your boys, even if it's one that didn't listen to his brothers or his mother's warnings."

"I see your point there. So, tell me how soon will this plan come into play?" Barbette asked. "Sooner than we hope or not to soon?"

"Once I have settled it with the other guys, the plan should begin to unfold." Ray said. "But, once the plan begins, we must take out Hoyt and afterwards, we'll deal with those marshals."

"I've heard the history between you and the blonde one." Barbette said. "I also heard that she's the one who shot you in the shoulder a few days ago. So, I figure that you'll handle her and leave the Instinct Marshal for me. My two boys will deal with those other marshals they have backing them up."

"I'm up for that." Ray said. "So, do we have a deal?"

Ray extended his hand and Barbette looked at it. She shook his hand in agreement. Ray smiled.

"Let the process begin." Barbette said smiling.

In downtown, a meeting is being held at City Hall, concerning the economy and how they should increase jobs across the city. The room is entirely full, from left to right of over a dozen citizens. Every seat is taken as some extras stand in the back because of it. As one of the lead gentlemen stand in front of them, behind a podium, he talks about the cause and says that they should increase jobs across the city, therefore there won't be any problems to cause someone to turn to a life of crime.

As he continued saying his speech, the doors opened up and everyone looked toward them. The gentlemen behind the podium looks straight and in comes Hoyt, Billy, and Russell. Hoyt, holding his arms out and hands open, smiling as he looked down at the gentlemen.

"My, my. It's been a very long time, since I've stepped foot inside of a crowded location such as this." Hoyt said. "Usually, I'm the one who brings in the big crowd. For parties of the rightful ones of course."

"Sir." The gentleman said. "Who are you and what concerns you about the economy? If you may ask?"

"If I may, I'm the guy that will change the foundation of this city's economy for years to come." Hoyt said. "Ladies and gentlemen of New Haven, Connecticut. We are all trying our hardest to find jobs and to work. Some of us have families to take care of, while some of us are only in it for ourselves just to make a buck or a name for ourselves. I am here to say that there's something new coming to New Haven and it will bring happiness across the entire landscape of this city. Once the dark cloud that's currently above us, passes along. A new and brighter cloud will emerge, and the sun will shine down upon us and we will have succeeded against this broken economy and its vile operators."

The audience began to clap as they started to agree with Hoyt. He walked up to the gentleman at the podium. The gentleman stared at him as Hoyt smirked toward him and extended his hand toward the podium.

"May I?" Hoyt said to the gentleman.

The gentleman moved away from the podium, letting Hoyt take

his spot. Billy and Russell stood behind him, watching the gentleman and his associates.

"Don't try anything funny." Russell said. "I mean it."

"He won't." Billy said. "He's too afraid to do anything. He could barely speak when we walked in here. So, don't expect anything from him."

Hoyt grabbed the microphone and looks out toward the audience.

"Now, since I have a microphone, I don't have to raise my voice to speak the truth." Hoyt said. "Now, when the time comes when we all have jobs and this city is out of the economy's path, that will be the start of a new era for New Haven. Now, the rich folks and the crime lords that surround this city will also learn of that new era. An era that will bring them down to our level. A level that will show them that there no better than the rest of us. A level that will stand the test of time against crime in the city. Once, they feel that era upon them, they will look at us all and fully understand the true ways of life."

The audience continues to clap, as some of the civilians start to yell in joy. Hoyt smiles and looks back at Billy and Russell.

"This is going better than I hoped." Hoyt said. "Just keep your eyes on these guys right over here. I got the crowd in my hands."

Russell and Billy turn around and stare at the gentleman and his associates. They sit back and just look on at the audience, seeing how they're accepting Hoyt when he just walked into the building. Hoyt continues his speech.

"Now, I know some of you are asking yourselves, how is this man, who just walked in here a few minutes ago, knows so much about the economy and how to fix it. Well, for those of you that don't know who I am, my name is Hoyt Randall Bennett. The younger son of Ory and Loretta Bennett and the younger brother of Darren Bennett, who's currently in Hartford, obtaining his psychology doctrine. I was born and raised in this city and so, I'm currently stating that this city, with my profound help, along with my two partners, who are currently standing behind me, Billy Bronson and Russell, also known as Leader, will stand together to wipe out this depression upon our city and will restore the good inside of it and inside of us all New Haven citizens."

The audience began to clap louder. More cheers of joy began to pour out of the civilians. Russell looked out towards the audience and looked at Billy.

"Looks like he's got them." Russell said.

"Hoyt sure loves to talk." Billy said. "You can clearly see that."

Hoyt smiled and looked back at Billy and Russell. They smile as well.

Hoyt nodded toward the crowd of people and continued smiling at them.

"We got them on our side now. They won't accept or take anyone else's word except for mine."

CHAPTER 28

Preston walked into Eldon's office, as Eldon reads some documents. Preston sits down in the chair. Eldon looks up at him. Preston just stays quiet.

"Something on your mind, Preston?" Eldon asked.

"May I have a word, Eldon?" Preston asked.

"Sure." Eldon said. "As long as it doesn't involve anything to do with your personal life, I'm all ears."

"Nothing to do with my personal life." Preston said. "I heard that Hoyt was present at a City Hall meeting today. Thought, you knew about that."

"I didn't know, Preston." Eldon said. "Though, if you look on the bright side of things, it seems that nothing's been blown to shit, so, what's the problem?"

"I'm only wondering what he's told the people." Preston said. "He could've said anything to them and they probably fell for it. Not knowing that they're being used as his pawns. It just aches me to see that."

Eldon gets up from the chair and walks toward Preston.

"We'll just have to see what comes up next, Preston." Eldon said. "That's the only way we'll know for sure what Hoyt and his boy band are up to with the city."

"Yeah." Preston said. "As long as he's not recruiting them just to blow their shit up, I'll have no problems. Well, its Hoyt. He's known for doing this kind of shit and later doing even worse shit."

Meanwhile, Coover and Rusty sat inside their rental house, sitting on the couch watching the Outdoor Channel. They hear a knock on the door, they look at each other.

"Well, go answer the door, Coover." Rusty said. "I'm busy at the moment."

"Fine." Coover said. "But, if its Hoyt, Billy, or one of those marshals, you're dealing with them. Not I."

Coover opened the door and its Barbette. She walks inside and Coover closes the door. Barbette grabbed the TV remote from Rusty and turned off the television. Rusty looked at his mother, questioning.

"What was that for, mama?" Rusty asked. "I was watching that."

"There's something more important than watching animals get hunted down." Barbette said. "I've spoken with Ray and I'm going to tell you what he told me."

"What did he say, mama?" Coover asked. "Is it a raise? Is it about Hoyt and Billy?"

"Let me talk and I'll tell you what it's about." Barbette said sitting down in a chair. "Me and Ray have come up with a plan that will bring Hoyt and the marshals down."

"Really?" Rusty asked. "This already sounds great."

Later during the day, Karen and Richard sit in a living room, watching the TV. The doorbell rings and Richard takes a look back at the door and turns to Karen.

"Should I answer it?" Richard said.

"Yeah." Karen said. "Why wouldn't you."

Richard gets up from the couch and walks toward the front door. He opens the door and sees Preston, who's leaning against the wall, staring a hole through Richard.

"Detective." Richard said nervously. "Marshal. Detective Marshal."

"Richard." Preston said. "Richard Rogers."

Karen sees Preston standing in the doorway. She gets up and walks toward him and Richard. Preston looks behind Richard's shoulder and sees Karen approaching him.

"Preston." Karen said. "What are you doing here?"

"I'm here to speak with you." Preston said. "If you don't mind."

"Oh, I mind, Detective Marshal." Richard said.

"I was talking to Karen." Preston said.

Richard walks off to the kitchen as Karen allows Preston to enter their home. Preston walks to the living room and sits on the couch. Karen walks in and sits in the chair in the corner.

"Why are you looking at me like that?" Preston said.

"Because I find it quite strange to see you here." Karen said. "I spoke to you at the restaurant the last time we crossed paths. What more do you want?"

"I don't want anything." Preston said. "I just came by to see how you were doing with Richard."

"Why do you care?" Karen said.

"I don't care about Richard." Preston said. "I care about you and your safety."

"Don't see why you do." Karen said. "We're not together anymore. So, no feeling should be attached."

"You're telling me that you don't have feelings for me anymore?" Preston said. "Is that it?"

Karen gets up from the chair and walks toward the front door. Preston does the same, following her to the door. She opens the door, but Preston presses his hand against the door, closing it. Karen looks up at him, while Richard peeps through the kitchen.

"It's a yes or no answer." Preston said. "You seem not to tell me."

"Because it doesn't matter, Preston." Karen said. "If it did, I would not be married to Richard, nor would I be speaking to you about this matter."

Preston paused and stayed quiet for a quick second.

"Fair enough." Preston said.

He opened the door and walked out toward his car as Karen watches him. Once, Preston leaves, she shuts the door and turns back to Richard.

"Everything alright, honey?" Richard said.

"Everything's fine." Karen said. "Just something to get off his chest, that's all."

CHAPTER 29

Hoyt, Billy, and Russell are all waiting in their trucks, looking dead ahead at the warehouse. Hoyt looked at his watch and turned toward Billy.

"It's time." Hoyt said. "Let's get this party started."

"Are you sure about this, Hoyt?" Billy said. "I'm positive that there's another way we can do this. My brothers are in there for Christ's sake!"

"Then, it's their fault." Hoyt said. "Besides, I've been waiting for this moment for a long time now."

They get out of the truck and mark their positions. Russell has his AK ready for use as Billy carries his machine gun. Hoyt goes to the back of the truck and pulls out a rocket launcher. Billy and Russell look toward Hoyt.

"Holy shit, Hoyt!" Russell said. "A rocket launcher! That will do the trick perfectly."

"That's the reason why I chose it." Hoyt said. "A grenade launcher was alright. But, a rocket launcher is even better. Gives you a greater aim as well."

Preston, Emily, Eldon, Cody, and Darius arrive at the warehouse location. Preston and Darius head toward the western side of the trees as Eldon and Emily stay at the eastern side of the trees. Cody walks up a nearby hill and sets his sniper up there. Cody looked down and was able to see the entire location. Preston looked to his right and saw two trucks, he knew for certain that those were Hoyt's and Billy's. He also knew that Russell was along with them.

"What do you see, Preston?" Darius said. "Colby and his pals?"

"No, I see Hoyt and Billy's trucks over there to the right." Preston said. "Looks like this will turn into a show for us."

Preston pulled out his communicator and contacted Eldon.

"I see Hoyt and Billy's trucks, Eldon. You want us to take them out right now or wait? Because, from the way this is all being set up and placed, we're in for a major shootout."

"I hear you clear. Just wait for now. I called the SWAT team for a little assistance. They'll give us all the help we can get on this one once they arrive on the scene."

Emily looked at the surroundings of the warehouse with all types of vehicles parked in front. From Corvettes to Chargers to even Lamborghinis. The area looked as if a party was going on. Emily turned to Eldon.

"So, what do we do once the SWAT teams arrive?" Emily said. "Go straight in and take them out?"

"That's a good plan." Eldon said. "But, let's see how Colby and his gangbanging friends handle it first. Don't want them to get too startled by our arrival."

Eldon contacts Cody through the communicator.

"Hey, Cody. How's the view from up there" Eldon said. "Is it looking great or what?"

"The view's just great up here, chief." Cody said. "I can see the entire location from this point of view. If I wasn't here for this moment, I could come out here on a good and have me some good hunting."

"I'm sure you would. Just keep us posted on anything you see that's unusual, alright." Eldon said.

"Sure thing, sir." Cody said.

Inside the warehouse, Ray is continuing a meeting with the crime lords that he spoke to while he was in Jersey. They continue speaking about their drug shipments and how they can transport them across the state and country.

"By doing the transporting on that trail, we will have no problems moving our shipments across the state and across the country." Ray said.

"If that's the case, Mr. Colby." One crime lord said. "How do we make sure that we don't get caught in the process?"

"You getting caught by the officials is not on me." Ray said. "It's on you."

"I agree with Colby on that one." Another crime lord said. "He has a point with that. If you get caught, it's your fault. You let yourself slip out for them to find and capture you."

Coover and Rusty lean forward towards Ray and the crime lords.

"That's good thinking, sir." Rusty said.

"Yeah, that's a great thought." Coover said. "But, none of us, should get caught. Unless we're either drunk or high."

"The chief has demanded that we take more and charge directly into the promise land." Ray said. "It's what he wants us all to do."

"I don't take orders from the chief, Colby." One crime lord said. "I do what is best for my alliance. Most of the chief's orders are inexplicably erratic."

"Which is why he gave me the choice of taking you gentlemen out." Ray said. "So, what will you do? Will you obey the chief's commands and live? Or will you follow your own path and die? Make a choice, pal?"

On the outside, Hoyt is slowly moving closer toward the warehouse with the rocket launcher on his right shoulder. Billy and Russell watched Hoyt as he continues getting closer.

"What are you trying to do, Hoyt?" Billy said. "You trying to get yourself caught or killed?"

"I'm only getting a closer shot, Billy." Hoyt said. "Gives me an adrenaline rush and makes for more entertainment."

"Does he know exactly what he's doing?" Russell said. "He could be seen, captured, or even killed by Colby and his gun thugs."

"I have no idea." Billy said. "He's trying to get us captured by Colby. Because, I don't want to deal with my mama at this point. She'll kill me."

"She'll kill us before she'll get to you, Billy." Hoyt said. "Just relax and prepare to enjoy the show."

Preston looked over and sees Hoyt with the launcher. He looked at Darius, who's keen on the warehouse.

"Darius, you continue your watch on the warehouse." Preston said. "I'll be right back."

"Where are you going?" Darius asked. "Though, Eldon wanted us here?"

"I've got something to finish here." Preston said. "Won't be too long."

Preston crouched down behind the bushes as he slowly walked over toward Hoyt, Billy, and Russell.

Hoyt continued to aim the launcher and moves his hand toward the trigger. He starts to smile as Billy and Russell started backing up behind the trucks nearby. Hoyt's eyes light up.

"INCOMING CALL!!!"

"Don't think so, Hoyt." Preston said across from Hoyt.

Hoyt looked at Preston, but also fired the launcher. The rocket flies across the ground and hits one of the crime lords' vehicle. A blue and white Charger. The Charger exploded and flies into the air, covered in flames. Debris starts to fall and inside the warehouse, Ray and the others hear the explosion. They walked toward the front door and debris falls in front of them, a few of them back away from the door as others run out the door, heading toward their cars.

Hoyt looked at Preston with an angry glare. Preston stared at Hoyt, with his right hand to his side.

"What the hell have you done, Preston?" Hoyt yelled. "I had them right where I wanted them. You've just destroyed the entire event! I even gave you a warning that you should not come here, but you didn't listen to that either!"

"I lied, Hoyt." Preston said. "You, of all people, besides Eldon, should know I do that for a reason. The right reasons actually."

Billy looked up from behind the truck and seen Preston. Preston turned and saw Billy's head peeking out from the back of the truck.

"Aw shit!" Billy said. "He caught us! We're all caught! We're going to jail! We're going to jail!"

"Yeah. Aw shit is right, Billy." Preston said. "You're all headed to prison and Hoyt, you just got out of the cell. Looks like you're going back for another vacation."

"Preston, I'm not going anywhere, until those men inside that warehouse come with me and the price of their consequences." Hoyt said. "If not, I'll have to pull some drastic measures to make sure of that. Either they come to prison with me or they die here on the spot. Your call, Instinct."

Preston grinned.

"I'm sure they'll be headed to prison, along with you, Hoyt." Preston said. "You and your boys here. You'll all fit just fine, behind bars."

As they stand completely in the open, a gunshot is sounded as Preston and Hoyt duck down around the trucks. Billy decided to dive into the front of the truck, laying under the windshield. Russell laid under his truck, looking around the area. Preston pulled out his communicator and contacted Eldon.

"Eldon, what the hell's going out?!" Preston asked. "Who's doing the shooting at us?"

"It seems that the crime lords have taken matters into their own hands." Eldon said. "I suspect that they're trying to kill us."

"You think?" Preston said.

The crime lords and their thugs continue to fire at Preston and the rest of the group. Eldon and Emily are hiding under the bushes as Preston and Hoyt hide behind the trucks. Billy is still laying down inside the front of the truck, so does Russell under his truck.

"Hoyt, what the hell do we do, man?!" Russell asked.

"We'll have to fire back." Hoyt said. "Just like the cabin. But, this time, we fire until we fall."

Preston continues speaking with Eldon through the communicator.

"Eldon, what should we do?" Preston asked.

"It looks like we're going to have to fire back." Eldon said.

"Straight shots, no misses."

"Now you're talking." Preston said.

Preston stood up and began shooting toward the warehouse and its front door. Hoyt does the same and fires as well. To the left of them, Darius is also firing at the warehouse, so do both Eldon and Emily. Atop of the hill, Cody is firing down and aiming with his sniper rifle. Through his aim position, he sees one thug with an AK. He fires the sniper and the bullet goes clean through the thug's chest and out through his back. The thug falls dead.

"That was very sweet." Cody said.

The warehouse door slammed open, pouring out dozens of thugs, all carrying AKs, shotguns, machine guns, and even handguns. They run out through the door and start firing back at them. Most of them shoot towards the trucks. Billy hears the bullets hitting the truck and he screams in fear. Hoyt looked at Billy inside the truck.

"Billy, get out here and shut the fuck up!" Hoyt yelled. "You're part of this too."

"I'm staying in here, Hoyt!" Billy yelled. "I'm not going out there and getting my head blown off!"

Preston and Hoyt moved from the trucks and crouch behind the metallic fence close by. They hear the bullets bouncing off the fence. Eldon, Emily, and Darius are continuing their share of firing back.

"I haven't done something like this before!" Emily said.

"As I've told you before, Emily." Eldon said. "Its New Haven. I suggest you get used to it."

They continue to shoot and duck from the incoming shots. Cody is still firing his sniper from atop the hill. He pulls out his communicator and its Eldon on the other end.

"Eldon." Cody said.

"How are things on your end?" Eldon said. "Or should I say, below you."

"Very good, actually." Cody said. "I guess they don't even know that I'm up here. You can still see me, though?"

Eldon looked up towards his left and he could still see Cody, atop the hill, firing down at the thugs.

"I can see you clearly, Cody." Eldon said.

"Appears that the thugs and their bosses aren't minding their surroundings." Cody said. "Shows their intelligence."

"Yeah." Eldon said. "Shows it alright."

Preston continued firing back and so does Hoyt. They notice that the two of them haven't missed a single shot at all. They looked at one another, impressed.

"I've always known that you were good with a weapon." Hoyt said.

"Yeah. I proved that at the cabin." Preston said. "You're not so bad yourself."

"I do what I must to survive." Hoyt said. "That's what my father always told me."

The gunshots continue to sound as the thugs continue to fire. Ray and his men leave out of the back door of the warehouse, leaving the other crime lords and their thugs to defend for themselves. As soon as they reach the outside, they hear sounds in the sky, as if something's is coming. They look up and see a SWAT helicopter flying over the area. Preston looked up and sees the helicopter. From the left, arrives a SWAT van and over six police cars. The thugs stop firing and run toward their vehicles.

SWAT members pour out of the van and tackle the thugs by the cars, knocking them to the ground. Some of the thugs run into the woods, not able to track down. One thug gets into a car and drives toward the exit, but a police car drives in the way and the thug rams into the police car, knocking himself unconscious.

Cody looked at the SWAT surrounding the scene.

"Finally, they've arrived." Cody said smiling.

Eldon looked at the scene as SWAT members run past him. Eldon smiles.

"It's about time they showed up." Eldon said. "Business has now been picked up."

Russell and Billy noticed the SWAT officers. His men run off into the woods, Russell looked back at Billy.

"If you see Hoyt, tell him we went for cover." Russell said, as he ran off into the woods with his men.

"He did not just leave me here with a SWAT team." Billy said. "Oh, the days that will come."

They walk over to the warehouse and see that the SWAT members have handcuffed all the thugs around. Preston walked over and looked to his right, seeing Ray running into the woods.

He proceeds to chase him, Hoyt looked over as well and followed Preston into the woods. Ray runs through the woods and as he dodges the trees, he runs into Hoyt, holding his pistol. Ray began slowly to back up as Hoyt walked closer.

"Now, Hoyt. Let's just talk this over." Ray said. "We can make a deal here."

"No, Colby." Hoyt said. "There's no need for talking, because I've already made my decision to take you out. You've taken my men, you've destroying the city with your corruption. So, I believe it's time for you to go, my friend."

"Not that way, Hoyt." Preston said from behind Hoyt. "Now, move away from Ray before I have to put one in your back."

Hoyt moved to the left. Smiled as he turned over toward Preston.

"You really going to shoot me, Preston?" Hoyt asked. "Because, if that's the case, I would love to see you try."

Ray stood still with his hands over his head. Quiet and not even moving an inch.

"Looks like the two of you are busy." Ray said. "So, I'll just leave you guys alone to speak among yourselves."

"You're not going anywhere." Preston and Hoyt both said.

"Don't mock me." Preston said to Hoyt.

"Mock you?" Hoyt said. "Don't mock me is what you mean."

"My point exactly." said Ray.

Ray looked to run but was stopped by Preston, who jumped in front of him. Ray slowly turned back around as Hoyt aimed directly at his head.

"Preston, I think you should just leave please." Hoyt said. "We have so much business to discuss."

"I'm not leaving him here only for you to murder." Preston said. "He's coming back with me to the agency."

"Well, I believe we should let Colby, here decide his own fate" Hoyt said. "What will it be, Colby?"

"Would it be alright if I were to make up my own option?" Ray said. "It would be a much fair deal."

"No." Hoyt said. "Either option one, you go along with Preston to prison or option two, where he leaves you here for me to finish the job that needs finishing."

"My god, this isn't happening." Preston said.

Preston moved over quickly to Hoyt and smacked him in the head with his gun. Hoyt fell to the ground, knocked out from the collision. Preston looked down at him and turned around, where Ray is nowhere in sight.

"Shit." Preston said. "Damn it!"

CHAPTER 30

Back at the warehouse site, most of Colby's crime thugs were arrested and taken to jail by the SWAT team. Preston walked back to the site from out of the woods with Hoyt in tow, handcuffed. Eldon thanked one of the SWAT officials and turned, seeing Preston with Hoyt.

"I see you have him." Eldon said. "Great news there."

"Yeah I do." Preston said. "Wasn't an easy task, you know. Had to deal with him constantly talking on the way over here"

"You keep telling your fairy tales, Preston. We'll see who's living in reality, who's waiting for his chariot to arrive."

"Could you please take him over to the SWAT van. That way we can't hear him speaking."

"I CAN TALK LOUDER IF YOU WANT, CHIEF! HOW DOES THIS SOUND TO YOU?!"

Eldon fanned his arm as the SWAT members walked over and grabbed Hoyt, dragging him to the van. Preston smiled as he turned and focused on Eldon. Eldon shook his head as he watched Hoyt being dragged off.

"From what just transpired, I'm sure it wasn't easy for you to deal with."

"I manage as much as I possibly can."

Emily walked over to Preston and Eldon. They turned toward her as she looked around to see who was being arrested and placed in police cars and SWAT vans. Her face began to change as didn't see Colby being placed or sitting in any of them. She looked at Preston with a slight concern.

"Something wrong, Weston?" Preston said.

"Have you seen Colby anywhere?" Emily said. "You can't tell me the bastard got away."

"Last saw him, he was in the woods. I caught up with him and Hoyt came in right after. It was between him or Hoyt. I couldn't risk Hoyt of escaping, so I went for him first and as I turned around, Colby was gone. He ran off as I was apprehending Hoyt. Hoyt was very close to killing him."

"So, what you're saying is Ray's still out there. Free and at large? No one to chase after him."

"Afraid so. I would believe he shouldn't be too far along from this location it would seem. I mean, the forest where he was is right behind me. Probably if you take some steps, you could find his tracks and follow them to the finish line."

"Thanks for information." Emily said. "I'll go ahead and do that."

Emily went to walk into the forest as Eldon raised his arm in front of her. She glanced over and faced him as Preston held his head down for a second before raising it up and facing Emily himself.

"Fine. I'll wait until when we have an appropriate time of doing the task. Contact me when its settled."

She walked off as Eldon looked at Preston, uneasy.

"You do realize that the emotion she's currently in that she's going to go on a hunting spree now." Eldon said.

"Yeah." Preston said. "Wasn't much I could do except to shoot him."

"Good thing you didn't. Otherwise, we would all be looking at another "Jonny Cartel event" with you killing another elite crime boss in New Haven."

"It would've given us some media attention time. That would've helped us in some way of having an advantage."

"I prefer we don't have any of those kinds of people running over to the agency, asking for a god damn interview about our jobs. When they can't even do their own damn jobs."

"I feel your pain, Eldon and it's a cold one indeed."

"You'll be feeling something of that caliber if you continue to piss me off in such a manner."

Nearby Preston and Eldon, Coover, Rusty, and Billy were all being arrested and taken to jail. As Eldon went to answer his cell phone, Preston walked over to them and placed Hoyt inside the truck. Coover and Rusty stared at Hoyt, which he does the same to them.

"You have something to say to me?" Hoyt said. "If so, I would like to hear it please."

"I've got a lot to say to your ass. You and Billy. The two of you don't know who you're dealing with here by causing all of this."

"It doesn't matter who we're dealing with. What matters is showing Colby and his group of lapdogs that Hoyt Bennett is in town and is here to stay. You understood all of that, Rusty."

"Don't play smart with me, Hoyt." Coover said. "Because, I'll show you what I can really do and it doesn't involve me using my mouth."

"Is that right. I assumed you used your mouths for countess things. Who's to tell exactly what for when you walk around with stains across your face."

Coover lunged at Hoyt, ramming his shoulders into Hoyt. Rusty and Billy tried pulling Coover off as Hoyt kicked him in the knee. Coover yelled in pain as Hoyt laughed at him. Preston walked over to the van, gaining the attention of the four men.

"I suggest to the four of you. No fighting in here guys." Preston said. "One mistake could put an extra charge on your timeslot."

"You've made a big mistake, Preston." Hoyt said. "I could've taken them all out and would have done a great service to my city."

"I have to say, you were doing a good thing." Preston said. "You just went about it the wrong way."

SWAT officer walked by and closed the back door of the truck, as Hoyt smiled at Preston when the last door was shut. Preston watched as the SWAT truck drove off from the site. Emily walked back to Preston, looking at the truck.

"It's a shame really." Preston said.

"How is that?" Emily said.

"Because Hoyt just came out of prison and now it looks like he's going back in."

"He made his choice to do what he does." Emily said. "Nothing could've changed that."

Eldon walked toward them, placing his cell phone back into his pocket.

"I just received a phone call from the coroner's office that contained information regarding the double homicide in that neighborhood." Eldon said. "Appears they were also responsible for blowing up the bank as well."

"May we know who you're talking about here?" Preston said. "At least on a job extent."

"The DNA and witnesses' descriptions added up and lead to Coover and Rusty Bronson. The two older Bronson Brothers."

"No wonder they were the first suspects that many were expecting. It was obvious to a certain degree."

"At least they were in that truck and are heading to prison. Where they can settle their losses and find a way to move on with their lives or better yet, just rot in prison"

"You couldn't have said it any better." Preston said. "Job well done I say."

"We'll deal with the rest of this in the morning." Eldon said. "Because I'm tired and I need some sleep."

"Same here, Eldon." Preston said. "See you tomorrow then."

"I'll see you at the office tomorrow. Good and sound."

Eldon walked away as Preston approached Emily.

Preston turned to Emily.

"I figured we'll search for Colby right away, first thing in the morning." Preston said. "That way, we'll have enough energy in our systems to track him down long term."

"I very well could use the energy." Emily said. "I'm up for the task."

Late in the night, Richard and Karen are sleeping in their bed as the front door's bell ringed. Richard raised his head from his pillow, believing that the TV was still on. From his point of view, he knew for certain that the TV wasn't on. The doorbell ranged again as he got up from the bed and walked downstairs toward the door. He took a slight peek through the blinds next to the door. Seeing no one as the bell continued to ring. He opened the door and Preston stood before him.

"Jesus Christ." Richard said. "I couldn't see you through the blinds."

"You're that paranoid that someone would come over to your house and try to do what exactly."

"Never mind, Mr. Maddox. May I ask what you're doing here?"

"I need to speak with Karen. It'll be a quick word and I'll be out of your hair's reach."

"I don't know if she's awake."

"Well can you go ahead and check. Just to make sure. If she's asleep, I'll go ahead and leave. If not, I just need a word."

Richard nodded as he let Preston enter into his home. Preston looked around at the interior of the home. Glancing at his museum-like qualities and the fireplace that sat in the living room near a large flat-screen TV.

"If I may ask, how many TVs are in this home?"

"What's it to you?"

"Just curious is all. I've seen one of those TV's before. Though, it was inside a store weeks before the Black Friday fiasco took place. I decide I shouldn't get one because I would have to worry about the possibility of someone coming over to my place and trying to kill me over a damn flat screen."

"I'll tell you. I was lucky to get one of those."

"Really. When did you get it?"

"Black Friday. Last year. Had to fight through an entire mob just to put my hands on it. Luckily, I checked out before the police arrived and nearly electrocuted everyone inside the store with their taser guns"

"Sounds like a crazy morning that was."

"It was around eight or nine in the evening."

"Holy shit. Stores are opening on the day of the supposed thanks."

"Yeah. These are some crazy times when you have people nearly killing each other over TVs."

"Can you imagine how'll they react when there's no food or water available for them to purchase. They'll turn into pure savages."

"When that day comes, I will be ready for certain."

"Same goes here, Richard."

Preston glanced up and saw Karen coming down the stairs. She looked at him as if he stole something from the house and returned to take even more of the items. Preston smirked a bit before Karen approached him up close.

"You can leave us here, Richard." Karen said. "I'll be just fine."

"Are you sure, sweetheart? I mean, I could join in on the little conversation you two are having."

"No need, Richard. It'll be quick and savvy."

"If I may ask you, why are you here at my house after midnight?"

"I just needed to have a word with you and like I told Richard, I'll be out of your hair. Just a word is all I need from you."

Uncertain of Preston's motives, Karen agreed to speak with him as they entered the kitchen. Preston pulled up one of the wooden stools from the counter and sat down as Karen stood on the other side of the counter. She opened the refrigerator.

"You want anything to drink while you're here?"

"No thanks. I don't want to take any of your water or soda or alcoholic beverages."

Karen closed the refrigerator as she walked over to the counter and faced Preston.

"So, what did you want to talk about? Especially at this time of night. Just unusual to me that you would do this. Well, not too unusual."

"I just came from a massive shootout in the outskirts of town and I just need some word comforting is all."

"Word comforting?"

"Yeah. That sounds about right I believe. Shouldn't be so difficult I suppose. You used to give me a lot of word comforting back when we were together."

"I did that because that was the only way to get you to relax about anything and afterwards you wanted physical comforting."

"I didn't come here for anything physical. Just some small words of advice and that would be all."

"Ok then. How about these words of advice? You just came from a shootout in which you could've been killed and currently lying down on the table in a morgue. But, you didn't die and you're not lying down on the morgue table. So, the words of advice are you're still alive and you're able to correct any mistakes you've made in your life to move forward. You know, continue saving people's lives and giving them hope for a better world or at least a better city.

"Same sort of frame I get it. I understand what you're saying"

Preston looked at his watch and his eyes grew as he stood up from the stool and tucked it beneath the counter. He walked over to Karen and hugged her. He kissed her on the cheek.

"It was nice speaking with you, Karen. It really was. The word helped in their own way."

"Glad I could help out in some sort of way."

Preston walked to the front door as Karen walked behind him. He opened the door and took a step out before turning toward her.

"Oh. Richard seems like a good man. Just try to keep him home on Black Fridays can you."

Karen laughed as Preston smiled.

"I'll manage my best on that one. it's a big task."

"I'm sure it is. Well, nice speaking with you and I'm out of your hair now."

Preston exited the home and walked toward his car. Karen watched him leave the area as she went back upstairs to bed. Richard waited for her in the bedroom, guessing to himself if she would return to bed.

Preston drove back to his apartment, he opened the door and walked in. As he laid down on his bed, placing his hands onto his chest and slowly closing his eyes, prepared to go to sleep, his cell phone began to ring. He grabbed it and answered the call.

"Hello." Preston said. "Who's this?"

The voice on the other side was mumbled. Preston couldn't understand what they were saying.

"Who is this?" Preston said. "Hello? Is anybody there?"

He hung up the phone and began thinking. He noticed that the caller sounded like a woman.

Around close to midnight, Emily arrived at her apartment. She placed her bag and other gear onto the desk nearby the counter. As she took off her leather jacket, her cell phone began to ring. She glanced over and looked at the number. Knowing it from her past, she knew it was from New Jersey, so she answered it quickly.

"Emily Weston speaking." Emily said.

"This is the Newark Marshal and Detective Agency." The caller said. "We wanted to make sure we contacted you straight ahead. Detective Gloria gave us your number, so we could speak with you on this urgent matter?"

"Yes, ma'am." Emily said. "What is it that you would need to speak with me and why is it such an urgent situation?"

"We contacted you because your father was found dead." The caller said. "We figured you were the first to call on this matter."

Emily paused as she cannot even continue to talk. She shakes a bit before placing the phone toward her ear. She tried to catch her breath and she started breathing calmly before she spoke on the phone.

"My father's dead?" Emily said. "May I ask what the cause of death was?"

"From what we understand here at this moment, it appeared he was murdered."

Three weeks total have passed since the incident that occurred at the warehouse between Ray Colby and Hoyt Bennett. Preston stayed calm and to himself as he's seemly sat in a courtroom, reviewing a case involving his old friend. The Judge is recommending that Hoyt stay in prison for a total of six months. Preston agreed with the judge to a certain extent, but insisted on visiting Hoyt at the prison.

Within a couple of days, Preston traveled to Washington D.C. to visit Hoyt and arrived at the prison to speak with him in person. Preston awaited Hoyt's presence in the calling room as took a glance to the side and spouted Hoyt, wearing an orange prison suit coming towards him being guarded by security officers of the prison. Hoyt sits in front of Preston, smiling.

"What a sight to see for myself. I am highly surprised to see you here in my presence, Preston."

"Just came to visit." Preston said. "To see how you were, really. Being back behind bars to where no harm can come from your hand."

"So, if I may ask, what's been going on in New Haven so far? What have my allies been doing in this spare time they possess? Have the people forgotten who I am or do they still remember the actions that I've taken?"

"They still remember what you've done to the city and its innocent residents." Preston said. "But, they don't want to remember you or see you, for that matter. Your line of guys are not really in the limelight these days. Seeing how they beloved and devoted leader is currently behind bars and won't be able to speak with them until his six months of jail time is officially off."

"Funny, how you speak about me directly toward myself. Good stuff you're pulling here. Though, overall, I don't blame them at all one bit for staying out of the spotlight. In time, they will return under that light with me by their side and we will continue what we started. Only this time we won't have any interferences from either side of the law."

"From the sound of your voice and how your body reacted along with it, I can tell you're being completely serious about what you just said. Least they won't have to worry anymore about you or what you've got conjuring up in that head of yours that could put the rest of them behind steel bars. I figured that your time here would give you enough hours to clear your head of that ruckus that goes around. Try thinking of happy thoughts. While you're here, you could write a book of your own or some music lyrics like other inmates have done."

"Funny. Hoyt Bennett writing a book or even a song in prison. Crazy shit and even I would say no to that kind of offer. No matter how much money were thrown in my face for such garbage that was created. While I have you here, let me ask you a question, Preston. Have you ever heard of the theory? A theory that involves someone like myself to corrupt someone such as yourself to do unspeakable things to his co-workers and loved ones."

"Can't say that I haven't." Preston said. "Does this supposed theory have a name exactly? Something that I can keep my attention toward if it ever comes across."

"Well, I'll just say this. Preston, you need to always remember flat out that I'm your equal. The Yin to your Yang." Hoyt said. "Take it how you want. But, believe it or not, I am."

"We'll see about that when or if you're released from prison once again, Hoyt."

Preston left the booth as Hoyt watched on and continued to speak. He raised his voice so Preston could hear him. Preston turned around, he stared at Hoyt, who smiled. Preston shook his head in shame for Hoyt.

"I am your equal in pure magic, Preston Maddox! Remember that phrase and keep it in your head for a long time to come. I am your equal in pure magic!"

"Maybe in pure madness."

"That one was great, Preston. Really good job on that one."

Preston turned back around toward the front entrance and walked out. Hoyt smiled as the police grabbed him by his arms and returned him to his prison cell.

"I'm his equal. It's funny." Hoyt said.

Hoyt sits inside the prison cell laughing hysterically as Preston left the premises and headed toward the airport, returning to New Haven.

THE PLEASURED KILLING

An array of marshals and police officers walk throughout the office building. Many spoke with each other. Others were in the boardroom with detectives discussing cases which culminate between Point Hope and New Haven, Connecticut. In the distance, a desk covered with files containing information on fugitives, murderers, and con artists. The phone rang, the fellow detective at the desk answered.

"This is Brant Harper. United States marshal and detective agent speaking."

Brant is a young detective. Somewhat early in the field. Sitting quietly, listening to the other individual on the phone.

"Yes ma'am. I'll look into that right away. Thank you."

He hung up the phone and looked around the office area. Few detectives and marshals pass by in the office. Brant stood up from his desk, walking toward the filing room. He entered the filing room and went into the system of files. No one else was in the room as he entered. Searching and looking through the file system labeled "*Codenames*" While searching through the files, he stopped upon one, taking the information and printing it out. He approached the printer, waiting for the papers to release. The papers were printed and Brant exited the room. Brant returned to his desk and begun reading the files. He noticed the codename listed above. "*Codename: The Pleasure Man*".

"The Pleasure Man?"

He continued reading the file before stacking it, placing it inside a manila folder and putting it in his desk drawer. He looked at his watch, packed his gear, and left his desk. Brant walked through the area until he was stopped by a fellow detective.

"Sorry to bother you before leaving, Harper. From what I understand, you weren't involved in the warehouse incident that occurred over in New Haven a week ago?"

"No I wasn't." Brant said. "Heard about the incident. Crime bosses meeting in secret. Discussing plots to shake down New Haven. The warehouse being attacked by a vigilante congregation lead by Hoyt Bennett. Last I heard of anything, the agency took care of it."

"Sure they did. The *Instinct* Marshal was one of the leading officials there along with Emily Weston."

Brant looked at his watch again before facing the detective. Time is moving.

"Why are you telling me this?"

"The Chief informed me to tell you you're needed over in New Haven in about another two weeks."

Brant shook his head in disagreement.

"What do you mean I'm needed over there? I have duties to take care of here."

"The Chief's aware of that. Which is why he placed your time slot to the next two weeks. He knows you're currently on a case here."

The Detective walked off as Brant turned his head toward him and back.

"Take care, Harper."

"Same to you."

Brant walked and exited the agency building.

In an undisclosed location elsewhere, a pair of mannequins sitting on a shelf, covered in blood that appeared to have been smeared upon them by a human hand. The sound of laughter echoes from behind. A man walked into the room, rubbing his hands together. Blood rested on his hands. Wet and warm.

"Only time will tell if they'll ever enjoy the pleasure of my wonderful work."

Brant drove down a street. Passing by homes as leaves fly off the ground as the car passed by. Brant reached over to the passenger seat, pulling up a map. He gazed at the map while driving. Glancing down the areas marked in red ink. The marks indicated locations of which the Pleasure Man was once located. The research was done due to left-behind messages and victims he murdered.

"He's been around."

Inside his home office, Brant sat at his desk, studying the map trying to decipher the Pleasure Man's next possible location. He rubbed his head as he continued staring at the map.

"Only if I could find your next move without you even noticing me. Would it go as planned."

Brant pulled some folders from the drawer. Placing them on the desk next to the map. He searched through the folders, revealing files. The files contain other information on the victims and the locations where they were killed.

He glanced over at the map and to the files and realized that the map was a definitive tool in searching for the Pleasure Man. Brant picks up the phone and contacts his Chief.

"Chief, yes, its Brant. I have discovered some information on the Pleasure Man and I would like to search these locations. If its fine with you."

A slight pause as Brant listened to the Chief.

"Thank you, Chief. I'll get to it immediately."

Brant puts the phone down as the Chief hanged up on the other line. Brant stared at the map and the files.

"If I find these spots, I'll find the Pleasure Man."

The following day, Brant entered through the door of an abandoned home. The home was one of the dotted locations on the map of where the Pleasure Man has once been spotted or sometimes located directly. The electricity of the home was shut off. Brant pulled out a flashlight to search the home, spotting for anything that could be a signal of the Pleasure Man.

Brant walked into the living room of the home. Holding the flashlight in his left hand while his right hand is holding the map and near his weapon on his side. He sees the living room completely cleaned out. No furniture, no home equipment. Just the walls and the floor.

"There has to be something here that could lead to him."

He continued searching, heading into the kitchen. Entering the kitchen, Brant saw the stove, a counter, drawers, but no table for anything to sit on. Not even a dining room table.

"I should check the upstairs area."

He left the kitchen, turning toward the staircase.

He walked up the stairs, seeing three doors. One in front of him, another to his right, and the last one down a hallway near a bathroom. He enters the room in front of him.

Upon opening the door, he saw the room is completely spotless with nothing inside. However, he did notice the room was very clean as if someone was previously inside the home.

"Someone cleaned up well."

Brant left the room and went into the second room, which was to his right.

He opened the door slightly and saw the room was filled with a wooden table and some old furniture. The room appeared to be a storage room. Brant searched the room and was unable to find anything.

He exited, staring down the hall toward the last room. Walking down the hall to the door, he caught the sound of a slight creak from the bottom floor. He decided to take a look back and didn't see anything. He focused his attention back toward the last room. Taking a small glance in the nearby bathroom. Nothing was there to indicate evidence. He opened the last room's door and Brant saw the room was set up as if someone was living there. There was a bed, clothes racked in the closet, and even a flat-screen TV rested on the wall. He scratched his head before walking to the closet. Moving the clothes in the closet and searched them. Finding nothing but old receipts and tissue paper. He searched the drawer, finding nothing but old newspapers and magazines.

"Appears this place isn't the spot."

Brant left the house.

The next location Brant arrived to was an old theater in Point Hope. Seeing no one around as he approached the doors. He enters the old, abandoned theater and looks at the map. The theater is placed as the number two location to where the Pleasure Man was last seen.

"Hopefully I can find something here. This looks like his kind of place."

Brant entered, searching the theater in every spot possible. He then opened the double-door room and revealed it was an auditorium with a stage. Used for plays. He walked down the long aisle of the auditorium. Seeing only empty seats and hearing nothing but his footsteps, he approached the stage and walk up the stairs. He took a look at the seats and thought in his mind of how many people would be sitting in those seats while watching a play or a musical. He approached the back rooms. The rooms where the actors and crew would be preparing themselves for their roles in the musicals or plays.

Brant noticed the room was recently used. He's unsure of the reason due to the theater being closed. He did notice the costumes in the closets and the amount of make-up tools that were sitting on the tables along with wigs and hairbrushes and combs. Brant looked at his watch.

"Almost time to return to the office. I'll take one last look."

Brant came up to another room nearby, opening the doors. The room was pitch black with only the light from the sun coming in from the other room. Brant took out his flashlight and saw a pair of mannequins atop a table. The mannequins' faces have been decorated with sinister and creepy smiles, frowns, anger, confusion. Brant pulled out his gun, aiming it toward the mannequins.

"The hell is this?" Brant questioned.

He approached the table, seeing the red coloring on the mannequins. He shined the flashlight on the mannequins, all have been decorated with a red substance. Brant pulled out a cloth, wiping some of the red material and put it in a plastic bag. Brant caught a strange smell, which came from within the room. Tracing the odor, he realized the smell came from the mannequins themselves, particularly the red substance. Brant recognized such a stench.

"Blood."

Shining the flashlight on the rest of the mannequins and seeing that they're all covered with the blood and looked at the one with the smiling face, seeing it has a handprint on the chest made from the blood itself. He spotted a note on the table in front of the smiling mannequin.

The letter said, "*Without pleasure, there can be no true satisfaction.*" Signed, The Pleasure Man. Brant took the letter and threw it onto the table, resting in a small puddle of blood.

"I have to find him."

Brant left out of the auditorium after seeing the blood-covered mannequins. Outside, he approached his car as his cell phone rang. He looked at the ID, seeing it's the office.

"Harper." Brant said.

"We have some major news for you, Marshal."

"Does it relate to the Pleasure Man case?"

"A family of five are being held hostage in their home."

Brant stood next to his car as he listened. He unlocked his car, opening the door. He entered into the car while listening to the office over the phone.

"Where is their home located?"

"In the suburbs. Not far from where you are."

"I'll get there as soon as I can."

An electrical cracking sound came through the phone, interrupting on both ends. Brant looks at the screen, seeing it begin to warp and twist. A glitch? He continued to hear the official on the other side, cracking up.

"I can't hear you clearly through this disturbance. Hello?"

"Is this the marshal that is currently tracking my whereabouts?" Another voice said through the cracking.

"Who is this?" Brant asked. "Who's hacking through this line?"

"By now you should know full well who I am. I'm the guy you're looking for."

Brant paused.

"You're him. The Pleasure Man."

"It's about time we spoke."

"How'd you get this line?"

"I wouldn't concern myself with such pettiness. You're speaking to me, aren't you?"

"Where are you?"

"I'm currently sitting in a suburban home with a family of, about five. Two adults and three children. That's about right."

"I hope you're ready for the two of us to meet in person because I'm on my way there now."

"While, your on your way over here, let's see how fast you can get here to save this family in despair. I feel like teaching them some pleasurable techniques."

"Don't you dare place your hands on that family. If I see a scratch or a slight bruise, I will not hesitate."

"I'm counting on it, Marshal. I'll see you very soon. Don't be late."

Brant heard the screeching screams and hollers in the background.

"You better not harm them! You hear me!"

The phone clicked off with complete silence.

"Damn it!"

Brant started the car, driving at quick speed. Brant speeds down the road, heading towards the suburb home where the Pleasure Man is holding a family hostage. Passing by other vehicles and driving pass stop signs and red lights, nearby causing collisions between cars. He continued to speed up, until he saw a series of suburb homes ahead. Brant took out his phone, pressed speed dial to contact the office.

"Someone pick up." Brant clamored.

Within the office, the ringing echoes as many detectives move continuously through the office. At one desk, an officer picked up the phone.

"Yes."

"I need to speak with the Chief, please. This is Marshal Brant Harper. On pursuit of the Pleasure Man's location."

"The Pleasure Man?" The officer said. "Right away."

The office gets up from his chair and runs toward the Chief's office. The officer knocks as the Chief looks up.

"What can I help you with?" The Chief asked.

"Brant's on the pursuit of the Pleasure Man as we speak. Do you want me to call in the officials for follow?

"Wait till Brant calls back for details."

"Why?"

"Just do what I say. Brant knows how to operate in these matters."

"Are you sure, sir?"

"He's fine."

Brant drove down the road of the suburban area. Scouting the homes for the exact one, he took small glances at a map and back toward the homes. Seeing no sign, impatience brewed within him. Up to that point, he saw a man standing outside of one home waving in the air. Brant knew such a sight.

"This must be the place."

He pulled up his car and stormed out of it. Running toward the front door. He rammed through the front door, seeing a family. Husband, wife, two sons, and a daughter sitting in the living room. Their hands tied behind their back with duct tape placed on their mouths.

"I'm here to help you."

Brant moved over to them, only to be stopped by the sound of the click of a gun behind him. He froze, slowly turning around to see the Pleasure Man standing in front of him with a gun. The Pleasure Man wore a white mask. No emotion. No life present. Giving himself the appearance of a doll or a walking mannequin.

"It's about time we've come face to face. Now, remove your weapon from your side and slide it over to me."

Brant pulled out his gun from his side slowly, leaning slowly toward the floor. He slid the gun across the living room floor. The Pleasure Man picked it up and set it on the counter. Brant stood still with his hands in the air.

"Isn't this a sight to see. A marshal holding his hands up in the air in the presence of a fugitive."

"I only ask that you do not hurt the family. That's all I-"

"I believe that's the usual cliché we've always heard someone say. Wouldn't you agree, young man?"

The young boy's voice muffled in fear. The Pleasure Man nodded.

"I thought so too."

"This is only between us now." said Brant. "Not the innocent family that's sitting in their own living room tied down and taped."

"The only reason they're here is because I needed a suburb home to use and I love an audience. It gives me great pleasure."

"What would you want? Pleasure or satisfaction?"

"I prefer both." he Pleasure Man chuckled. "The more, the better."

Brant slowly reaches behind his back and pulls out another gun and aims it toward the Pleasure Man.

"Oh!" The Pleasure Man jumped. "Another weapon."

"I will ask you again. Let the family go and it will be settled between you and I."

The Pleasure Man nodded slightly, snatching Brant's other gun from the counter. Holding it up.

"I have a different agenda, Marshal."

He slid the gun back toward Brant, who slowly reached down to pick it up, watching the Pleasure Man stand still. Brant now had both his firearms and only one aimed at the Pleasure Man.

"Looks to me that you've lost this one."

"The show isn't over just yet."

The Pleasure Man reached behind his back, revealing a kitchen knife. He knelt down toward the young boy. The parents attempted to scream, they moved the bodies like tremors, but the duct tape held in their voices. Brant held his gun tightly, aiming at the Pleasure Man.

"Leave the kid alone!"

The Pleasure Man slowly slid the knife across the young boy's throat. Laughing at the scenery.

"You've seen my mannequins. The work I displaced upon them. I believe that

I will need a younger one's blood to complete my next one."

The Pleasure Man pulled back the knife, inching closer toward the boy's throat. The family trembled in horror as Brant fired a shot through the head of the Pleasure Man. He fell to the ground with blood pouring from his head.

Sometime later, the other officials arrived at the scene. Brant walked out of the home, approaching his car. The Chief came over toward him.

"How did it go in there?"

"It went into a necessary cause for action."

The Chief nodded.

"I knew you could handle matters like this."

Brant entered his car.

"So, where's the Pleasure Man?" The Chief asked.

Brant's car backed up into the street as a coroner van pulled up in the driveway. The Chief's face went still.

"Never mind."

The Chief entered the home with other officers at the scene. The coroners came out of the van, taking out the stretcher and the body bag. Brant drove down the street. He glanced at his mirror, seeing the home from behind. He focused his attention back to the road. Ending his mission of the Pleasure Man.

INSTINCTS POINT HOPE

1

Two months after the case of the Pleasure Man was solved, Brant Harper continued his work into other cases which many of his colleagues deemed peculiar to solve. The town is aware of Harper's contributions to them ever since he's been out solving cases and finding more evidence toward unseen killers. The town deemed him a hero. Suggesting he settle on the common cases within the boundaries of Point Hope, Connecticut. Harper often ignored his colleagues regarding the choice of cases and always wanted the ones the others deemed out of the ordinary.

On a foggy day in Point Hope as it occasional is on a clear day, before entering the file office, Detective Smith approached Harper with caution. His hands up near his shoulders with a smirk across his face. Harper stared with a shrug.

"Finally found you." Smith said with a smile. "Others said you would be heading into that room. Even though you're not supposed to go in there."

"What did the Chief tell you to say to me?" Brant questioned. "Did he tell you to watch me if I go ahead and enter the room?"

"Nothing. Other than to stay out of those case files. You know he said they're off limits."

"Off limits? Then, if that was true, the Pleasure Man would not exist and he wouldn't have murdered those people."

"I know you're doing this for the good of the town. Between you and I, this place is already filled with a negative energy. Unlike New Haven, this town is where nightmares are real."

"Nightmares." Brant said with an exhale. "Every place has its round of murderers. It's commonplace."

"I'm not talking about average serial killers or drug lords. There's something different here. Some otherworldly."

"You're thinking of becoming a paranormal investigator or something?"

"No. I know when something's off. As do you."

Harper collected Smith's words before placing his hand on the doorknob. Smith sighed. Harper stood and waited to see what Smith's next motive would be. Would he attempt to stop him from entering the room? Would he let him pass and enter? Or? Would he tell the Chief of Harper's disobedience to the rules? Harper waited and Smith gave him a nod before taking three steps back.

"Good choice." Harper replied.

Searching through the case files, Harper paused on one in particular. Titled, "*The Head-Collector*", Harper grabbed the file and left he office to see Smith standing at the exit, somewhat waiting for him.

"Did you tell the Chief?"

"No. figured you know what you're doing. No reason for me to report this to the Chief."

Harper smirked with relief as he held the file. Smith's eyes turned toward it as Harper waved it. In one glance, Smith caught the tab of the file and read the title. Smith's head went back as he laughed.

"You're not seriously taking on that one are you?"

"It'll be no different than the Pleasure Man."

"I think it will be. Haven't you heard of this Head-Collector?"

"Figure I will once I read what's in this file."

"One thing from me. He's not like the Pleasure Man or any of the average thugs we encountered out in the field. This guy, he's something else."

"He's just a man and this is just a case. Waiting on someone with bravery to solve it."

"You're sure about that?"

"I am." Brant said with confidence.

Brant went and double-checked to see if there were any more files pertaining to the Head-Collector's murders. His purpose for searching is known amongst the officers as there have been multiple files found on certain suspects. As if someone wanted them scattered throughout the office building. Seeing as there weren't any other files on the Head-Collector, Brant left the station to head home.

Once he was home, Harper opened the folder and read everything there was on the Head-Collector. A mysterious individual. A serial killer who decapitates his victims and keeps their heads as his trophies. The history of the Head-Collector intrigued Harper. So much so to the point of uncovering the killings in decades past. Point Hope had always been the residing place for the Head-Collector and somehow he was never caught by the authorities. The same was said of the Pleasure Man, yet, Brant had proved him wrong upon his discovery.

"Alright. Now where do I begin."

Within the file were case photos from the crime scenes. Photos of evidence of potential weapons used in the killings. Photos of the victims. All decapitated and left on the ground either outside or within a building. The records within the file had detailed a number of officers have tried to stop the Head-Collector. However, through some strange mystery they never succeeded. It was as if the Head-Collector would appear at will and vanish without a trace. Such is the known around Point Hope, Connecticut.

Brant had often heard the stories from the older locals of the town. Rumors of paranormal occurrences to vanishing suspects. As if they were to disappear without a trace and could never be found in other cities or towns outside of Point Hope. Point Hope was like a vacuum to them or a black hole, whichever the locals prefer. Harper never delved into the stories of the locals as deep as the other officers. He was always focused on the cases. Completing the task and going into the next case. Every so often would he hear the tales spoken by his colleagues of strange activities happening across the town. Some even suggested the crimes in New Haven were more tolerable than the strangeness hovering over Point

Hope.

"I'll never get over the stories of this town. The people here, they truly believe there's something otherworldly here. As if it dwells under the concrete streets and the green fields. Maybe they're right. Maybe not. However, it is none of my concern. Only this case is."

Still sitting at the desk for several hours, studying every photo and document on the Head-Collector, Brant paused on one of the pages. Discovering an address. The details under the address stated the location was the home of the Head-Collector. Rumored to have been abandoned over ten years ago. Harper nodded and stamped the address, keeping a record of it. Brant collected the pages and photos and closed the folder. Leaning back in his chair and exhaling with relief as the touch of tiredness encompassed him.

"Tomorrow. Tomorrow, I'll head out to the home of this Head-Collector."

2

The next morning Brant awoke and began work on the case. Traveling out into the outskirts of Point Hope to the address. The drive was long. Even he wasn't aware as to how deep Point Hope rested in the midst of the wilderness. When you're in the town, everything seems open. As if the land is cleared for the view. Yet, when you're outside of the town, everything feels as if it's all closing around you. Like a door you can't fight. A looming shadow overlapping the solid figure in which it's made.

Within a twenty-minute drive, Brant looked ahead and could see a chimney. He knew it was the house as the map indicated the path of the address. Coming closer as the trees began to move past him as he drove closer, he could see the house. An old wooden home. Two floors. Stopping the car in front of the home. Brant exited. Seeing around him old barrels of wood laying around the ground. The grass buried under the covering of melting snow. Taking steps closer to the stairs of the porch. The scent of charred wood swift past him. The direction of its origin was unsure to Brant as he questioned the possibly of someone being inside the old home.

"No vehicles. No sign of any transportation of any kind. Strange. Yet common here."

Stepping onto the stairs of the porch. Brant walked until he heard the breaking of a branch behind him. Pausing, Brant turned quickly with his handgun raised toward the cause of the noise. Only to find himself staring at a man dressed in old rags and ripped clothing. The man held his hands up in fear of the gun. Brant sighed, slowly lowering the weapon. Not a complete lowering.

"I didn't know there was someone out here." The man said. "I heard the sound of a car and I came quickly to see who it could be."

"Do you live out here? Do you live in this home?"

"I live out here. Just not inside that home. It is a place of dread. Many people have died inside those old wooden walls."

"How are you aware of that?"

"Because. It is the home of the Head-Collector."

Brant nodded. It was indeed the Head-Collector's home. Just as the address indicated.

"Do you know if he's inside?" Brant asked. "Is the Head-Collector inside this home right now?"

"I do not know."

"Well. Can you tell me what I should know. I'm U.S. Marshal and Homicide Detective Brant Harper. I'm out here on a case. A case to find the Head-Collector and end his trail of blood from continuing."

The man's eyes widen as he pointed toward Brant.

"You. You're the man who stopped the Pleasure Man."

"I see my work goes around. Didn't realize people outside of Point Hope would be aware."

"You shouldn't be here. We shouldn't be here."

"Why not? Because of the Head-Collector?"

"No. The owner of this land."

"The land? Who owns the land?"

"She does."

"I'm sorry." Brant said, shaking his head with confusion. "Who is she?"

"The Lady Abigail."

"Lady Abigail? I've never heard of a Lady Abigail. Does she live around here?"

"Yes. But, I would advise you not to go to her home. Many have done such a thing and have never returned."

"She's another murderer. Probably a helping hand to the Head-Collector. Where is this woman's home?"

"You should not go there. You should leave. Return to Point Hope. Remain there."

"I have a job to do. First, I need to know if the Head-Collector's inside. I'll deal with this Lady Abigail later."

"No one's been here in weeks. Maybe months."

"So, you don't know why there's the stench of burning wood out here?"

"Many places burn wood during the winter months. It's commonplace."

"Out in the middle of nowhere." Brant said with a straight face.

"They're people out here. In places."

"Where are they?"

"They're around. Most don't walk outside the boundaries of their homes often."

"How come?"

"They abide by Lady Abigail's laws. She is their leader. She protects them when in need."

"Seems she didn't do much of a job with the Pleasure Man. Best leave the protecting to the authorities. It helps some better."

"I'm not trying to bother you, Marshal. But, you're on her land. She would not want you here. No matter if you are working a case or not."

Brant became annoyed by the man's words. Not a sense of seriousness in him he thought. Brant placed his gun back into the holster, turning away from the man as he focused on the home. The man yelled like a wounded dog as he stepped forward. Brant turned back to the man whit his gun on his side.

"What?" Brant asked with a hint of anger.

"Do not go in there." The man said. "It's not safe."

"I have a job to do, sir. I expect to see it through."

"Don't! Lady Abigail will not be pleased of your trespass."

"Sir. Leave me to my business or else I'll take you in for custody."

The man went silent. His face emotionless. With a slight nod of the head, the man turned and walked away from the home. Brant watched as the man left and somewhat vanished through the snow-covered trees into the wilderness. The man didn't even bother to walk on the road to have a better view of his path. It seemed strange to Brant. However, he turned back toward the home and approached the front door. He knocked three times and waited for a answer. Nothing. Brant held his gun tightly as he went to open the door. Only to find it locked. A sigh came from Brant's mouth as he stepped back, kicking the door open. The swing of the door echoed through the home and the outside. Brant stood still as the stench of blood poured out of the home. To the point where Brant had to cover his noise to avoid the smell.

"He was here. This is his place."

Brant entered the home, hearing only the sounds of creaking beneath his feet. Taking a thorough search through the home. On the first floor, Brant found nothing but old furniture, broken utensils, and used cigarettes. A filthy home to dwell in. Brant was disgusted by the scenery. Looking at the staircase, Brant walked slowly up the stairs. Seeing three rooms ahead. He searched them with ease. Two rooms had no furniture. They were simply empty. The third room had a bed. Worn out from time. Stains of a sort rested on the sheets and pillows. Even the room itself had a smell of its own. As if water flowed through the room without a break. It reminded Brant of the gym and shower in his academy days. Finding nothing worth of evidence on the second floor, Brant returned to the first. Taking the turn toward the back of the home, Brant was surprised to see the wooden floors with specks of blood. Brant knelt down. Wiping the blood with a piece of tissue from his jacket pocket.

"Droplets fell here."

Brant looked and noticed a pattern of the blood. Moving in a line toward the backdoor of the home. Approaching the backdoor, he opened it with his gun raised. Standing in the backyard as the ground is covered in snow. He knew no one had been there due to the amount of snow. Nearly three feet in height from the ground. What Brant did notice was the smell of decay near him. Looking around for the origin of the smell. He realized the snow near the gate was higher than usual. A chance Brant took by removing the snow with his own hands as he could not find a shovel to dig. As the snow fell, the stench grew stronger. Once he moved enough snow, Brant stumbled back as he saw what was causing the odor.

"Ah shit." Brant said with a quickening setback.

Brant stood still. Gazing down at a decaying deer. A large buck. What was strange about the animal's body was it had no head. By the look of it,

Brant could tell the head was chopped off. The wound on the body was a clean cut. Whomever had decapitated the deer knew how to cut perfectly. Brant took the notice as pure evidence of the Head-Collector's presence being in the area. This was enough evidence of the home belonging to the Head-Collector.

"I'm getting closer. Closer than I thought I would in such a quick amount of time. Point Hope is a small place. I only thought it would take some more digging for me to discover more."

3

Returning to his home, Brant went back to the map of Point Hope and the wilderness around. Going from the home which he had just returned from and moving the pen down a trail. Leading deeper into the forest. Brant knew there was something deep within the woods. Perhaps it was the dwelling place of the Lady Abigail the wanderer warned him about. However, Brant noticed the Head-Collector's movements across the map. Each path led him closer to the exit of the town. If the Head-Collector were to escape Point Hope without being caught, he would be in the boundaries of New Haven. Something Brant could not let happen. With no other options available for Brant to take upon. He took a moment of thought.

"This Lady Abigail. I wonder. I wonder if she's aware of the Head-Collector's workings throughout the area. Within the town. I must ask her."

Brant gathered the files and headed out into the woods once more. Now on the trail leading into the unknown. While driving, he noticed the same homeless man wandering around the road. The man waved as Brant slowed down.

"You again." Brant said.

"You aren't going to her home are you?"

"Why not? I believe she may know something about the Head-Collector."

"Do not trespass on her home. She will bring forth dark forces to take you out."

"Dark forces? What are you talking about?"

"She's not as you think. She isn't ordinary. She's beyond our understanding."

"Either way, I need answers. She may have them."

"Please, Detective." The man begged. "Do not go there. No one ever returns!"

Brant stared at the man and could sense he was honest about his words. He nodded.

"I have to try." Brant said with a calm voice.

Brant drove away as the homeless man watched on as Brant's car took a left turn, heading down the path toward the home of The Lady Abigail. The homeless man shook his head. Not in shame. But in despair as what Brant will encounter. Down the trail, a long trail, Brant drove. Nothing but trees on every side. Only the front and back are clear aside from the snow-covered grounds and the whistling cold air. The trail seemed to grow longer by the moments as Brant drove. Looking somewhat at an endless road into the unknown. Behind him appeared the same.

"Where is this place?"

Driving up, Brant noticed an end to the trees on the sides. Once past them, his eyes caught the sight of a castle. A large castle. Such castles aren't known to the people of Point Hope. Perhaps even to those in New Haven and beyond. The castle appeared grim. Made with Victorian sculpture. The road led to the front of the castle grounds and Brant went ahead and drove toward it. Passing by an old vineyard and stable. No horses. No husbandmen or maids to tend the vines. Although Brant was aware of their uncertainty due to the wintry weather. The car stopped as Brant exited. Standing before the monument which was the castle.

"When the homeless man said a home, I didn't think he meant a castle."

Brant looked to his side, checking his firearm. Making sure it was loaded. He also carried a small blade attached to his pocket. In front of him were the stairs to the entrance of the castle. No gate Brant thought to himself. No matter, he went ahead up the staircase, approaching the large double-doors without a hint of concern as to what may be on the other side. Brant stopped at the doors and saw their height. Standing nearly twelve feet in length. He knocked. Waiting for a response. After the second time knocking, Brant looked toward the windows. Seeing if he can get a peek. Once he reached the nearest window, he couldn't see anything due to the blinds within and the painted murals which were upon the windows.

"This place is old. Very old."

Brant wondered if the castle had any phone service. Seeing how there weren't any phone lines of any kind in the area where the castle stood. Returning to the door to knock once again. His hand raised as the doors themselves creaked open. Causing Brant to pause in his place as he watched the doors grant him entrance.

"I see."

Brant walked into the castle as the doors closed behind him with an elegance. Brant looked forward, seeing the red carpet glinting by the daylight. The murals brightened with their colors of emerald and ruby. The walls and ceiling appeared as solid gold with a slight scorch. The sight was impressive to someone like Brant who's never been in a place such as this. Nor in a land where a castle would be standing.

"Is there anyone here? Anyone besides me?"

Brant walked into the lounge room where he saw several couches and recliner chairs sitting alongside a fireplace. There were a fire. Brant knew something wasn't right about the castle. How can there be a fire when they're no one home? Or so he assumed by the image of seeing no one during his entrance. Brant continued his walk as he took a seat in one of the chairs facing the fireplace. While sitting, a quick touch of air rubbed his neck. The touch felt as if ice was placed on him. The feeling caused him to turn around with a quickness. He knew something or someone was inside with him.

"Who's here?" Brant asked. "Show yourself."

At the entrance where Brant walked in, he caught a glimpse of a shadow. A shadow cloaked in darkness. From that moment, Brant stood up and took out his firearm. Walking near the sight of the shadow figure. Turning to the corridor on the right side of the entrance, Brant saw nothing. No one. Only an empty hallway. He nodded and proceeded to walk into the hallway. Within the hallway, there were barely any light as the windows were small. Only a glimmer of sunlight could enter the hall for a better view. Knowing this, Brant took out his flashlight and walked down the hallway. Gun in one hand. Flashlight in the other. The air in the castle began to have a presence of its own. One Brant could feel as he stepped deeper into the hallway.

"Who's here?" Brant questioned. "I know there's someone in here."

Within the end of the hallway, Brant caught the image of a figure. Same cloaked in shadow. His gun raised ad flashlight pointing toward the figure, which unveiled its bodily presence. Yet it had no face. The hands were as pale as the falling snow. Nails blue as the sky.

"Who are you?" Brant asked. "Are you the Lady Abigail?"

The figure did not respond. Brant took several steps forward toward the figure. His gun steady as was the flashlight. He asked the same questions once more to another moment of silence from the figure of shadows. Brant became tired of the non-responsiveness. Proceeding to approach the figure, Brant lowered the gun and went to grab the figure's arm. Discovering his hand moving through it as if the figure were fog. To Brant's shocking expression, a creepy giggle exhaled from the figure as it vanished from his sight. Brant looked around the hallway to catch the figure. Only he was standing in the hallway by himself.

"What was that? Was that a ghost?"

Returning to the front. Brant noticed a change in furniture. The couches and chairs were switched in positions. Now all of them were facing their backs against the fireplace, which the fire was out. Only smoke reached above the burnt wood. A sound of wind moved through the home as he lights began to flicker. Raising his gun up, Brant went and stood against the wall as he had a good view of his surroundings.

"I am not afraid of you. Whatever you are. Now, I will ask once more? Where is the Lady Abigail?"

The intensity of the flickering lights increased as did the wind. The doors rattled in chaotic fashion as the furniture began to move on its own. Bouncing on and off the floor. The fire combusted once again in the fireplace, mixed with the smoke of the past. With all the commotion taking place, Brant was not afraid. He was ready to strike whatever was coming for him. As he could feel the presence of a figure within the castle. Its unseen eyes watching him from every corner. Ahead of him on the other end of the living room, the two doors open to Brant's surprise. Silence entered the living room. The furniture ceased. The doors paused.

The fire steady.

"Show yourself." Brant commanded. "I'm wasting my time here."

Through the silence muffled the sound of footsteps. Echoing within the darkness of the opened doors. The steps of heels approached as through the shadowed entrance entered a woman. A peculiar one dressed in a black gown. Coated in white linings. Hair dark as crows. Lips as red as blood. Her eyes matched the emerald in the murals. Brant saw as she entered the living room and the doors behind her shut by themselves. In her left hand, she held a rose. Something which was seemly strange to Brant. The woman saw Brant and stared at him with a grin on her face.

"Are you the Lady Abigail?"

"I am. And who might you be? Aside from a trespasser in my home."

"I am Brant Harper." He said, walking toward her. "United States Marshal and Homicide Detective."

"And why has a detective come to my domain? Is there something here in which you desire?"

"Because I believe you may know something about the killer lurking around the area. The killer known as the Head-Collector."

Abigail's eyes widen with a much larger grin growing on her face. A small hunt of laughter exhaled from her lips. Brant stood in confusion at the scenery. It itched him.

"The Head-Collector's nowhere to be found. He died many ages ago."

"Ages ago? No. he is alive and well and is on the trail once more. I'm investigating his murders. He's still at large. Killing people. Decapitating them and collecting their heads. I need to know if you have some details I can gather to find him and end his spree."

"Detective Harper, let me give you some words in which you may understand or may not understand. The Head-Collector is nothing more than an urban tale told to the wrongdoers of this land. The town you know of as Point Hope is only a beacon to such stories.

Brant disagreed with Lady Abigail. He knew she possessed some knowledge on the Head-Collector and he was going to get it out of her by any means of interrogation.

"Ma'am. I'm sorry to have come to your home. A castle of all places. Here in Connecticut. It's something else. I must know if you're aware of anything related to the Head-Collector? Anything."

Abigail gave Brant a nod. He nodded back in reply. With a sigh breathing from her mouth, she took a seat in one of the recliner chairs. Taking out a pipe and smoking it. She exhaled slowly. Brant waited for an answer.

"Ms. Abigail, I'm sorry to rush you on your response. But, I do not have a lot of time. I need some information and I'll be on my way."

"Information you say?"

"Yes. On the Head-Collector. I need to know something that I may find him."

Abigail nodded as she exhaled once more. The smoke levitated through the living room, past Brant.

"And what will you do once you find the Head-Collector? Will you bring forth the justice the dead sought? Their loved ones seek? What will you do once you've achieved your mission?"

"I will bring him to the authorities, and he'll be placed in prison. Potentially for life. He'll no longer be able to harm those of the innocent."

Abigail laughed greatly to Brant's displeasure. The words he spoke were as dung to her ears. She exhaled as she clapped her hands together in the humor she heard in Brant's words.

"What is funny to you?"

"Your view of justice, detective. Your ideal methods of punishing those who have done harm. Such harm as murder cannot go unpunished."

"He'll be locked up in prison. He won' be able to harm anyone else. Justice is done."

"Is it? Or when the time comes, shall he be let loose to bring more harm onto the world? Shall he inspire others to continue his work. To become more than just a murderer. To become a god amongst men."

"You speak as if you're aware of his purpose for killing. That means you know something. Tell me now."

"Very well. The Head-Collector was once a student of this castle. This castle is not just my home. It is the dwelling place of many souls who have come and gone. This castle has been standing in the wilderness of this and for centuries. As have I."

Brant shook his head as he stepped back from Abigail's presence. Her words did not add up to him. Her eyes however told something different from the words which came forth from her lips. They were strange. Mysterious. Peculiar.

"You see, Detective. I must tell you. The things you encountered while inside my castle, they were no mirage. No illusions. It's real. All of it."

Through the doorways came forth more of the shadow figures. Brant turned and raised his gun to them. Seeing over a dozen of them surrounding the living room from every entry point. Abigail smiled as she saw them.

"What is this?"

"This is reality, detective. There are things in this world the masses have yet to encounter. Yet to believe."

"So what? Are these ghosts? Demons?"

"They're spirits. Spirits of the past. Souls that have been slaughtered to keep me alive."

"You killed people."

"Others did it for me. My servants. However, they're long gone. My last servant was the murderer you seek. For that reason of his loyalty to me, I cannot give him up. No matter his actions outside of my castle grounds."

"You've admitted to aiding a murderer. You're part of his crimes. For that reason, I must take you in to the authorities as well."

Brant stepped forward to grab Abigail's arm. Yet, while reaching one of the spirits rushed toward him. Standing between him and Abigail. The cold air touched Brant's face as Abigail grinned.

"I am not going anywhere."

Brant nodded, stepping back as his eyes were on Abigail and the shadow figures. His gun was raised.

"I don't want to shoot in here."

"Go ahead. Surprise me."

One of the shadows lunged toward him, Brant fried a shot and the shadow vanished. The others followed as Brant continued to shoot them to Abigail's pleasure. His eyes showed no fear as the shadow continued followed by Abigail's dark laughter in the distance. After the shots were fired, Abigail stood up and applauded Brant for his bravery. With a wave of her hand, the front doors opened, startling Brant as he looked back to them.

"Take your leave from my castle, detective. I give you this one blessing."

"I will report you to the authorities. They will come here and bring you in."

"I'll love to see them try."

Brant stepped back with his eyes on Abigail as he went for the doors. On his way out, Abigail called out to him. He turned back slightly with his hand ready to go for the gun.

"I give you this one warning. If I ever see you again on my grounds, I will set foot upon your little town of Point Hope and I will show the world what truly dwells beyond the scales of their eyes."

Brant nodded and exited the castle. The doors closed behind him as Abigail watched his every step down the staircase.

4

The next day, Brant arrived back the office in a hurry, barging into the Chief's office to his displeasure. Brant begged to explain himself as the Chief simply agreed to let him talk as the visitor who was sitting inside the office decided to leave. Giving the Chief a moment with one of his detectives. The door closed behind Brant as the Chief's full attention was on him.

"Now, what do you need to tell me?'

"It's about the case I'm working on."

"Which case besides the one I've placed everyone on?"

"The Head-Collector case."

The Chief sighed.

"Tell me, you did not go back inside that office and pick another file. I told you those are not meant for you or anyone else here. All those files are confidential. Nothing more. Nothing less."

"Sir, it is important. He's still on the loose and I've uncovered his trail. I know where he's going."

"Very well. Humor me on everything you've learned about this Collector?"

Brant nodded as he laid the file atop the Chief's desk and sat down in the seat. Opening the file for the Chief to get a look.

"Ever since I started on this case, it's led me to some disturbing places. Both physically and mentally."

"How disturbing are you talking?"

"Very disturbing. The first thing I learned what an abandoned home on the outskirts of town. Found nothing but a decapitated buck and a wanderer who told me the land belonged to some Lady Abigail."

"No way." The Chief chuckled.

"What is it?"

"Lady Abigail? This homeless guy told you to beware the Lady Abigail?"

"Yes," Brant paused. "Wait. How do you know?"

"Everyone in this town has heard the folktales of the Lady Abigail. A mysterious woman. Dressed in black who lives in an old castle within the wilderness of the land. She controls an army of shadow spirits. Ghosts basically under her thumb. It's an old wives' tale told to spook children and weak men alike."

Brant stayed quiet. A little too quiet for the Chief.

"You know something, don't you?"

"Sir, she's not a folktale. She's real."

The Chief sat up in his seat toward the desk. His eyes locked on Brant as he slid the file over to the side.

"Tell me how you know this."

"I saw her. I spoke with her. The castle is real. She is real."

"And you came back here alive? Huh. Just this one time, I'm impressed with you. Now, why go and bother the woman?"

"She knew about the Head-Collector. Said he was one of her students in the past. She knew where he was going."

"And where's he off to now?"

"New Haven." Brant said, pointing down toward the map on the desk.

The Chief sighed as he leaned back in the chair.

"Very well. If this Collector is heading off to New Haven, it is no longer your concern."

"But, sir. I'm onto this. I can stop him if I find him before he enters their jurisdiction."

"No need. Let the Marshals and detectives of New Haven handle this guy. Besides, some of their own problems have leaked into our territories."

"What's happened?"

"You're familiar with that Vigilante Congregation in New Haven. The one that was led by that infamous Hoyt Bennett?"

"I'm aware."

"Well, those bastards have come here. Into our town. A few of them at least. From what we've learned from the New Haven branch, remnants from the Congregation have fled into our land, seeking a place to dwell before they leave for Hoyt's return."

"Is that why all the officers here are on alert?"

"That's right and I need you to work this case. They'll need you on this one. Every hand-on-deck at the most."

"Chief, there's plenty of officers and detectives that can handle a few renegades from New Haven. Let me find this killer before he enters New Haven and brings forth more trouble for them than this Hoyt Bennett ever did."

The Chief disagreed with Brant's proposal to remain on the case. Instead, the Chief continued to tell him to lead the other officers on the trail for the remnants of the Congregation. Brant sighed in annoyance, taking the file and exiting the office as the Chief continued on about leaving the Head-Collector to the detectives of New Haven. Walking out in the lobby, Brant watched as the other officers headed out in mass to search out the Congregation's followers. Brant followed them outside to the vehicles. Entering his own, he made his leave. Taking an alternate route than the officers. Brant wasn't concerned about a small group of men from New Haven. Hs concern was the Head-Collector and him alone.

Driving out near the area where Interstate 95 rested, Brant followed on a small note of information which he discovered buried within the file toward the back. The details indicated a small cabin deep in the woods near the interstate. It seemed like the perfect spot for a killer to make his escape and Brant knew it for sure. Driving down the open road similar to the road near the castle, this time Brant saw the cabin ahead and it was clear. There was no other vehicle besides his own. Exiting the car at the gated entrance, Brant scouted the location for anyone. Including the Head-Collector. Brant believed the killer could be hiding inside the cabin, planning his move to escape.

"Seems like there's no one here. Dammit."

Brant went to open the door until the sound of rustling came from the trees behind him. Near the entrance onto the cabin grounds. Brant took out his firearm and walked steady near the sight of the sound. Seeing no one, yet hearing the cracking of wood in the distance, Brant yelled out orders to come out from the woods and face him. Hearing the branches crack coming closer, exiting the woods were two Caucasian men. Dressed in jeans and jackets. One had a beard. The other was clean-shaven. Brant didn't recognize them, yet they appeared to have been on the run due to their dirty attire.

"Who are you guys?" Brant asked.

"We're just passing through. That's all." The bearded man said.

"Hey, this cabin yours?" The clean-shaven man asked. "I'm curious because if it isn't, perhaps my friend and I can use it while we're here. For just a rest stop."

"First off, this cabin isn't mine. It belongs to a killer. Second, both of you will stay put until you answers my questions."

"Questions? What are we? Arrested or something?"

"Where are you both from?"

"We come from New Haven. Just looking for a place to stay while our homes are being renovated."

"You decided to come into Point Hope because your homes are being renovated?"

"Yeah."

Brant shook his head.

"I'm not buying that shit."

"Look man, we're not trying to cause trouble or anything. We just need a place to stay. After our situation back in New Haven is settled, we'll be out of this land before you can say stop, drop, and roll."

Brant sighed. His gun still aimed toward the two strangers.

"One more question then."

"Go for it."

"We you part of the Congregation?"

"I'm sorry?" The bearded man said.

"You heard what I said. Were either of you part of the Congregation? The one led by Hoyt Bennett?"

The two men stood paused. Their eyes moving back and forth

between themselves.

"Answer my question and I'll let you go."

"Afraid we can't do that!" The bearded man said, raising up his gun.

Before he could take a shot Brant fired his own, shooting both men in the head. The brief moment of silence cleared the air after the echoed gunfire. Brant sighed with displeasure as more footsteps were sounded from the woods. Listening closely, Brant could hear the voices of more men. He knew they were part of the Congregation as well. Once they stepped out from the trees, Brant saw them. Nearly over a dozen of them. Wielding firearms of their own. Dressed in jeans and big coats. The first ones looked down at the bodies of their comrades.

"Who did this?" Their leader spoke.

"Must be those guys from back home. They've followed us here."

"Nah. I'll see that to be true once they arrive. Right now, this was the cause of someone here. Perhaps they're inside that cabin."

Looking around, they saw Brant's car. Brant looked out from the cabin window, seeing them approaching the car.

"Shit."

Brant bolted from the cabin door with his gun raised. Gaining the attention of the Congregation. Their leader looked, seeing Brant standing at the cabin door.

"Did you kill my brethren?"

"They brought it on themselves. Now, why don't you guys take your leave and return to New Haven. This land is under the jurisdiction of Point Hope. You don't belong here."

The leading vigilante scoffed at Brant's words.

"You believe we're just going to let you live after you killed two of our own in cold blood? I don't think so."

The leader commanded his men to take fire at Brant. Their firearms raised just as Brant jumped back inside the cabin. The guns go off, blasting into the cabin. Brant moved the furniture around to hide as the bullets pierce through the wood. Brant kept his head ducked, hearing their leader shouting over the gunfire to bring vengeance upon him. Looking around toward the back, Brant saw a door and rushed to exit the cabin. Running through the gunfire and blasting himself through the back door, he found himself back on the outside. The Congregation could not see him as the cabin covered him. He sighed and turned around toward the trees. Only to see six individuals standing before him. Dressed in black and Kevlar. Carrying firearms. Four men and two women. The man in the middle stepped forward as the gunshots continued.

"Are you with them?" Brant asked.

"We're here to stop them."

"And who are you guys?"

"We're United States Marshals. From New Haven. These guys are our concern."

"I'll help you guys."

"No need." The man said. "Let us do our work."

"You don't understand. I'm a U.S. Marshal as well. From Point Hope. I'm here on a case and these men surrounded me after I killed two of their own."

"I see. Very well. Continue with your case. Leave these guys to us."

"Mind if I get your name?"

"Preston Maddox. Now go."

Maddox and his team of Emily Weston, Cody Aries, Darius Conway, Gloria Hunter, and newcomer Leon Thompson walked past Brant toward the cabin, taking looks out toward the Congregation. As they prepared themselves, Brant looked over to his left, seeing the bodies of the two men he killed being pulled into the forest.

"The hell?"

Brant ran after the bodies. Meanwhile, Preston and his team prepared themselves as the gunfire ceased. Loading their weapons. Unlike the others, Cody carried a sniper rifle and Leon wielded a bow and arrow. A weapon he preferred in the field.

"Didn't expect to find other Marshals out here." Preston said. "For what? I'm not concerned."

"Never knew there were Marshals in Point Hope." Cody mentioned. "Town's so small for one I suppose."

"How's it looking?" Preston asked.

Cody took a look, seeing the Congregation regrouping as they slowly approached the cabin.

"They're on their way to the cabin. Any second now."

"Any adjustments?" Darius asked.

"No. Terminate the Congregation. Clear Hoyt's residue. That's the mission. Eldon expects us to finish this."

"Very well then." Leon said, holding an arrow. "Let's have some fun with this."

Preston nodded.

"Everyone take your positions."

Preston looked over to Emily, seeing her with no expression on her face. A sheer moment of solemn came over him.

"Are you sure you can go through with this?" Preston asked.

"I'm here aren't I."

"Yeah." Preston nodded.

Preston turned the corner, gaining the attention of the Congregation.

"Take your shots!"

The shootout commenced as Preston fire toward the vigilantes in front of him. On the other end of the cabin, Darius and Gloria took their shots. Atop the cabin, Cody laid low, sniping vigilantes near the tree line as Leon fired arrows through their legs and arms. The vigilante leader looked out toward the cabin from behind the trees, seeing Preston and Emily in particular taking fire toward them.

"It's them. The same ones who put our leader behind bars."

Preston and Emily reached the front of the cabin, taking out the vigilantes with ease. On the other end, Darius and Gloria approached, standing beside Preston and Emily as they fired.

"How many are left?" Darius questioned.

"It's like there's no end to them." Gloria said.

"As many until there are none." Preston said.

Seeing a clearing of vigilantes standing, the Marshals continued to finish off the remaining ones. Once the area was silent, the leader stepped forward. Holding two shotguns in his hand.

"You can't take us out. Hoyt will be free again and his vision will come to pass."

"I'm afraid not." Preston said.

The shotguns clicked as Preston took the shot, killing the leader. The snow covered in bodies, bullets, and blood as Preston and the Marshals circled the area.

"Hope that's the last of them." Cody said.

"As do I." Preston replied.

5

Hearing the faint gunfire, Brant continued to chase down the two bodies of the Congregation as they were pulled through the woods. Following the trails of blood in the snow, Brant moved quicker than he had done before. Nearly reaching the end of the wood line, Brant stumbled out of the woods to find no bodies. Only the fact he was standing in a cul-de-sac of a suburban neighborhood. Confusion grew on his face. How could the wilderness where the castle stands be so close to a neighborhood? Brant didn't take the moment to think.

"They're inside one of these homes."

Brant went and checked the homes. There were ten of them in the neighborhood. Built the same. Outer structure were exact copies. Brant searched the homes for blood and didn't find any. Neither was there any sign of blood in the snow. While walking toward one of the last three homes, a stench caught his attention. A smell similar to what he found in the abandoned home.

"Blood."

Brant turned to his left as he walked in the center of the road, staring at a home. The stench increased as he approached the front door. Grabbing the door handle, the door was locked. Brant scoffed as he stepped back, kicking in the door and rushing in with his gun aimed.

"What died in here?"

Brant covered his nose from the odor, which was stronger than it appeared outside. The musk of the air was dosed in blood and water. He searched the home, finding nothing related to his cause. While walking near the back door, Brant turned to his right and noticed sitting next to him was a set of stairs which led into the basement. Brant believed it would be the spot to find the bodies. Stepping down on the stairs, the smell grew stronger. Reaching the floor of the basement, the dim light bulb was already on, giving Brant something to keep an eye on. The ground was wet from melted snow and flowing through the water was the sight of blood. Brant knew he was in the right place. Looking around the basement, Brant saw a refrigerator sitting against the wall. Opening the refrigerator as the cold air burst toward him. What Brant saw caused him to freeze for a moment.

"The hell?"

Looking into the refrigerator, Brant saw the head of the deer he found at the home as well as other heads from victims. He shut the door out of panic. Taking a second before opening up the freezer at the top and seeing the two severed heads of the vigilantes he killed. Brant shut the freezer door and breathed.

"This is his place. He's here."

"You're right. I am." A low voice said behind Brant.

With a quick turnaround, Brant stood and saw him. The Head-Collector himself. Shrouded by the darkness of the room with his face hidden by his dark brown fedora. His body hidden with his long trench-coat. The Head-Collector's hands rested in his coat pockets. Brant raised up his gun, ready to take the shot.

"I've been looking for you."

"I know. And you've come to take me in."

"I am. You're under arrest for the murders you've committed."

The Head-Collector chuckled.

"I'm not going to the authorities. I'm beyond such laws of man."

"You're just a man." Brant said. "You're under the jurisdiction of Point Hope, Connecticut. Thereby, you're coming with me."

"You really don't understand the reality of such things. Do you, boy."

"I'm not wasting anymore time. I've found you and I'm taking you in."

"Just like you did with the Pleasure Man? Do worry yourself. I know all about your past case. Saving the family from such a treacherous man. A pity he died the way he did. Hopeless. Without anyone there to help him see the terror in his ways."

"Terror in his ways? What you're saying surely doesn't fit the things you've done. Killing people and animals. Keeping their heads in your collection like trophies."

"They are trophies. Accomplishments of my work."

Brant coughed with disgust.

"Part of me is saying I should just kill you and end this."

"Well then, what's taking you so long. You have two options set before you. Take me down and bring me to the authorities or kill me and end my journey of hunting."

"I can't just choose from those choices. This is life and death we're talking about."

"By that case, I will make the choice for you."

From the Head-Collector's right hand, he reached into his coat and pulled out a machete. Smeared in the blood of his victims. Brant's eyes caught it by the glinting of the light.

"Let's see what you're really made of, Brant Harper."

With a quick jump and lunge, the Head-Collector swiped hematite near Brant, stepping back to avoid the attacks, Brant ducked and dodged the blood-covered blade as the Head-Collector laughed after every attack. Moving around the table, Brant used it to duck and jump past the machete swipes. Ducking past the coming slash, Brant turned around and shot the Head-Collector in the shoulder. The machete dropped as the Head-Collector shouted in pain and in anger.

"Oh, you've done it now, boy."

Picking up the machete with his left hand, the Head-Collector smashed the light bulb. Causing the basement to be shrouded in darkness. Brant, unable to see what's happening, hears footsteps going up the staircase. Finding the stairs with the help of his flashlight, Brant ran up to the first floor as he caught the snippet of the Head-Collector bolting through the front door. Running outside, Brant chased the Head-Collector down the road. Every step became heavier due to the amount of snow which was built up. The Head-Collector rushed into the woods and Brant followed. Brant ran and ran until he heard the sound of vehicles on the road. Stepping out of the woods to find himself on Interstate 95 with a sign pointing in the location of New Haven. Brant looked around and there was no sign of the Head-Collector. A sigh of anger exhaled from his mouth.

"He's entered their jurisdiction. I can't. I can't stop him now. Shit."

With the Head-Collector vanishing from the area and no one else to track down, Brant made his return back to the cabin, finding the landscape empty with only blood in the snow. No bodies. While walking to his car, Preston waited for him. Startling him for a bit.

"No need to get scared."

"Thought I was the only one out here. Where did your partners go?"

"Back to New Haven to bring forth the news. The Vigilante Congregation is no more. What of your mission?"

"Mission failed."

"How so?"

"My target is no longer in my jurisdiction. He's on his way into New Haven."

Preston nodded.

"Huh. I see. So, what will you do now?"

"I'm not sure. I can speak with my chief. See if he gives me permission to work in New Haven. Track down this killer."

"How about this. Since New Haven is my territory and you're saying there's a killer on the loose. Let my boss speak with your chief. Make an arrangement to get you working out there."

"That's possible?"

"You must be young in this field. I understand. Yes, it is possible."

Brant sighed with relief. Nodding.

"Thank you. I don't know what else to say."

"Once you arrive in New Haven, contact the Marshal service there. I'll like to tag along with you on this one."

"Are you sure? This killer might be a handful."

"I've dealt with my share of killers. One from Point Hope won't be much of a difference."

"How are you so sure of that?"

"Call it an *Instinct*."

INTERESTED IN MORE CRIME-FICTION STORIES? HERE'S ANOTHER ONE!

AVAILABLE WHEREVER BOOKS ARE SOLD!

ABOUT THE AUTHOR

Ty'Ron W. C. Robinson II is the author of several works of fiction. Including the *Dark Titan Universe Saga, The Haunted City Saga, EverWar Universe, Symbolum Venatores, Frightened!, Instincts,* and more!

More information pertaining to the author and stories can be found at darktitanentertainment.com.

Twitter: @DarkTitan_
Instagram: @darktitanentertainment
Facebook: @DarkTitanEnt
Pinterest: @darktitanentertainment
YouTube: Dark Titan Entertainment

www.ingramcontent.com/pod-product-compliance
Lightning Source LLC
LaVergne TN
LVHW091636070526
838199LV00044B/1089